THE OUTLAW HEART

Vivian Knight-Jenkins

Bestselling Author of *Love's Timeless Dance*

RECIPE FOR LOVE

"You taste wonderful," Caycee whispered in his ear.

"Men don't taste wonderful," Zackary said, gallantly cushioning her back against the hard ground with his arms.

"You do. It's the chemistry," she insisted, tilting her face so that her lips slid across his beard-shadowed cheek, ending in a tender collision with his lips.

"The chemistry?" he muttered against her mouth.

The sable hair on his chest teased at her ivory breasts as he stretched his warm, aroused body across the length of hers.

"Yeah, the chemistry between us," she said. "It makes everything—"

"—wonderful," he finished so softly that she sensed rather than heard the word. "Easy. We have time," he rasped, smoothing her hair from her forehead in a caring caress.

"I'm not so sure about that," she managed.

THE OUTLAW HEART

VIVIAN KNIGHT-JENKINS

LOVE SPELL   **NEW YORK CITY**

This book is dedicated to my beamish boy.

LOVE SPELL®

March 1995

Published by

Dorchester Publishing Co., Inc.
276 Fifth Avenue
New York, NY 10001

Copyright © 1995 by Vivian Knight-Jenkins

Printed in the United States of America.

Prologue

The old warrior could hear the three young braves camped below the mountaintop burial place as they discussed the grand adventure they were about to embark upon. The same breeze that teased at the pony's tail flying from the holy man's wooden scaffold carried their words to him.

The old warrior frowned into the moonlit darkness, deciding the braves must have been improperly raised. Even though the fine possessions he was buried with might seem extremely attractive to the living, most children learned from their parents that it was

9

unwise to disturb a man's final resting place.

So be it. The braves appeared determined in their mission as they stealthily crept up the hill toward the scaffold. But they were in for a surprise they hadn't counted on. It was his mission, for as long as the Great Spirit allowed his life to continue, to protect the burial place of his brother.

Covered from head to toe in white clay he had gathered at a nearby riverbank, the old warrior advanced toward the braves even as they quietly discussed the powerful magic the holy man's personal things must surely possess. Waving his arms wildly about his head, he challenged, "Who dares to interfere with my final resting place? You should all be ashamed. What kind of men would disrupt my peace in this manner. And who, in his right mind, would steal from a powerful medicine man like me?"

Much to his satisfaction, the braves recoiled in unison.

"A ghost," one of the three whispered in a strained voice.

"Perhaps this was not such a good idea after all," a second chimed in.

The third fainted when the old warrior reached out to grasp his arm.

"The ghost has killed him!" the first brave grasped in a panicked voice.

"He is not dead, merely sleeping," the old warrior assured them. "Your friend will awaken soon enough. Carry him away with you. Remove your camp farther down the hillside where your voices will not disturb me," he advised. "Remember this night and what has happened to you here. Spread the word among your people. And never return again to this burial place!"

The braves nodded, hurriedly gathered up their fallen compatriot, and scurried down the hillside out of sight.

The old warrior smiled to himself in silent satisfaction. When his life was done and he had traveled on to meet the Great Spirit, he held no doubt that someone would finally visit his brother's scaffold, ransack his possessions, and scatter his bones. But only those who were pure of heart would ever witness the full potential of the holy man's magic.

Chapter One

Hollywood, California
Spring, 1995

"I've planned this down to the last detail. I promise, it'll work like a charm," Caycee Hammond said. Reaching up to touch the polished bone talisman suspended from a thin chain around her neck, she smiled brightly at the rotund director fidgeting beside her.

"It'd better." Henry Lawrence shielded his eyes and squinted up at the noonday sun. "We're way overschedule on the picture. One more take on this stunt thing and we'll be as overbudget as—"

Annoyed at his dismissing tone, Caycee

cut him short. "The gag is called a crouper. It's a routine mount. All you do is position your hands on the horse's rump and vault into the saddle."

"If it's so damned simple, why did the other guy wind up with a broken jaw?"

Caycee squared her shoulders and straightened to her full five-foot-nine height. "Because he was an amateur. I'm a professional, even if I am a woman. Big difference." She glanced beyond Henry to the bay gelding pawing the ground 20 feet from the doorway of a false-front bank.

"Is that a subtle way of saying I should have called you first?" Henry asked.

Caycee chuckled. She'd never been accused of being subtle. "No, it's my way of telling you it's easy to get kicked unless the horse's feet are together when the stunt is performed, and that I know my stuff. Track records don't lie, Henry."

He studied her for a moment, then sank into his canvas director's chair. "Okay. You win. Enough with the chitchat. Time is money," he said.

Henry motioned toward his assistant, standing in the open doorway of a banged-up utility trailer stationed on the far side of the studio back lot. "Get someone over here—ASAP." He pointed to Caycee. "Have

14

them dirty her up a bit before we get started."

While the costume designer adjusted Caycee's Stetson to cover her blond bob, makeup powdered her cinnamon corduroys, crimson chamois, and khaki duster with fuller's earth. Caycee suffered the dirty-up with cool grace.

"That's good enough," Henry said finally.

He cued her, and Caycee stepped to her mark.

"Saunter through the bank's entrance, exit at a run with the bulging wheat sack held prominently, and jump on the horse," he directed. "When you reach the edge of town, spring from the saddle as if you've been shot. And mind you, I want to see some authenticity here today."

Caycee nodded. She was an accredited stuntwoman, and the things he'd recounted were all in a day's work. Besides, with the stunt coordinator's help, she'd planned the crouper down to the last letter. Her saddle had a special stirrup called an open-L, which enabled the rider to make an acrobatic leap from a horse without being caught and dragged. And the soft pile of dirt which she'd personally inspected would cushion her landing so she wouldn't wind up sore and bruised.

Caycee felt confident. Exhilarated. Alive in the broadest sense of the word. She loved the rush of adrenaline, the hammering of her heart in her throat, the acute satisfaction of a job well done.

"If authenticity is what you want, authenticity is what you'll get," she vowed.

"Let's do it then," Henry said.

Following his lead, the script supervisor called for quiet. A pulsating hush fell across the back lot.

Henry yelled, "Roll 'em."

A crew member marked the scene with the resounding click of a black-and-white clapper.

"Action," Henry called.

Filled with a heady sense of anticipation, Caycee sauntered across the threshold of the Missouri Cattlemens' Savings Bank. She immediately felt as if she'd smacked headlong into a brick wall . . . and then somehow moved through it without displacing a single block.

Caycee gasped as excruciating pain racked her body. Her throat felt suddenly parched, her mouth as dry as desert sand, the chain around her throat suddenly acting like a hangman's noose. And as if a camera flash had exploded in her face, a bright white light momentarily blinded her.

Westport, Missouri
March 29, 1872

The light subsided by degrees, leaving Caycee
with a kaleidoscope of spots gamboling
before her eyes, and her confidence frag-
mented by the hangoverlike pounding in her
head. She instinctively reached up to mas-
sage her temples with her fingertips. As the
pain lessened, she made a hasty assessment
of her surroundings.

Thoroughly disoriented, Caycee blinked
several times. The spots before her eyes disappeared, but the bank's interior remained.

She glanced down at the uneven plank
floorboards beneath her scuffed leather
boots, then upward to the ceiling, and
finally over her shoulder toward the front
entrance. She stood in the middle of a room
with a wagon-wheel chandelier suspended
from an exposed beam, brocade drapes
parted against a quintet of double-hung
windows, and a counter partially caged in
wrought-iron grillwork.

Something was terribly wrong! The bank
she'd sauntered into possessed no old-world
decor because it was a false front. At least,
there wasn't supposed to be a core to the

facade. . . . No, she was sure it hadn't been there when she'd stepped across the threshold moments earlier. But it most definitely existed now. The set even smelled different. Like perspiration and saddle leather and fear, instead of the smog-tinged California odor of the studio back lot.

Caycee slowly lowered her hands to her sides, gazing blankly at the costumed people that stared back at her. A tall, well-built man sporting a slouch hat and clothed in a broadcloth sack coat, charcoal-colored linsey-woolsey shirt, and indigo-blue Levi's held a clerk and cashier at gunpoint. A second gloved outlaw with an annoying blink filled a wheat sack with gold coins from a cash drawer. Both men wore cotton bandannas tied like Halloween masks around their lower faces.

Caycee wanted to blurt, "What in the Sam Hill is going on here!" But she remained silent. She had no speaking lines in the script. It was mandatory she keep her lips buttoned until the director yelled *cut*, she reminded herself. Otherwise she might ruin the take.

Still, Caycee couldn't help wondering if the supervisor had changed the script without clueing her in. Could the set dresser have asked the grips to reset the scenery, and then forgotten to warn her about it? Or could the whole thing be an elaborate prank? Henry Lawrence was notorious for setting people up for laughs. But surely even he wouldn't jeopardize a major project with a deadline staring him in the face.

More importantly, where had all these extras come from? Supporting cast didn't materialize out of thin air, Caycee reasoned.

The man with the muscular physique pivoted to focus more fully on her. Caycee read the surprise in his piercing steel-gray eyes as he gave her a quick once-over. Then he aimed the muzzle of his Colt .45 revolver at her forehead, saying in a smooth-as-silk voice flavored with the faintest hint of a Southern drawl, "Kid, you sure picked a helluva time to make a deposit."

Caycee suspected that even without his mask and weapon, he would project a certain dangerous intensity that fascinated women. Filmmakers called it sex appeal. Writers called it the intrinsic bad-boy quality, or male magnetism. She preferred a more simple term—charisma.

Clearly viewing her arrival as some sort of cue, the clerk hunched into a crouching run and eased from the bank's rear entrance.

Caycee watched as the outlaw clutching the wheat sack withdrew one of four guns from his waist belt, but he wasn't fast enough to nail the escaping clerk.

"Son of a schoolteacher," the outlaw exclaimed. "The weasel's squirmed out of here clean as a whistle."

As the clerk rounded the side of the building, Caycee heard him yelling that the bank was being robbed. She glanced out the window and watched him disappear down the dusty main street toward a weathered clapboard. The sign above the door read WESTPORT SHERIFF'S OFFICE.

Within seconds a handful of concerned citizens swarmed like bees from their homes and businesses, rifles in hand. Caycee assumed the crack of gunfire and the brief bursts of light punctuated by smoke billowing from their weapons were harmless blanks and flash powder. Then a lead bullet shattered a window and slammed into the cedar-paneled wall above her head. Instead of clear plastic and cork, shards of glass and chunks of wood flew through the air.

Unable to remain silent a moment longer, Caycee gasped, "My God! They're firing live ammo."

Had Henry gone crazy? Or had she? Either way, she wasn't getting paid enough to act as a human target for a bunch of trumped-up, trigger-happy vigilantes.

Her father, a veteran stuntman, had taught her that fear plus a healthy dose of good old-fashioned levelheadedness kept a stunt-person alive. She sure hoped he was right.

Another bullet sailed through the window and whizzed past her ear. Caycee scrambled over and behind the counter, bumping heads with the outlaw in the broadcloth coat who had dived to safety ahead of her. They grappled for a moment, his hand inadvertently brushing her breast as he attempted to subdue her flailing arms.

Caycee's eyes widened at the intimate contact.

Startled, he slackened his grip.

She pushed his hands away.

His eyes narrowed to glittering gray slits and he reached for her again.

Caycee blocked him, knocking his broadbrimmed slouch hat from his sable hair and snagging his bandanna in the process. The flimsy mask slipped down around his neck and she glimpsed his clean-shaven face— model-handsome if not for a slightly off-center nose which suggested a badly mended break sometime in his life. She was sure she hadn't seen his face around Hollywood before. She'd remember a hunk like him.

He pointed his Colt .45 so close to her nose she smelled the gunmetal. He studied her for a long moment.

"I don't know what you're up to, but—" he began.

Clicking back the hammer of his six-shooter, his partner rounded the counter, interrupting him. Hurriedly, the outlaw snatched up his black felt hat and readjusted the bandanna across his cheeks.

"We've got what we came for, Zackary." He raised the wheat sack high in the air and shook it, smiling triumphantly. The gold coins clinked together like metal wind chimes in a storm. "Let's get out of here!" he urged before turning his full attention toward Caycee. "Zackary was right, son. You picked a poor time to pay a visit to the bank. Looks as if it's going to cost you your life."

He raised his revolver hip-high, squinting and gazing down the barrel's length.

Caycee swallowed against the lump in her throat. Pull yourself together, she admonished herself. Realizing her hands trembled, she curled her fingers into fists.

"Wait!" Caycee finally managed. Despite her best efforts her voice sounded thin and pale. She consciously lowered it an octave. "You have no right to—"

"Keep quiet," Zackary growled. Stepping between them, he hauled Caycee to her feet by her duster collar as if she weighed no more than a foam-filled rag doll.

"The, uh . . . boy isn't armed, Dingus." His voice, flavored with the faintest hint of a Southern drawl, sounded strong, sure, and authoritative. "The other day you wrote a letter to the *Democrat* swearing you weren't a cold-blooded murderer. Are you planning on going back on your statement? Let the journalists have a heyday making you out to be a liar?"

"But he's seen your face. Next thing we know there will be wanted posters with your picture tacked all over the territory," Dingus argued.

"Let me worry about that," Zackary told him.

Using his gun as a pointer, Zackary motioned the shaken cashier into the vault. Dragging Caycee along beside him, he kicked the iron door shut. Then he steered her toward the bank's splintered back door.

"The kid's more use to us alive than dead," Zackary said.

The men exchanged knowing looks. It was obvious to Caycee by their calm deliberation in the face of danger that they had played in action scenes like this before. Either that, or they had nerves of pig iron.

"So . . . what do you propose to do with him?" Dingus asked. He nodded at Caycee.

"Use him as a shield to make good our escape," Zackary said in a matter-of-fact tone.

Caycee blanched from the roots of her hair to the tips of her toes as Zackary nudged her closer to the door. There was no way that this was part of the same script she'd previewed with her father yesterday!

Caycee's steps faltered.

Zackary caught her under the elbow and steadied her.

"Keep moving," he suggested evenly. And she did—because she had no alternative. At least for now.

Once outside the bank, the trio dashed to a pair of horses hidden in a shadowed alley. Trying to keep up with Zackary's ground-eating strides as he hustled her along beside him, Caycee experienced the intuitive sensation that he shielded *her* from possible assault rather than vice versa.

Why would he do that? Surely she was wrong.

Upon reaching the Black Hawk Morgan, her suspicions were dispelled when he abruptly released her arm and brushed past her. Unsure what to expect, Caycee pirouetted in a circle, attempting to gain her bearings while she wondered why the gunfire had died down, and tried to decide what she should do next.

Dingus stopped her in midturn, thrusting Caycee back into Zackary's deliberate embrace.

"I've decided to take the kid with us." Dingus scrambled into his saddle. "Put him up double with you."

"What the blue blazes has gotten into you?" Zackary demanded sharply. "He's served his purpose. We don't need a kid dragging us down." He scowled at Caycee. Her stomach churned and she found herself wishing she hadn't eaten that second all-the-way hot dog for lunch.

"We need him—at least for now," Dingus said.

"He's still wet behind the ears. Let him go, Dingus," Zackary said.

Caycee didn't think it was because Zackary objected to kidnapping her that he protested, but because he didn't want the responsibility thrust on him by Dingus.

Reining his chestnut thoroughbred toward the light at the end of the alleyway, Dingus tossed over his shoulder, "We'd best hightail it out of here before they have time to reload.

We can parley later, unless you have a yearning to participate in a necktie party, Zackary Reece Butler."

Zackary's scowl intensified and Caycee realized that Dingus, in an attempt to tip the scales in his favor, had purposely supplied a name to fit the handsome face she'd glimpsed. Zackary wasn't far behind her.

Caycee felt thankful when he transferred his stormy gaze from her to Dingus. She saw his jaw tighten, noting the telltale twitch, before Zackary visibly relaxed. And though he shrugged as if he'd come to terms with Dingus's orders, she sensed he seethed inside.

"You're the boss. Have it your way," Zackary said in a gruff tone. His arm lashed out and he hauled Caycee backward against his muscular torso, promptly jabbing his revolver in her side. He was rough with her, but not too rough. No rougher than she could handle.

Why did she have the strangest suspicion he knew that?

"You heard Dingus. Step lively," Zackary said.

Caycee twisted in his arms and glanced directly into Zackary's eyes—eyes that looked beyond her surface calm to the turmoil beneath. For a moment, she could have sworn she glimpsed quiet desperation in them before it scurried behind a cloud of grim determination.

With the cold revolver riding her rib cage, Zackary forced Caycee to turn and mount the Morgan.

Don't think about his gun, she advised herself, even if it does feel like the genuine article. Worry about that later. For now, just do as he says.

Chin up, Caycee obeyed Zackary without challenge.

Since there was no saddle horn, she threaded her fingers into the prancing horse's mane as Zackary mounted with an easy grace behind her. He reached around her to gather the reins, clamping his arms about her waist, though whether to support her or himself Caycee wasn't certain.

Following Dingus's lead, Zackary spurred his Morgan into a smooth, rocking-horse-like gallop. They lunged from the alley into the stark daylight and down the main street of Westport like flesh-and-blood whirlwinds. Intensely aware of the heat of Zackary's encircling arms and the impressive manner in which he handled his frisky mount, Caycee dug her knees in and settled in for what she feared would prove the ride of her life.

Issuing yipping rebel yells and waving their guns above their heads, the outlaws raced toward the edge of town. A fresh volley of gunfire finally erupted from the rooftop of the general store. Caycee felt Zackary recoil. Within seconds, he dropped the reins and slumped heavily against her. Sensing his rider's distress, the skittish Morgan executed a curt little buck.

Caycee felt Zackary slide from the horse like the cherry from a melting sundae. In a last desperate attempt to cling to the agitated animal he almost yanked Caycee off with him. As she righted herself in the saddle, she glanced over her shoulder in time to witness Zackary perform a choppy shoulder roll onto decidedly hard-packed earth.

Her heart constricted. She'd done that once—hit the dirt like a human missile. It hurt like hell. She'd rather have a tooth extracted without novocaine than endure a fall like that again.

Still half believing there were hidden cameras somewhere and thinking their wild ride through town some sort of wacky stunt gone haywire, a scene concocted by Henry Lawrence for impact and authenticity, Caycee leaned across the Morgan's neck and firmly gathered his dragging reins before he could tangle his legs in them, fall, and injure them both. Peering uncertainly up at the general store's now quiet rooftop, she urged the Morgan into a circling canter as Zackary rose drunkenly to his knees, eventually finding his feet.

Caycee noticed he had lost his hat, and that his crimson bandanna rested once again like wadded cotton rope around the strong column of his throat. She watched him tug the swatch of cloth off and press it to his chest with his right hand. He brandished his Colt .45 threateningly in his left while rapidly scanning the narrow street.

Caycee could see for herself there had been no watering troughs strategically planted by the set designer, no overturned wagons, no barrels, nothing to adequately protect a man of Zackary's size. He stood spread-eagled, exposed to the elements with nowhere to run and no place to hide.

What happened to Zackary when the men on the rooftop reloaded again? Would they finish him off? Was that how this new scene went? Caycee wondered. Why did the idea bother her? This wasn't real—was it? And if by some weird twist of fate it was reality rather than the surrealistic fantasy it felt like, could she stand by and witness Zackary Butler's death at the hands of a group of angry vigilantes?

The answer came to Caycee with driving force—absolutely not. There was no justice in that, even if Zackary was a criminal.

Courage is like a black dress—always appreciated, and never out of style, Caycee reminded herself.

Sucking a deep breath into her lungs and slowly exhaling, she reined the Morgan from its spiral canter and into a horizontal gallop toward Zackary Butler. She didn't ponder further. She didn't analyze why. Boosted by a rush of adrenaline, she simply reacted.

Caycee heard the gunfire cease behind her and realized Dingus had stopped to watch her wrestle the Morgan under control. Positioned in a stand of camouflaging oaks, he covered her rescue mission from a safe distance.

As Caycee reached Zackary's side, she pulled the horse up short and leaned down to extend a helping hand. His astonished expression told her that was the last thing he had expected.

Caycee felt a surge of unexpected feelings wash over her. Anger. Elation. Concern for herself. And him.

Caycee silently acknowledged that Zackary

stirred the ashes of her emotions by courting the daredevil in her. The feelings frightened and yet intrigued her.

She'd help him, like it or not, if it was the last thing she ever did, Caycee decided.

"Step lively," she commanded firmly, mimicking his words.

His eyes sought and held hers. Their gazes connected.

"There's nothing wrong with your ears. You heard me correctly," she said boldly.

Zackary gripped her hand in his larger, callused one. With a pain-filled *humph* that sounded terribly authentic to her, he struggled into the saddle behind her and pressed his chest against her back.

In a heartbeat, he'd appropriated the reins from her tense fingers. Caycee could feel his warm breath fan her ear as Zackary rasped, "Ma'am, I hate to be the one to tell you this. But I think you just made the worst mistake of your life."

Determined to have the last word, she said, "My name is Caycee. Caycee Hammond. I prefer it over ma'am any day. Best remember that."

Chapter Two

"You know the old saying. If I didn't have bad luck, I'd have no luck at all," Caycee responded to Zackary's taunt.

She sounded flippant. Zackary wasn't in the mood for flippant. Nor had he heard of such a saying.

He gritted his teeth and tightened his embrace around her trim waist. Not a cruel touch, just an insistent pressure to convey in no uncertain terms that he wasn't pleased with the latest sequence of events.

Spine stiffening, she instantly lapsed into silence. Zackary nudged the Morgan into a full-fledged gallop. A trail of dust billowed behind them as his mount dug in, hooves churning like the wheels of a locomotive engine on the Hannibal and St. Joseph Railroad as he made a beeline for the stand of oaks where Dingus awaited them.

Glory above, the hole in his back burned as if he'd been seared with a branding iron! Zackary thought. He'd almost forgotten how a bullet lodged beneath the skin felt. He had a scar where one had once grazed his thigh, another that distorted the muscular calf of his right leg. Old wounds. War wounds. Wounds long healed.

Now, at 35, he realized he was getting too old to dodge gunfire. Besides, he'd been assured this job would be easier than rolling out of a flea-infested cot; he hadn't spent three months in the Minnesota penitentiary at Stillwater to watch something like this happen. All his careful plans, shot to damnation. The Westport bank robbery bungled because of a self-proclaimed jinx with nothing but bad luck. Luck that seemed to be rubbing off on him—much to his chagrin.

If only the Jackson County sheriff had curtailed the vigilante attack from the rooftops. If only he'd had a few more minutes before Caycee Hammond had stepped across the threshold. If only he didn't owe the success of this venture to his kid brother, Adam. If only he could shake his guilt and get on with life and living.

But he couldn't. Not until he successfully settled the score.

If only Caycee Hammond hadn't reminded him so much of Adam in the first place. Her exaggerated swagger. Her spunk. Her bravado. The cocky angle of her broad-brimmed Stetson, which shadowed her prominent cheekbones, pert nose, and the adventuresome twinkle in her daring hazel eyes. The way she turned her duster collar up at the throat.

Even before he'd realized she was a woman, he'd felt a surge of protectiveness toward her. An innocent caught in the backwash of the robbery, she was too young, impressionable, and vulnerable. He didn't want to feel responsible for her, and yet he did despite himself.

Frustrated and feeling suddenly light-headed, Zackary cursed beneath his breath. Caycee stiffened. He used her body as a crutch, leaned into the solid wall of her back, and forced the reins into her hands as they galloped past Dingus, who had by now removed his bandanna as well. Dingus reined his thoroughbred into action, quickly catching up with them as they reached the safety of the converging trees.

"Let Dingus stretch out in front," Zackary said.

Caycee glanced over her shoulder. "But I—" she began.

"Dingus knows the way. Follow him!" he commanded. "And for the love of . . . Watch where you're going!"

Caycee turned. A low-hanging red cedar branch swiped at her cheek, the harsh sting of the needles bringing reality into sharp focus as a cloud of birds lifted skyward from the uppermost limbs.

"Glory hallelujah! They'll catch us for sure if the kid scares up another flock of bluebirds . . . good as smoke signals. Do something with him," Dingus flung back at them.

"I'll set him down here. He can walk back to town," Zackary said.

Caycee felt momentarily grateful. This scene was getting way out of hand. Where in the heck were the cameramen hiding? She'd never dreamed the property line of the studio back lot ran this far. And why hadn't Henry yelled *cut* when she reached the edge of town—a town that appeared so authentic it was downright scary? She glanced at the bulging wheat sack tied to Dingus's saddlebags, for the first time consciously marking the telltale jingle of coins.

Strange—her wheat sack had been stuffed with Monopoly money.

Dingus pulled off his hat and wiped the

perspiration from his brow with his shirt-sleeve. "No. Can't afford to set him down."

Caycee's attention rose from the wheat sack to rest on the back of Dingus's head. She'd rarely seen such a poor haircut—it looked as if it had been styled with a soup bowl and a dull kitchen knife.

"Just keep moving till we reach the junction of the Independence and Lexington wagon roads," Dingus responded, repositioning his hat on his head.

"You plan to take the Blue Mills ferry," Zackary commented—rather weakly, Caycee thought.

"That I do, clear across to the other side of the Missouri."

Feeling progressively more uncomfortable, Caycee frowned. "The Missouri? Henry never said anything about crossing a river. Why in the world would we want to—"

Zackary interrupted her. "I don't know anyone named Henry," he said solemnly.

Caycee's eyes widened involuntarily. "He's the director. I thought you guys were extras."

"The ride's rattled the kid," Dingus commented dryly.

"You talk too much . . . ask too many questions," Zackary cautioned in a tight voice. His warm breath touched her check as he leaned in closer. "You keep digging yourself in deeper and deeper."

"He sure does," Dingus interjected. "But the worst of it is that the kid's not only seen your face, Zackary; he's seen mine too now. You know what that means once we've crossed the river. I can't take a chance on him supplying an accurate description to the authorities."

Caycee waited with bated breath for Zackary's response. Seconds drew into minutes and yet he made no comment.

Suddenly the Morgan, lathered and understandably exhausted, stumbled over an exposed root, and Caycee tipped forward. A soft moan escaped Zackary's lips. He abruptly slipped a hand from around her waist as the horse's gait smoothed, leaned back in the saddle, then relinked his fingers securely around her middle. Caycee glanced down at his hand. His fingertips were slathered in crimson.

Caycee swallowed heavily, momentarily stunned by what she recognized as honest-to-God blood. If Zackary was oozing real blood, then there was only one explanation—something she had suspected and vehemently denied—that she had somehow traversed time and space.

Having studied physics in college, she recalled the theory that every hundred years or so the present catches up with light particles emitted long ago. The result was reported to be a random gateway to the past. She'd rejected the theory as impossible until now. But it was becoming apparent that during filming she'd somehow stumbled through that bright white gateway as she'd stepped from her mark through the false-front bank's doorway . . . and eventually into Zackary Butler's arms.

Caycee's lips felt suddenly dry. She ran her tongue across them and lapsed into silence, a silence so intense the honeybees sounded like chain saws; so profound that the muffled clop of the horses' hooves across beds of dried pine needles seemed to reverberate within her like minor earthquakes; so acute she could almost hear the gears of her own brain grinding out: For your own sake, believe it. This isn't a movie! Your life is at stake.

Glancing back at Zackary, Dingus fingered one of the guns tucked in his waistband. "Maybe the kid should get down here . . . probably as good a place as any."

Refusing to panic, Caycee nonetheless tensed.

Zackary reacted automatically to her body language.

She sensed him gathering strength, felt his

muscles tense, heard him bring his breathing under control as he sat up straighter in the saddle. In the smoother-than-smooth voice she'd heard him use during the bank robbery he said, "The kid's fine for now right where he is."

Dingus smiled and eased his hand away from his gun to rest it on his thigh. "Makes a good prop, huh?"

"Makes a helluva prop," Zackary said. "Good thing you suggested we bring him along."

"For a spell," Dingus reminded him.

"Yeah, for a spell."

Caycee forced herself to relax. She'd been in life-threatening situations before. True, they'd been stunts that had been planned down to the last detail, but she had known anything could go wrong at any time. And often did. Granted, this was an extreme scenario, but she could handle it. She hoped.

Though perspiration beaded on her forehead, Caycee rallied like the professional she was. Physical, mental, and emotional flexibility were a must in stunting. Taking a deep breath and holding it to combat her building anxiety, she counted on her strong character along with her indomitable spirit to see her through, forcing her mind to reason coherently.

Even though Zackary Butler obviously knew she was a woman, Dingus still thought her a young man, and now, through no fault of her own, her life was at risk.

Her time to make a break would come. She wasn't sure how to proceed once she won her freedom, but proceed she would. There would be time to think of the consequences of escape once she accomplished the deed. For now, she must spend her time mentally marking their trail so she could find her way back to Westport and hopefully the portal to her own time.

Caycee estimated by the sun's movement across the sky that they traveled for over an hour, stopping only long enough to allow the horses to drink from a woodland stream. They joined the horses in quenching their thirst, though they drank from wooden canteens which were promptly refilled by Dingus from the same stream.

Caycee followed Zackary's previous suggestion and made no comment, though she wondered about the purity of the water. During a camping trip, her father had once explained that people often acquired hepatitis by drinking from streams. Of course, that seemed to be the least of her worries at the moment, Caycee reasoned.

41

After quenching their thirst, they continued on until the forest thinned significantly, petering out into a grove of budding dogwoods that bordered a wagon-wheel-rutted trail. They walked the horses single-file along the shoulder, shortly reaching a sloping riverbank edged with cottonwood trees. In a clearing stood a weathered shack not much larger than the outhouse perched behind it.

"Ferry should be here in a minute," Dingus commented, nudging his horse down the embankment toward the outhouse. Caycee wasn't surprised when Zackary collected the reins from her hands and with a click of his tongue urged the Morgan forward. She was surprised, however, that his fingers trembled as they brushed hers. She glanced over her shoulder to see a flicker of pain skitter across his face before he quickly concealed it behind a disgruntled frown.

"Best make use of the necessary while you can. Won't see another one anytime soon."

Caycee shook her head, intending to tell him she didn't need to "make use of the necessary." But it took all her concentration to keep her body from being pushed up along the Morgan's neck as Zackary leaned heavily into her.

No doubt about it—Zackary Butler's condition was worsening. As was hers with each passing minute.

Zackary dismounted near the ferry landing, demanding that she do the same.

Caycee complied, watching the log ferry poled by a bearded man and young boy dip back and forth in the river like a bar of soap as it floated languidly toward them from the landing on the opposite bank. Keenly aware of the dragonflies lighting on the water and the bass breaking the surface to consume them whole, Caycee refused to panic. A strong swimmer, she instead began formulating a plan.

She weighed the odds of successfully diving off the raft beneath the river's surface and allowing the current to carry her downstream and out of harm's way. And then what? Strike out on foot? In the middle of nowhere?

No—strong swimmer or not, she needed one of the horses. The Morgan was stoic, but winded from carrying double weight. The chestnut thoroughbred, tied a hundred feet away on a hitching post outside the outhouse, made the most likely choice if she intended to make it back to town. Forget the waning afternoon light. Forget that if she waited to make her move until they boarded the ferry, she would have to recross the river at some point in time. Forget that she'd be forced to backtrack through territory she'd traversed only once. Forget everything except the necessity of escape.

Caycee glanced at the far riverbank, gauging its height. This wasn't the movies. They would shoot her if they got a chance. It was steeper than the bank on this side, which might work to her advantage, she decided. If she could safely make it over the top, she'd be home free.

Well, maybe not home, but free.

The ferry bumped against the landing, breaking into Caycee's thoughts with a wooden thud.

The ferryman motioned with a wave of his arm for Zackary to board, pointedly ignoring the blood crusted on his jacket.

Caycee hesitated. Zackary nudged her firmly on the arm. "Let's go. We're burnin' daylight."

She'd heard that line before. From her father.

A twinge of homesickness assailed her, and try though she might, Caycee couldn't seem to repress it. She found herself wondering how her father was doing. By now he'd be watching for her from the kitchen window, expecting to see her steer her Ford pickup into the driveway after a day of shooting.

Though he was confined to a wheelchair, he'd already have the dinner table set when she walked through the door. By the time she finished her shower, the meal would be prepared. One of them would say grace. They'd break bread together, and then talk out the trials, tribulations, and accomplishments of the day over a plate of paella. Or Cornish hens and wild rice. Or spaghetti with dandelion salad and garlic toast. Her mother, an elementary school physical education teacher, had made dinner an adventure. Due to their varied and busy schedules, it was the one meal a day they'd always shared. After her mother's death from cancer, her father doggedly carried on the ritual through her mother's recipe box.

Of course, there had been times when tradition had been broken: during the last few months of her mother's lengthy illness; later, during Caycee's disastrous two-year marriage to a Florida-based stuntman whose ego couldn't compete with her rising popularity and professional expertise; and still later, when her father had undergone rehabilitation after his near-fatal fall.

Caycee admitted that because of her status as a beloved only child she was probably outrageously spoiled, yet the rigors thrust on her by life had made her strong willed, competent, and compassionate as well.

Compassion momentarily chased all other thoughts from her mind when she saw Zackary wince as he dug a copper coin the size of a half-dollar from his inside coat pocket and tossed it to the boy. She actively suppressed the desire to reach out and assist him. She could ill afford concern for his well-being at this point, she advised herself.

Dingus shortly joined them on the ferry. Caycee noted that the horses appeared calm, as if they were accustomed to the rigors of river-crossing. Good. It made things easier.

Caycee remained outwardly relaxed, leaning against the railing as the ferry eased from the bank. She gathered her energy as she awaited an opportune moment. How would she push Dingus out of the way and mount the chestnut without mishap as they reached their destination? she worried.

Her chance came unexpectedly when they reached the other side. Dingus handed the chestnut's reins to the boy and offered Zackary a leg up in mounting. Caycee made her move. Splintery-rough against her back, the railing caught at her duster as she lifted away from it, wresting the reins from the boy's hands, springing into Dingus's saddle, and giving the mount a swift kick of her heels.

She was halfway up the embankment when, to Caycee's amazement, a long, low whistle stopped the horse in its tracks.

Trained! she thought, realizing instantly that she'd miscalculated and chosen the wrong horse.

Positive she'd seen her last sunset, Caycee reined the chestnut around, facing Dingus squarely. As she'd assumed, he'd drawn his gun.

"Give me one good reason I shouldn't put a bullet through your skull here and now," he said.

The ferryman and his helper looked like human statues, frozen in place, fearful of breathing lest it should attract undue attention to them. Zackary remained perfectly quiet. Watching. Waiting, Caycee surmised. Second-guessing. Anticipating her next move. So that he might make another appropriate countermove as he'd done in the alley? she wondered. Her father was fond of checkers—this reminded her of the game. Only the consequences of a wrong move in checkers weren't life-threatening.

"I'm waiting and none too patiently," Dingus prompted.

Think quick. "Because I could prove invaluable to you," Caycee responded.

"You've outlived your value. Besides, I don't need your kind of trouble," Dingus said.

"Your horse . . . it's trained," Caycee said.

"Yep. What of it?"

Although she was proficient in a variety of stunts, her father had been from the old school when Westerns were all the rage. During his career, he'd dealt primarily with mounted stunts. He'd maintained a stable on their property throughout her adolescence—she'd even helped him train the stunt mounts until he'd become disabled.

"I know horses. My father maintained a stable."

"A smithy?"

Caycee hesitated. "Sort of."

"Can you shoe?" Dingus asked curtly.

Caycee could tell she'd piqued Dingus's curiosity. She played on that.

"No, but I can ride."

"I know plenty of men who can sit a horse," he said.

"Not like me. I never intended to make a bank deposit. I wanted to, uh . . . join your gang. That's why I walked into the bank when I did. I thought I could talk to you about—"

Dingus cut her off short. "'Fraid I'm not interested."

With a sinking heart, she realized she'd lost her advantage with Dingus.

For Caycee, time seemed to draw out toward eternity. And then Zackary coughed and the Morgan shifted its weight, jostling Dingus's hand. His gun went spinning off into the river.

"For God's—Hold that blasted Morgan still, Zackary," Dingus exclaimed, staring at his gun glistening up at him through the shallows.

"Sorry. My hand's going numb," Zackary replied evenly, his gaze never wavering from her face.

Caycee's eyes met Zackary's in a brief exchange of acknowledgment, for she realized he had shifted the Morgan into Dingus's hand on purpose. If only she could figure out why he kept protecting her. He was a ruthless outlaw; she'd been someone in the wrong place at the wrong time. She was nothing to him, and yet . . .

Disgust evident on his face, Dingus stomped off the raft and sloshed out into the Missouri shallows to retrieve his gun. He tugged his shirttail from his pants and, critically examining it, dried off the dripping weapon.

"You owe me, Zackary," he grumbled, slipping his shirttail and gun back into the waistband of his pants.

"More than you can ever know," Zackary

replied, reining the Morgan beside the chestnut.

"Hold on to his mane," he ordered, snatching the reins from Caycee's fingers and leading the chestnut up the embankment to level ground. While Dingus stomped after them on foot, Zackary leaned over and suggested in her ear, "You'll get shot sure as hell if you run. Best show the man what you can do in the saddle while I can still sit upright."

Caycee wasn't exactly sure what Zackary meant, but she wasn't going to let the opportunity pass her by. She promptly treated them to a dazzling, circuslike performance of professional expertise and horsemanship that she felt sure Ringling Brothers would have been proud to showcase in one of its three rings. And she did so without even losing her hat.

Dingus actually applauded.

"I never would have believed it! Almost as good as Wild Bill . . . and to think I almost shot you," he said, his good humor restored.

"Flat-out wondrous," Zackary agreed in a tone laced with what Caycee recognized as forthright admiration.

"So . . . ?" Caycee asked tentatively as she handed the chestnut over to Dingus.

"So I suppose you can tag along. But not with me," he said as he mounted.

Zackary's eyes narrowed. "What are you getting at, Dingus?"

"Plain truth, you're going to slow me down and you know it. Heck fire! You're already slowing me down. What with my family depending on me, I'd be a fool to ride any farther with you, Zackary. For Zee's sake, I can't give the law a chance at me. You know that."

Dingus turned to Caycee. "You take care of him."

"Me?" Caycee croaked. She hadn't planned on this! "But I don't—"

"You manage to keep Zackary alive long enough to meet up with me at the end of next month, and I'll consider letting you join the gang—as a horse-holder, mind you. At least until I get to know you better. It's not much, but it's a start."

Caycee felt flabbergasted by the unexpected turn of events. She glanced at Zackary, noting the increasing cloudiness of his eyes and the bloodlessness of his cheeks.

"How am I supposed to find you?" Caycee stuttered.

"Zackary knows the answer to that one. Consider it added incentive for you to take good care of him," Dingus said with a self-satisfied grin.

"You're pressuring the kid," Zackary said.

"You bet I am," Dingus replied.

"Who wouldn't want to ride with a gang for a spell? It's preferable to death any day."

"Right again," Dingus conceded.

Caycee suddenly realized Dingus's ploy was twofold—a way of leaving the dead-weight behind without paining his own conscience, and a test of loyalty for her. Dingus was crafty. No doubt about it.

"The kid doesn't owe me anything," Zackary said in an increasingly weak voice.

Don't I? Caycee wondered. Then she silently answered her own question. Certainly not. It was his choice to intercede on your behalf.

He interceded twice, her conscience argued. Once in the alley, and once just now.

Your chances of returning to your own time are better without him dragging you down!

But she was a woman who paid her debts, she reminded herself. Besides, at the moment she seemed to have few options, Caycee thought, feeling herself being involuntarily sucked deeper and deeper into the past.

Chapter Three

Zackary watched as Dingus adopted the breakaway guerrilla tactics learned during the war and disappeared into the forest. Knowing Dingus was headed toward St. Joseph to melt within the protective bosom of his family, Zackary pointed the Morgan in the opposite direction.

"Mount up," he commanded.

"I don't suppose I have any choice," Caycee said grudgingly, placing her foot into the stirrup and easing into the saddle.

Zackary almost smiled. He imagined her rear was sore. And even if she *was* flat-out wondrous on a horse, he sensed she was unaccustomed to the rigors of a hard day's ride. Her face told him she felt exhausted.

Worried. Definitely frightened. Yet she remained plucky.

Thank the good Lord for small favors!

Zackary admitted to himself as Caycee silently settled in behind him that somehow their roles had reversed. At the moment, he needed this woman. More so than any woman he'd ever known.

During the holdup, his first instinct had been to somehow protect her without appearing suspect himself. The kid's ready-made clothes showed he was dirt-poor—Zackary had witnessed more than one man, too proud to be caught in store-bought goods, sneaking home to iron the creases from his trousers.

But before he could determine a safe course of action, fate had intervened. The clerk escaped, bullets flew, and he discovered the kid was really a woman who smelled like apple pie . . . good enough to eat . . . soft in his arms . . . inviting. He'd attempted to protect her with his ruse of using her as a shield. Much to his chagrin, the suggestion backfired. Dingus had taken charge in the alley, and she'd wound up a hostage.

To make matters worse, within minutes of clamoring onto his Morgan, he was shot by an irate citizen as they galloped away from the bank. Zackary figured he was as good as dead, until Caycee surprised him by reining the Morgan around and rescuing him.

Feeling increasingly light-headed, Zackary acknowledged that as little as he liked the notion, it now seemed this woman was the only thing protecting him from an untimely death.

"I'm no more pleased by this than you are," Zackary said. It hadn't been part of his plan.

"If you only knew how . . . inconvenient this is," she said. Her words sounded almost wistful.

"If *you* only knew. This was the last thing on my agenda."

"Or mine," she stated in an even tone. Her voice rang deeper than most women's. Truer. He liked that.

And she was direct—vehemently so at times. This was no wishy-washy miss, no simpering female, subject to vapors. He discovered, much to his astonishment, her strength of character intrigued him. Through what trials and tribulations had she gone to attain such self-control?

"So . . ." Zackary began, scanning a tree line that seemed to undulate before his eyes. He blinked. His vision cleared somewhat, but not entirely to his satisfaction.

"So, what now?" she finished for him as

she placed her hands gingerly on his hips. He grasped her hands and intertwined them around his waist, as much to keep himself in the saddle as to secure her seat.

"I figure the Westport posse is still trailing us."

"I haven't seen anyone," she said, glancing around.

"Neither have I. But it seems logical that they'd be out there. Most men don't take kindly to their life savings being withdrawn by strangers. To throw them off, I've decided we're going to do a bit of circling." It was another tactic the troops had often implemented during the war. "Eventually we'll be following the posse instead of vice versa."

"You can't go on like this much longer. You need a doctor," Caycee commented tentatively.

Zackary cleared his throat. "Yeah. I know."

"What are you . . ." Her sentence trailed off and she began again. "What are we going to do about it?"

Her use of the plural surprised him. He paused for a moment, taking into account the fact that she was verbally linking them as a unit. He wasn't sure he liked it; he wasn't sure he didn't. His brain felt as if it were made of goose down. He struggled to keep his thoughts together.

"I can't risk riding into a town. Not shot up like this. It wouldn't be any time before someone figured out what happened and wired my location back to the Westport sherriff's office.

"I'd most likely wind up in a jail before hard nightfall." The idea was at best unsavory. He'd have a mountain of explaining to do. It could take days. Weeks, even. He couldn't chance it.

"At the rate I'm going, I'd be right beside you," she said.

"I wouldn't rule it out."

"That's not to say it would happen, but there's no guarantee it wouldn't," she said as if considering her options aloud.

If she was asking for assurances, she was barking up the wrong tree. He couldn't give her any. Besides, he prided himself in being honest—up to a point.

"None," he said finally.

He thought he heard her sigh. Then she abruptly changed the direction of the conversation.

"The bullet's still in there, isn't it?"

He shifted in the saddle, wondering if the Morgan had a rock in his shoe. The horse's gait felt unnaturally choppy. Then again, maybe the Morgan wasn't the problem. Perhaps it was the wound in his shoulder making him feel wobbly. "I'd hazard a sharp guess it's stuck in there somewhere."

"But that doesn't mean you're going to die."

It was a statement rather than a question, emitted in a low voice that brooked no argument. Zackary felt renewed admiration for this levelheaded, agile-minded woman. He was also comforted by the knowledge that no matter how dire the straits, he was fortunate indeed to have landed in the company of such a capable if understandably reluctant companion. It didn't matter that her concern for him stemmed from the fact that his plight directly affected hers.

No doubt about it—Caycee Hammond was indeed a unique specimen of womanhood. Sometime when he felt more like himself, he supposed he might just have to tell her so. Sometime when he wasn't so damned weary. Right now the notion of a mattress and pillow had never seemed so good. Or a hay-sweetened loft with a cushioning mound of straw. Or darkness, a dry camp, and a bedroll. Any spot except jail would do, if only he could close his eyes and rest a spell.

Of their own accord, his thoughts veered to Adam's final resting place, a grassy knoll beneath an ancient Georgia pine. To his mother's tearstained cheeks, and his father's trembling hand as he read scriptures from the family Bible, shielding the pages against a fitful breeze that whipped them back and forth as if in protest of youth cut short.

Gaining strength of purpose from the mental picture, Zackary said, "I'll not go under without a fight." He had a score to settle. He couldn't rest. Not now. Not with his objective so close at hand. One more bank robbery, perhaps two and . . .

Zackary suddenly pulled the Morgan up short to glance at the sky. Caycee's gaze followed his.

"The weather's changing, and fast," he commented. "Hold on to your John B."

"My what?"

"Your Stetson."

"Oh." She'd never heard the hat called by that name before.

"Missouri's famous for this. Not like Georgia."

Not like anything she'd ever seen, Caycee thought. The sky seemed peculiar—yellowish gray and ominous. The air felt clammy against her skin. The wind had stilled to a dead calm and the birds, so raucous earlier when startled, had quieted in the trees as if steeling themselves against something.

Caycee glanced up at the sky and shuddered.

Now wait a minute. Somewhere in the back of her mind she knew what these signs meant. But what? Could it be something she'd learned on a movie set? Something she'd seen on television? Something to do with . . .

It suddenly hit her full force. She'd witnessed a violent storm system on the National Weather Channel. She'd never experienced one firsthand. Until now.

Scenes from *The Wizard Of Oz* flashed through her mind. What had Dorothy done when locked out of the root cellar? Dashed into the Kansas farmhouse? Well, she didn't have a root cellar or a farmhouse to use for shelter, Caycee thought.

On television they advised you to get out of the car and scramble into a ditch.

Or, when unable to move to a proper shelter, to take refuge in a closet, or the bathroom where the pipes blocked projectiles from penetrating the walls.

Both seemed good advice; they were utterly useless in her case.

"I'm not going to like this!" Caycee said, struggling to hold the alarmed horse steady as the wind suddenly picked up again.

"Don't know anyone who does," Zackary commented.

"Jeez! I'm not sure what we're supposed

to do. None of the options I know about apply here." She gasped as a funnel that reminded Caycee of an elephant's snaking trunk emerged from the low-hanging clouds.

It seemed to take Zackary a moment to collect his thoughts. When he did answer, his words sounded slurred. She glanced over her shoulder. She didn't need to be an M.D. to ascertain that his condition was deteriorating.

Great! The last thing she wanted was a body on her hands. Or to become a body on someone else's hands.

"Zackary?" Caycee prompted, tasting the grit the wind kicked between her teeth.

"There's a . . . an abandoned mine about a quarter-mile eastward. If we can make it there before we get caught up in—"

"East!" Fighting panic, Caycee pivoted first right, then left in the saddle. Given the option, she intended to get them both out of this alive. "Which way is east?"

Again Zackary hesitated, eventually muttering something unintelligible.

Caycee glanced toward the twister, gobbling up trees where it touched the ground as it churned in an unwavering path toward them.

"Come on, man!" She nudged Zackary gently yet firmly in the ribs with her elbow.

"We've got less than a Chinaman's chance unless you speak up. Which way is east?"

He pointed without answering, motioning for her to follow the Missouri downriver. It was enough for Caycee. She sank her heels into the Morgan's side, thankfully racing with the wildly howling wind rather than against it.

They reached the coal mine by sheer miracle. At least, it seemed that way to Caycee as she rode the Morgan through the vine-tasseled entrance into the timbered chamber's semidarkness. She tumbled out of the saddle and dropped the reins. The Morgan lowered its head and remained motionless as if thankful for the respite.

"Can you dismount without my help?" Caycee asked when Zackary failed to follow her lead.

He studied her impassively for a moment, then cast her a wan smile. "As much as I hate to admit it, I fear that's beyond me . . . at the moment. So, if it wouldn't be too much trouble—"

Caycee suspected that Zackary rarely asked anything of other human beings. That he was predominantly self-sufficient, emotionally reserved, and self-contained was evident. She also sensed that his pride smarted. He didn't want to ask for her assistance, yet he had no viable alternative.

Perhaps they had more in common than she'd once imagined, Caycee thought as she struggled to assist Zackary. He placed a hand on her shoulder and swung both legs to one side of the saddle, tucking her against him in a rough hug that tipped her Stetson from her head as he slid against her.

Funny, she hadn't realized he was so tall, Caycee mused, anticipating her immediate release as his feet touched solid ground. If anything, the hug intensified, transforming into a full-fledged embrace. His hard body cushioned itself against her softer one. Her cheek pressed into the smooth buttons studding his shirtfront. His breath faintly fanned her hair.

Caycee's stomach fluttered in a not-altogether-unpleasant manner.

Startled, she disengaged his hands from her waist and abruptly stepped back, realizing too late that she was the only thing holding Zackary erect. With an almost inaudible sigh his pain-shadowed eyes closed and he sagged to one knee, then slumped forward to sprawl face-first against the coal-dusted earth.

"Mr. Butler?" Caycee asked, wincing.

"Get the lead out," he slurred.

Caycee frowned. Get the lead out—what did he mean by that? She went automatically into her troubleshooting mode. Lead in gasoline. Lead in paint. Lead? What lead?

At a loss, Caycee prompted, "Mr. Butler?"

He didn't reply.

She tried again, and received no response.

As if it might help to rouse him, she touched his muscular thigh with the pointed toe of her boot and used his given name.

"Zackary?"

It was suddenly glaringly apparent he couldn't hear her.

Hoping he hadn't broken his nose, Caycee hastily squatted, grabbed a fistful of broadcloth, and tugged. He didn't budge.

"Honestly," she exclaimed. She didn't want to hurt Zackary, but she couldn't leave him unconscious and in such an awkward position, could she? With his coat twisted and his arm caught beneath his already abused chest? Besides, she must ascertain whether he was unconscious or—

No, she couldn't think about the alternative right now, she advised herself. It would hamper her ability to think coherently and perform appropriately.

Sinking her fingers more deeply into the fabric, Caycee rocked back on her heels and, using her 120 pounds for leverage against

Zackary's superior body weight, rolled him over on his back. His eyes remained closed, his chest still.

"I don't believe this; he can't be dead!" Caycee exclaimed. Her words echoed eerily against the slate walls of the mining chamber and she realized she'd voiced her anxieties aloud.

A nurse on a movie set had once stated to her that talking to yourself didn't mean you were crazy. It meant only that you had a lot going on in your life. At the time, she'd wondered about the comment's validity. She didn't now—it made perfect sense considering the predicament she now found herself in.

Caycee swallowed and hesitantly placed an ear against Zackary's sternum before she lost her courage.

The steady *ker-thump* of his heart sounded sweeter than any music she could call to mind, issuing her a meager measure of the comfort she sought. She rose slowly, running her hands up and down her arms. A pained expression marred her clear complexion as she gazed down at Zackary.

The 64-thousand-dollar question—what to do at this stage of the game?

She was by no means a paramedic, but Caycee had worked on enough emergency-oriented television shows when she first joined the business to know that loss of blood sometimes sent victims into shock. And that trauma victims should be kept warm.

Could Zackary be going into shock? Quite probably.

Caycee stripped out of her duster, rolled it into a makeshift pillow, and positioned it beneath his head. Then she turned to the Morgan, untied Zackary's bedroll from the saddle, and covered him from chest to toe with the woolen blanket. She unsaddled the Morgan. Then she lowered herself, back against the wall, into a lotus position to stare at Zackary's prone body and think.

She thought about the whirling dervish kicking up its heels outside. She considered her fantastically precarious position. And she studied Zackary Butler's scraped yet handsome face, pondering the measures she might be forced to incorporate to save his life.

She thought until her head hurt, until the weather cleared, and his rattling breathing told her in no uncertain terms that Zackary's condition had considerably worsened.

Caycee stood, flexing the kinks from her legs while acknowledging that the time for affirmative action had arrived. In her professional career, all the things that could go wrong were figured in advance. Efforts were made to surmount any problems before they happened. And if things *did* go haywire, backup men were available to instantly provide expert assistance. This was an entirely different scenario. Either she reacted positively and promptly with only her limited medical experience and instinct to guide her, or she figured out how to scratch out a man-size grave in the earth with her bare hands, because she'd finally figured out what he meant by "Get the lead out."

Chapter Four

Caycee couldn't say exactly what she wanted at this point. But she knew what she didn't want—she didn't want Zackary Reece Butler to die from lead poisoning. He was her only link to the twentieth century and a father who depended on her for emotional support. The people in her time didn't know how good they had it. In an emergency situation, they simply shifted the responsibility to 911, Caycee thought, noting the sounds of the birds trilling in the trees outside the mine.

She was a stunt double, not a surgeon!

The tornado had passed and thanks to Zackary they remained unscathed. But she felt cold, lost, and inadequate for the first time in her life.

Caycee moved to stare beyond the mine's entrance. The air smelled invigorating—of recent rain and tousled honeysuckle blossoms—yet the landscape had suffered. A path of uprooted and splintered trees scarred the forest, changing the look of the densely wooded area. She was suddenly turned around and hopelessly lost in the Midwestern wilderness. She also realized she held her teeth clenched.

Caycee relaxed her jaw. Her cheeks felt like stone. She worked her lips back and forth until her expression softened. Hands on her hips, she rolled her head on her neck to relax the tension in her shoulders.

Decisive action was needed, action only she could supply.

Fortified with those thoughts, Caycee struck out toward the downed trees to retrieve an armload of firewood. She returned to the mine with it and deposited the wood near Zackary's feet. She'd been careful to select cured branches rather than green, and she had flames cheerfully lapping at the wood in no time thanks to a pack of red-tipped book matches she'd filched from a twentieth-century restaurant where she had shared lunch with the director and crew the day before. After rummaging through Zackary's saddlebags and finding a currycomb and brush, a nose bag for oats, a lariat, and a tin plate and cup, but nothing adequate to the job at hand, she was also thankful her father had taught her the value of a pocketknife.

She dipped into her pocket and extracted her Swiss Army knife. She'd carried the instrument for as long as she could remember, she thought, rejecting the tweezers, toothpick, and scissors to peel out one of the stainless steel blades.

Caycee hunkered down and toasted the blade in the fire. Then, before she lost her nerve, she carefully untucked the long-tailed linen shirt from Zackary's pants and, bunching the cloth in an attempt to cause as little discomfort as possible, peeled away the material encircling his wound. With profound determination, she inched the blade toward the hole.

The moment the blade touched his flesh, Zackary moaned and reached for her hand. "Merry hell!" he rasped, squeezing her fingers in a surprisingly strong grip.

Did he intend to fight her? She hadn't expected that. After all, he had been the one to apprise her of the necessity of getting the lead out.

Unnerved, Caycee brushed his hand aside. Though his eyes remained closed, he persisted, capturing her hand again and entwining his fingers with hers, squeezing reassuringly.

"I wish I had a long nine," he said, his voice barely above a whisper.

"A what?" Caycee asked, noting the bruises darkening his beard-shadowed cheek—bruises she suspected he'd acquired in the streets of Westport when he'd tumbled from his horse.

"A panatela cigar."

"Oh. I'm sorry, but I don't have anything like that on me at the moment."

"I didn't expect you to . . . only wishing aloud."

"Yeah. I know what you mean," Caycee responded.

He sighed. "Go ahead. Do what you must."

Caycee swallowed. "I intend to."

"Good girl."

Zackary disengaged his fingers from Caycee's, angled his arms, and slipped his hands beneath his lower back. His lips were compressed, his eyes fluttered closed, and his dusky lashes fanned his pale cheeks.

Caycee couldn't help but admire his stoicism. She thought of the dramatic scenes in the cowboy movies in which the hero pushed the arrow through his body, broke off the head, and pulled out the shaft. She'd always considered it hooey—before now. If worse came to worst and there were no other alternatives, she sensed Zackary could and would do something similar.

Only he didn't need to. Not this time. Not while she was around.

Caycee expelled a breath she hadn't realized she'd been holding and forced herself to relax. It suddenly dawned on her that she felt the same way she did when positioning for a "suicide" fall. Though she'd done more of them recently because they meant easy money, she'd never cared for high dives from rooftops—she wasn't a bird. The sensation of leaning back and extending her legs straight out so she'd land flat on her rear rather than hit the air bag feetfirst and break her legs, of hurtling away from the security of a building and free-falling out into space, always took her breath away. To heck with the thin steel cable secretly harnessed around her torso. Those had never kept anyone from slamming into the side of a building and buying the farm. Or taking early retirement, as her dad had been forced to do.

Each time she did a fall, she told herself she wouldn't contract for that particular stunt again. Yet each time the offer came her way, she accepted the job.

She supposed that was what made her

a daredevil. She supposed it was a good thing for Zackary Butler she was one. Otherwise . . .

Caycee's thoughts returned to the job at hand. She couldn't afford to lose Zackary.

The handle of the knife felt slippery to the touch and Caycee acknowledged that her hands were perspiring. She wanted to wash them and couldn't. She made do by rubbing them on her corduroys and proceeding.

When it was all over, it surprised her how easily the lead was extracted. No fuss. No muss. Little bleeding. Regardless, it was an experience Caycee hoped never to duplicate. She was sure the sensation of Zackary's body going rigid beneath her ministrations, the sight his contorted grimace, the sound of his grinding teeth as he endured the pain would remain with her for weeks to come.

Afterward Zackary slept, much to her amazement. Caycee knew he slept, for he snored softly. She offered up a prayer of thanks.

The night hobbled past like an old man on crutches. Caycee watched the sun set, wakeful and concerned by the sounds of the wild and worrying all the while that there were no professional handlers around to control the coyotes and mountain lions she imagined stalking in the shadows just beyond the mine's entrance. She'd read recently that a jogger in California had been killed by a hungry mountain lion bent on feeding her cubs.

Caycee exchanged her pocketknife for the gun from Zackary's left-handed leather holster and set up a night watch. By dawn her eyes felt puffy, her skin chilled, and her stomach grumbly. Her mouth watered and she longed for the comfort of her favorite breakfast—a deviled-egg sandwich on white toast, peanut-butter-slathered graham crackers, and a glass of ice-cold milk to wash it all down.

But hunger seemed a mild concern when she faced the knowledge that she must find more accommodating shelter if Zackary was to survive his wound.

Caycee turned toward the Morgan. He represented their only transportation. In her day, one took care of one's car—polished it, checked the fluids and the tires, topped the tank. She'd better take equivalent measures for the horse.

Keeping in mind she must make it last, she fashioned a cup with her hand and poured a ration of water from the canteen into her palm to quench his thirst. Then, with the gun tucked in her belt, she encircled the Morgan's neck with the lariat and led him around the fallen trees to a sunlight-pooled spot from which she could watch the mine's vine-tasseled entrance. Careful of snakes, she waded into the three-foot-high star grass and allowed the horse to graze on the succulent perennials. She realized she could have used the picket she discovered in Zackary's saddle-bags to stake the horse out, but she was concerned about losing him. Besides, the sun felt good on her shoulders, the air was fresh with morning dew, the wild turtle doves were cooing pleasantly in the trees, and she needed space and time to think.

By the time the horse had eaten his fill, Caycee had considered and rejected several game plans. Finally, she decided that she couldn't think her way out of the situation alone—she hadn't the knowledge needed to do so. Her only recourse was to once again solicit Zackary Butler's advice.

Still conscious of predators, she led the Morgan back into the mine. Zackary was no longer sprawled near the ashes of the extinguished fire. He was propped up in a sitting position with his back to one of the mine's rocky walls.

"Figured you'd left me," he admitted frankly.

Caycee pursed her lips, pointedly eyeing the saddle. "You figured wrong. If I'd planned to leave you behind, I would have taken that with me."

A hint of a smile softened his lips. "I suppose you would have taken the hull at that."

Caycee could only surmise *hull* was slang for saddle. "You can count on it. I'm for anything that makes life easier."

He studied her for a long moment. "Is that why you walked into the bank when you did? Hoped to make life a little easier for yourself?"

Caycee avoided the question. "If that was the reasoning behind my appearance, I sure got fooled, didn't I?"

"Sure did," he agreed.

Caycee watched as, with a grimace, he shifted and dipped into the pocket of his single-breasted sack coat to extract a watch sporting a hinged metal hunting case, attached to a chain with a fob charm and a funny-looking key dangling from it. He inserted the key in a slot at the base of the watch, explaining as he did so, "My brother gave me this watch in sixty-seven. Got it from the National Watch Company. Has an eight-day movement. Needs winding on Sundays. The anvil fob charm is supposed to bring good luck." He paused thoughtfully before continuing. "If I don't make it, I'd appreciate it if you see that my kin get the watch. My parents live in Savannah, Georgia," he added quietly. "East State Street. The house overlooks Columbia Square."

Caycee realized three things immediately—that his Southern heritage accounted for the hint of an accent, that it must be Sunday, and that Zackary's dazzling eyes were clouded with fever.

Caycee frowned. Her father had tried to do this to her. After his fall from the skittish studio horse, he'd learned that if he survived, he would be paralyzed for life from the waist down. He'd wanted to give up, but she hadn't allowed her father to wimp out on her then; she certainly didn't plan to give her ticket home the option.

"Don't plan on me winding your watch for you on Sundays. I don't like traveling in the Southern states. And I've never cared for playing the delivery boy," she said with considerable determination.

"I don't suppose anyone has ever accused you of being subtle," he commented.

"Not that I can recall," Caycee said solemnly. Those were almost the same words her father had used. And her ex-husband when she'd informed him their relationship wasn't working. And most of the people who knew her well. Giving up meant giving in and settling for less than life had to offer. She wasn't about to do that.

"Are you thirsty?" she asked.

"Parched."

She handed Zackary the canteen.

For the next several minutes silence reigned as Caycee busied herself with saddling the Morgan. When she once again turned her attention to Zackary, she realized he had been watching her.

"Time to hit the dusty trail . . . miles to go before we sleep," she quoted.

He rose on unsteady legs, using the wall as a crutch.

She could tell by his wince that the effort cost him. She found herself wincing in sympathetic response to his discomfort.

"Which way?" he rasped when he could once again get his breath.

Caycee cleared her throat. "That's what I was hoping you could tell me. I'm new at this."

"Green," he muttered.

"As green as grass, and aiding and abetting a known bank robber," Caycee said almost to herself as she adjusted his arm around her shoulder and assisted Zackary onto the Morgan.

He momentarily resisted her. "You could

stop it here and now . . . leave . . . head on up into the Ozarks. There are farms up there, cool valleys. You'll find the people more than sympathetic to our kind."

If she stayed long enough, would she become like him? Would she be his compatriot in crime, surviving hand-to-mouth by robbing banks, living on the edge, running from the law, always looking over her shoulder?

It was a grim proposition at best, but at the moment it seemed she had no choice. Time had cast her in the role. Only time could right her precarious situation.

"I'm not going anywhere. Not unless you plan to go with me," Caycee said, all the while wondering if Hoot Gibson, Yakima Canott, Tom Mix, or Bronco Billy Anderson, one-time rodeo riders and stuntmen who had topped wagons, made transfers from horses to trains, broken and ridden wild horses, and leapt from cliffs into swift-flowing water, would respect her daring . . . or frown and shake their heads at the risks she felt compelled to take. Then, following Zackary's suggestion, she pointed the horse in the direction of the distant mountains.

Chapter Five

There was no doubt she could pass for a boy now, Caycee thought as she finally stumbled across a winding country road, tired, dirty, hungry, and smelling of perspiration. It was the first sign of civilization she'd glimpsed in days. It gave her hope. People blazed country roads. People meant food and shelter. Perhaps a soft bed for her and hopefully some form of medical attention for her charge.

Once again, she turned to Zackary.

"Which way?" she asked.

He surveyed not the road, but the topography of the land, the bushes and trees, the horizon, and a cloud of dust snaking down the road in the distance.

Wheezing, he shook his head as if to clear

it. "I'm not sure. Feels as if a Chinaman's hammering railroad spikes inside my head. Can't seem to think straight."

"Does that cloud mean someone is heading this way?"

"Most likely."

"The posse?" Caycee asked anxiously. She wasn't sure Zackary could sit the Morgan much longer. He looked totally done in. Not only that, Caycee suspected he was developing something more. The cough worried her as much as the wound did. Did pneumonia cause a cough? She wasn't sure.

"A wagon, by the looks of it. Probably a farmer. Wait here. Ask him to give us a hand."

She had her doubts about the farmer giving them a hand. In her era, it was dangerous to ask a passing motorist for a ride. Hitchhikers were often suspect as well. Still, what choice did she have?

"Maybe you're right. Perhaps we should wait here." Caycee paused, then added, "How are you feeling?"

Taking a deep breath, Zackary passed his forearm across his damp brow. "Don't forget about the watch. Savannah. Remember."

She didn't intend to discuss his watch again. He wasn't going to die and that was that. She wasn't going to allow it because

82

she had no intention of being stuck in the past. As far as she was concerned, the idea of roughing it was far more pleasurable than the reality. She missed drive-through restaurants. She missed flushable toilets. She missed her battered old pickup truck. Her head hurt, her feet felt like clay, and her stomach was eating away at its own lining.

No—the last thing she intended to discuss right now was Zackary's pocket watch.

"We'll wait here," Caycee reiterated.

As the dust cloud streamed from upwind toward them, she noticed that borne on the same breeze was a not-so-pleasant and definitely unfamiliar aroma.

"What do you suppose that is?" she wondered aloud.

Zackary surprised her by answering, "Hogs."

Within minutes, a wagon rounded the bend and Caycee heard the oinks of a pair of crated animals. The wagon's driver proved to be an intimidating, bearlike man with a round face, sandy-blond hair, and a handlebar mustache.

Crossing her fingers, Caycee stepped out into the middle of the road and waved her arms to flag him down. "Whoa, mister. I need your help."

The man reined in the horses, pulling his

wagon to a standstill. Caycee noticed that he rested his hand on the butt of the weapon riding shotgun beside him.

"What goes on here?" he growled.

Caycee immediately categorized his accent as German. She almost laughed aloud. Fate definitely had a sense of humor, she decided. She was stuck in the middle of nowhere, dragging around a wounded outlaw like a peg leg, and forced to throw herself on the mercy of an armed German-American pig farmer. What next?

She hated to lie, but she didn't dare tell him the truth. Chances were he hadn't heard about the bank robbery in Westport, since television coverage was a thing of the future. She supposed newspaper circulation was as sluggish as maple syrup. Word of mouth would probably be even slower considering the sparsity of the population between towns. Postal or telegraph information was always a possibility, but perhaps this man hadn't visited either of those offices recently.

When it came right down to it, she'd just have to buck up and have at it no matter how much prevaricating grated on her nerves. She certainly couldn't afford to risk telling him the whole truth—anyone who heard it would think her nuts! Caycee decided.

"We're"—she glanced toward Zackary—

"cattlemen, ambushed by rustlers a day or so ago. My, uh, partner, needs medical attention. He's been shot. They took our herd."

"Only two of you . . . on a cattle drive?"

"So, okay, it was a small herd."

"I'm not sure I believe this story. You're not thinking that you're going to rob me, are you? Because I'm not carrying this rifle for nothing. I know how to use it." He patted the gun for emphasis.

Zackary began coughing again. Caycee turned her back on the farmer to gaze uneasily at him, slumped across the Morgan's neck like a crash dummy.

"Caycee," he gasped, "tell the man we aren't going to bother him. Ask him . . . if he can at least see his way clear . . . to giving us some water."

Caycee pivoted toward the farmer, promptly relaying Zackary's request. "Look, mister. We're not here to rob you, but we need help in the worst way." She hated the pleading note in her voice. She never pleaded with anyone, but this time she couldn't seem to help herself. "Have you got any water on that wagon?"

Caycee could tell by his squint that the man was sizing them up. She could also tell he didn't believe her story. She wouldn't have believed it either. Still, she sensed he was

willing to give them the benefit of the doubt.
She was assured of it when he tossed her
his canteen. At first she felt elated; almost
immediately her hopes were dashed, however. She could tell by the sloshing of the
water within the canteen that it was nearly
empty.

Caycee administered a swallow to Zackary,
getting more water on him than in him.
Smelling water, the Morgan stretched his
neck around. She pushed his head away, feeling guilty that she couldn't share the water
with him and wondering what she would
do when the plucky animal finally gave out
altogether. Would she be forced to add horse-
thieving to her lengthening resume of crime?

After taking a sip from the canteen herself,
Caycee returned the container to its owner.

"Hope you don't have too much farther to
go. We didn't leave you much," she commented.

Unsure of what course to follow now,
Caycee had an overwhelming desire to sit
down in the middle of the road and cry.
Zackary was obviously in no fit shape to go
on. His skin burned with fever, probably due
to the haphazard surgery she'd performed
on him.

She'd once toured Europe with her univer-
sity gymnastics team. It was a pity this adven-

ture didn't come with a similarly detailed travelers' guide, she thought.

Making up her mind that there was only one course left for her to pursue, Caycee asked, "Would you mind pointing me in the direction of the nearest town?"

Zackary groaned aloud, an unmistakable "No."

Caycee's attention swung toward him, then back to the farmer.

"I . . . he despises city life," she said into the silent void that had descended around them, thinking how much her statement sounded like a line from the theme song for *Green Acres*.

"I can't say that I blame him. I've never cared much for the crush of a town myself. Give me some land and some good hogs and I'm fairly well pleased."

As if he'd come to an abrupt decision, the farmer levered his ample physique from the wagon. The closer he advanced, the more pronounced his squint became. Caycee realized belatedly that the farmer probably suffered from farsightedness.

"Well, for whatever reason you're out here, boy, I don't reckon I can leave a body in such a fix. Wouldn't be Christian."

Astonished by the sudden turn of events, Caycee stuttered, "I really appreciate this."

She glanced toward Zackary again. "Is your place far from here?"

"Just over the next rise. Probably make it easier on him if he rode in the wagon."

"I'm sure it would."

"You look done in. I'll help you get him down off that horse, son," he offered.

The farmer lifted Zackary from the Morgan, practically carrying him to the back of the wagon.

"Hogs," Zackary grumbled as he crawled in between the crated animals.

"Fine hogs," the farmer agreed cheerfully. He tied the Morgan to the back of the wagon, placed the rifle under the seat, and motioned for Caycee to join him.

"By the way, my name is Klaus Becker. What's yours?"

"Caycee Hammond."

He motioned over his shoulder with his thumb. "And his?"

Caycee had a vision of wanted posters with the name Zackary Reece Butler printed in towering black letters tacked to every tree for miles around.

"Mel Gibson," she said as she slipped gratefully into the proffered seat.

Caycee had to admit as Klaus hauled Zackary from the wagon and threw him over his shoulder like a sack of potatoes that the Becker farm was nicer than she'd expected. The cedar-roofed log house rose in two squat stories with a rubble chimney on one side and a corncrib on the other. A woodshed stood near the kitchen door and behind the cabin was a smokehouse where Klaus proudly pointed out he had pork curing in the smoke of a slow-burning fire.

"I raise chickens too," he commented as he strode through a flock of poultry to reach the house. Caycee hesitated. One of the roosters, a huge red one, thought nothing of running at Klaus, crowing, and pecking at his boot.

Klaus motioned her on, commenting, "Come on, son. Don't mind him. He likes playing kingfish. Make soup out of him one day for sure." Caycee nodded, outracing the disgruntled rooster to the porch.

Once inside, she trailed Klaus through a maze of hand-hewn furniture and up a narrow corner staircase to a loft above the living quarters. Klaus dumped Zackary unceremoniously on a quilt-draped mattress that covered three-fourths of the floor space.

"Mel is probably too heavy for you to maneuver."

. "Who . . . ? Oh, yeah, I'm sure he is," Caycee said. She'd nearly forgotten Zackary now had an alias, thanks to her.

"Why don't you go down and care for the animals and I'll see that he's stripped and bedded down properly," Klaus offered. "The barn is behind the smokehouse," he said, wrestling Zackary out of his coat amid muffled protests that did no more to defer Klaus than a small child's complaints would stop its parent.

"What's he saying?" Caycee asked.

"I'm not sure. Something about an eye that never sleeps," Klaus responded.

Caycee frowned. Though it sounded like a vision from a nightmare, the phrase rang a bell, if only she could remember where she'd heard it before.

Zackary groaned and all other thoughts save concern for her charge fled her mind. "He's not going to make it, is he?" Caycee said hollowly, suddenly fearful that despite the supreme power of her will, Zackary's life might slip through her fingers and she'd be trapped in the past forever.

His squint highly pronounced, Klaus eyed Zackary critically.

"Can't say for sure, but we'll do our best for him."

"How about a doctor?" Caycee suggested.

"There's no doctor for fifty miles or more and it will be dark soon."

"Oh," Caycee said, unable to keep the anxiety from her voice. In her world, one took streetlights and doctors for granted.

"But I've got some sulfur salve to go on that gunshot. And a potent herb remedy to bring down his fever and curb that cough. You'll see," Klaus said hurriedly, blocking Zackary from her view with his body. "He'll be as right as rain in no time. Now run along, see to the animals . . . and while you're at it, you'll find a mounded pit to the right of the barn. Get a pitchfork and dig around until you stir up a head of cabbage and some turnips. Later, I'll put them on for supper."

Grateful to turn Zackary over to Klaus, if only temporarily, Caycee did an abrupt about-face as his shirt joined his jacket on the foot of the mattress. Why hadn't she realized how muscular Zackary was? she wondered. Or how baby-fine sable hair patterned his chest, tapering down to his belly button to disappear beneath the waistband of his pants?

Not about to wait for his pants to join the growing stack of clothing, she scurried down the stairs and out into the hickory-scented air of the yard.

She returned 30 minutes later tired, yet triumphant, a bunch of turnips in one hand and a cabbage in the other.

Klaus was already bending by the hearth, filling a stew pot with water dipped from a nearby bucket.

"I've wrapped his wound, slipped him into my spare pair of unmentionables, and dosed him. He's settled in comfortably, if you'd like to go up now. I'll call you when supper is ready," he offered.

"I appreciate everything you're doing for us," Caycee said, thinking how unusual it sounded to be lumping herself with Zackary as if they belonged together. Which they didn't.

"No more than I'd do for anyone in your situation."

"Is there anything I can do to help?" Caycee offered, thinking, If only he knew how precarious my position really is.

Klaus frowned. "Naw. Goin' to add some potatoes and sweet corn to the pot. Slice some corn bread."

He retrieved a jar of pickles from the shelf, blew the dust off the top, and offered it to her. "Can do one thing for me, though."

"What's that?" Caycee asked, accepting the jar.

"Broke my glasses a few weeks back. Storekeeper in town wouldn't take the hogs in exchange for a new pair and I can't see worth a hoot without them," he said sheepishly.

"Read that label. Tell me the date marked on the jar."

"All right," Caycee commented, realizing the reason Klaus thought her a boy was because he couldn't see well enough to tell the difference. At least *some* things were running in her favor. Thank goodness.

Caycee raised her eyebrows as she read aloud, "Watermelon pickles. Spring 1871."

Her mind reeled. 1871! Who would believe it?

"I thought I put those up last year about this time. They should still be good. We'll have a jar with our supper as well."

She didn't want to be stuck in 1872. She wanted to go home. Now.

Concern for Zackary prompted Caycee to stutter, "I don't mean to make trouble for you, but I don't think, uh, Mel will be able to eat—I mean, that sounds great to me, but I doubt Mel will—"

Klaus nodded, interrupting her. "I understand and you're probably right."

He shuffled to the front door and out onto the porch. Caycee heard a commotion punctuated by squawking protests. Afterward, Klaus returned with a limp red rooster dangling by the neck from his huge hand.

"Said I'd finish him off one day. Besides,

Mel will probably do more justice to a bowl of chicken soup."

Caycee swallowed, unable to redirect her gaze from the rooster.

"Hey, you're looking pale."

Positive Klaus's observation was correct, Caycee wondered why it was so much easier to envision eating a chicken wrapped in cellophane and purchased from a grocery meat counter than the one held in her host's hand. Did grocery stores desensitize people to the harsh realities of life and death?

On the tail of that thought came another. Would Zackary survive?

Klaus turned toward the hearth, then back to her. Placing the jar of watermelon pickles on the table beside the unplucked chicken, he said quietly, "Seems I have something for you."

He dug into the bib of his overalls and extracted a folded piece of paper, pressing it into Caycee's hand. "This fell out of Mel's pocket."

Caycee unfolded the paper, realizing immediately it was a hand-drawn map, detailed in Spanish. She wondered if it was the directions to the rendezvous point. Torn by visions of leaving Zackary behind and striking out on her own, she jammed the map into the pocket of her corduroys.

Klaus shuffled around a moment, then extracted something else from his bib. "I found this too. Wrapped in the map. I thought hard about keeping it, but . . ." He placed the rectangular slip of paper on the table. It took Caycee only a moment to recognize it as a 50-dollar bill.

She picked up the money and turned it over and over to study the date and picture. Then, touched by his honesty, she pressed it back into Klaus's hand.

"You keep it . . . for all your trouble."

"I can't take this," he stammered. "I mean, I almost did, but I can't."

"You can and you will. I insist. Think of the things you can buy with that," she said.

"*Ja* . . . more hogs," he said. His eyes twinkled.

"And another rooster to replace that one." She pointed to the table.

"A more agreeable one, for sure," he said.

"And a new pair of glasses," Caycee added.

He grinned. "That too." He paused. "I don't know what to say."

Caycee smiled. "My mother always said thank you was enough. Say thank you, Klaus."

His face turned bright red. "Thank you," he said as he placed the bill in a tin can on the shelf next to a jar of pickled eggs.

Caycee entertained a fleeting notion that he should have placed the money in the bank. Then, reminded of Zackary, she reconsidered. Perhaps a tin can was as good as any bank—at least, with outlaws like Zackary running around loose.

"Now what?" Caycee wondered aloud.

"All things considered, I think the best thing you can do for now is get a little rest yourself, keep an eye on Mel . . . see he doesn't roll off the mattress and fall from the loft," Klaus said, concentrating on decapitating the turnips.

Fearing the chicken beheading came next, Caycee nodded, clambering up the stairs.

Too weak to do more than crawl into the back of the farmer's wagon, Zackary had thanked his lucky stars for Caycee. Frustrated by his inability to operate under his own steam, he'd found himself impressed with her capacity for compassion, her innate courage, and her ingenuity. Now, he was entertaining second thoughts.

"There's a fifty-dollar bill missing from my pants pocket," he said.

"I expected to find you unconscious," she responded.

Caycee's image undulated. Zackary blinked several times to clear his eyes. "Did you?"

"Yes. That you aren't is a pleasant surprise."

Not to be swayed, he persisted, "Do you know anything about the money, Caycee?"

"I gave it to Klaus."

Zackary scowled weakly. "Have you been eating loco weed? Fifty dollars is more than a top ranch hand makes in a month."

"Is it?"

Though he could hardly credit it, she seemed genuinely surprised by his comment.

"Don't play coy with me, Caycee," he warned.

"I'm not."

Again, she seemed sincere. It must be his befuddled perception, Zackary decided.

"You are . . . and don't try to cloud the issue either. Why did you give Klaus the bill?"

He watched her inhale deeply, watched the rise and fall of her chest. As she moistened her lips with the tip of her tongue, he wondered how he'd gotten tangled up with a woman like Caycee Hammond.

"Because, as far as I know, you weren't carrying anything larger."

If he hadn't been so weak, he would have laughed aloud.

"Thank the Lord. Are you always so generous?"

97

She frowned, her expression thoughtful. "When the situation warrants it. I've always prided myself on being fair."

"Fair? You went through my pockets," he said solemnly.

"I didn't roll you, if that's what you're saying. I don't do things like that," she responded just as solemnly.

Attempting to concentrate on what she was saying made his head hurt worse than it already did. "Roll me? What do you mean?" he asked despite himself.

She hooked a thumb into the waistband of her corduroys before answering.

"I mean that I didn't go through your pockets. The money fell out when Klaus undressed you. I didn't see it. I wouldn't have known the difference if he'd kept the fifty without ever saying a word. He didn't. You don't run across that sort of honesty everyday. I simply couldn't see letting it pass without offering him some sort of reward."

Flabbergasted by Caycee's audacity, Zackary exclaimed, "Most people have to die and go to heaven to earn that much money at one time."

In a voice as smooth as sipping whiskey, she asked, "Is that why you rob banks?"

Zackary cut her a glance that would have

cowed a lesser person. "Makes sense, doesn't it?"

He wasn't surprised when Caycee stood her ground.

"Don't be such a skinflint. There's more money where that came from. Besides which, if Klaus hadn't taken us in you'd probably be collecting your fifty right now the hard way."

"It's a traditional part of Western hospitality for farmers to offer food and lodging to traveling strangers. They don't expect payment," Zackary argued.

"Honestly, have you no heart! The man doesn't live in a mansion. He owns one change of, and I quote, unmentionables and he gave them to you without batting an eyelash."

Zackary frowned, giving the long johns covering his body a cursory once-over. The legs bunched in a wad at his ankles, the seat fell almost to his knees, and he'd folded the sleeves in rolls over his elbows to keep them from covering his hands. "They're two sizes too big."

Zackary watched a reluctant smile tug at the corners of Caycee's lips. She mastered it after a moment, saying quickly, "That's irrelevant. The point is that we were in desperate straits until two hours ago. Klaus took us in, gave the long johns to you knowing he'd be without a change of clothing, and killed one of his roosters to make soup when I mentioned I probably wouldn't be able to get anything else of nutritional value down your throat!"

"Soup?"

"Yes. Soup. Chicken soup. Soup you'll be eating when he's finished preparing it. What was I supposed to give Klaus in return for his kindness? I don't have a dime to my name!"

Sometimes she used the strangest terms. They cropped up when he least expected them. Usually when she was excited about something. Her unique vocabulary intrigued him and for once he singled out a phrase to question her about, hoping to catch her off guard and perhaps learn more concerning her background than she had yet offered him.

"What do you mean by nutritional value?"

For a moment she looked perplexed. But, as he'd come to expect in the short time he'd known her, she rallied almost immediately.

"Food, Zackary. Life-restoring food with vitamins and minerals and stuff like that. And don't try to get me off track. I know I did the right thing by giving Klaus the money, regardless of how it might look to you. The man needs glasses—"

Lowering his voice, Zackary interrupted her. "Lucky for you he thinks you're a boy."

Caycee threw up her hands, hissing in a hushed voice, "Lucky for me? Lucky for both of us, you mean. I can't imagine what he would think . . . what he might do if . . . how I would handle . . . well, I just can't. The explanation is too bizarre for words."

He couldn't stop himself from asking, "Is it, Caycee?"

"Yes," she said quietly, unhooking her thumb to dig the map from her pocket. She tossed the map on the mattress beside him. "Like Klaus, I thought about keeping this and using it myself, but decided against it. The Morgan is exhausted. And my appearance at the rendezvous point without you would have been difficult to explain to Dingus. Besides which, I can't read Spanish."

She seemed suddenly so small and frail, so feminine with her cheeks flushed in exasperation and her lips slanted in a disgruntled and yet unconsciously provocative pout.

Suddenly discomfited, Zackary unsuccessfully grappled with his pillow. Caycee seemed to intuitively know what he sought.

"Here, let me," she said. She took the feather pillow from his hands, punched it up, and gently eased it behind his head.

Yes, he had a heart, buried somewhere

deep inside his chest. And a conscience he tried more often than not to ignore. Merry hell! He must remember Adam; he had a job to do.

But since Caycee had dived headfirst into his life, both his conscience and his heart were letting him know in no uncertain terms that they did indeed exist. He couldn't afford them, or her, or this, and yet he found himself saying, "So be it. Fifty it is."

"Thank you, Zackary," she said softly, her gaze locking with his.

Zackary unconsciously sucked in his breath. "You're welcome," he muttered gruffly, adding, "According to what I overheard you telling Klaus, I guess it's safe to assume that I'm going by the name of Mel Gibson while we're here."

"Yeah. Looks like we're both in the same boat—hiding our identities and all."

"Looks like."

Though he hadn't figured out the motivation behind it, he understood why Caycee would want to pass for a man in a world where women were limited to the roles of wives, prostitutes, or downtrodden spinsters. What he didn't understand was why she affected him the way she did. He harbored an unsettling need that gnawed at his insides, a need he blatantly refused to put a name to.

Zackary dropped his gaze abruptly to Caycee's hands, thinking safety resided in studying them rather than her face. He noted that she wore no jewelry. That her fingers were long and tapered, her nails short, her knuckles small and unobtrusive, her wrists delicate.

The hands of a lady, he found himself thinking. A lady whose touch he'd felt when—

He chopped off the thought. Caycee wasn't the one that was loco. He was! Dingus and the remainder of the outlaw gang were waiting on him at the Gonzales place 300 miles from Liberty, Missouri; he was committed to finishing the job he'd started. There could be no ifs, ands, or buts about it. Caycee had no place in his life—none whatsoever. He'd best keep that in mind. His life, and hers, depended on it. God forbid! The last thing he wanted was to be forced to carry out Dingus's orders and put a bullet through Caycee Hammond's brain.

Best put her out of his mind, he thought, closing his eyes against her.

Best get well as quick as possible and be on his way.

Best figure out how he was going to duck out and leave Caycee behind.

Chapter Six

"How are you feeling today?"

Caycee stood at the foot of the mattress, a plate of crisp bacon, eggs sunny-side up, and a slice of bread balanced in one hand, a mug of black coffee clutched in the other.

"Hungry."

As crazy as it sounded, they had managed to establish a repartee he found acutely satisfying. They still didn't completely trust one another, and yet they didn't exactly distrust each other either.

A slow grin curved her lips. "So what's new?"

Zackary sat up, accepting the plate and mug she handed him and nodding appreciatively.

"Perhaps you were right in offering Klaus the money after all," he commented.

Her grin broadened into a perfect-toothed smile, enhancing a set of dimples on either side of her expressive mouth.

"Don't tell me you still have your doubts."

Zackary had spent much of the last week flat on his back, observing Caycee in action. He had learned that it was impossible for her to be casual about anything and that she maintained a serious expression 95 percent of the time. To pass the day, he'd quickly made a game out of making her smile. He'd gotten pretty good at it too.

He'd learned that she possessed a high level of concentration, even in the most difficult circumstances, and that she invariably looked people dead in the eye when she spoke to them. Known by the members of the outlaw gang for his unwavering stare, he was surprised how often he was the first to avert his gaze from her hazel perusal.

She was sometimes sharp-tongued, often pushy, and yet she possessed the ability to take instruction. She'd proven that early on. Spending seven days in her company had only reinforced his first impressions.

He'd also discovered something about her he hadn't expected. Despite her prickly exterior, she had a soft and gentle touch. When Klaus had nicked him with a straight razor while shaving him, Caycee had firmly steered the German to less tedious duties and competently completed the job herself. Now, after days of soul-searching, he could finally admit to himself that Caycee's intimate care of him that morning had stirred something deep within him. Something blessedly dormant since his younger brother's funeral.

Caycee would make some man a damned good partner—if he were looking for one. Which he wasn't, Zackary sternly reminded himself.

"No doubts about the money," he said, focusing his attention on his breakfast.

"I figured you'd come around eventually," she said.

Zackary stabbed at the eggs with his fork to break the yolks. Then, tearing the bread into pieces, he soaked it in the warm yellow liquid puddling on the plate.

Caycee muttered something nearly inaudible. Zackary glanced up.

"Will you join me?" he asked.

She paled, wrinkling her nose. "Uh . . . no thanks. I've already had my breakfast. Besides, I prefer my eggs hard-cooked."

"Best way I know of to ruin a good egg," he said between bites.

"I don't like the idea of ingesting salmonella incubators."

His fork stilled. The woman constantly used terms he'd never heard before.

"What?"

As if she'd said something she wished she hadn't, she responded hastily, "That's what my father calls eggs that are prepared sunnyside up—salmonella incubators."

Caycee rarely mentioned her family. His interest piqued, Zackary sat up a little straighter.

"He does, huh?" he asked.

He found himself oddly disappointed when, rather than continuing in the same vein, Caycee effectively shut him out by observing absently, "The hawthorns are in bloom."

She moved to stand at the side of the bed with her back to him, staring beyond the open window, out across the hedges and beyond toward the greening wheat fields.

"It's mid-April and high time for that, I suppose," he responded. He polished off his breakfast. Washing it down with a swig of hot coffee, he set the plate and mug aside.

"April . . . how time flies," she commented.

He understood what she meant. She felt restless; so did he. He'd passed the time drifting in and out of health-restoring sleep, with Caycee almost constantly by his side. She'd amazed him; he'd never awakened when she wasn't within calling distance. She was always there, reassuring him he was getting better, encouraging him to eat, speaking soothing words to him as if she genuinely cared.

"Do they have a fragrance?" she asked, turning toward him. A distant expression clouded her eyes. It was as if she'd been gazing beyond the immediate toward something beyond the fields. Something the normal eye couldn't see. Something that he could only guess at.

"What?" he asked.

"The hawthorns."

He couldn't keep his mind on what Caycee was saying for thinking of the way she smelled. He inhaled appreciatively. He could tell by the faint aroma of soap and her dampened tendrils that she'd recently bathed in the creek that, according to Klaus, ran the length of his property. The bath only enhanced the feminine scent of her. A scent her boyish clothes failed to disguise. A scent he'd come to recognize as peculiarly her own.

"I imagine they have a fragrance. Most flowers do," he said, tracing the contour of her lips with his eyes.

She shifted her weight, moving closer to

the mattress and to him. "Some don't smell so hot."

"Hot?" he asked.

Caycee stood close enough now for him to almost feel the heat radiating from her body. He swallowed. He wasn't sure if the sudden weakness he felt came from his recent illness or her nearness.

"Don't smell pleasant. Like marigolds, for example," she explained.

She was talking around something. But he wasn't sure what. He attempted to concentrate on her words rather than her physical presence.

"My mother has a garden full of them in Savannah," he said.

"Full of what?" she asked, and he realized she wasn't really listening to him either. It reminded him of a Saturday night social complete with square dancing—swing your partner to and fro, promenade left, promenade right, 'round and 'round . . . don't fall down.

"Marigolds," he said. "Mother said they helped keep the squirrels away from her tulip bulbs. I never noticed that they smelled unpleasant, however."

She turned away from the window and toward him. "Why do you think they keep the squirrels out of the tulip bulbs?"

He grinned. "Because they smell bad."

"Precisely," she said.

"I wonder how I missed that."

"Because you don't spend enough time stopping to smell the roses. Nobody does."

He sensed a sadness in her gaze and a hint of the child in the woman—a frightened child. Zackary felt the threads of compassion he'd knotted so tightly against the world slipping.

Something was worrying Caycee. The thought weighed heavily on his mind. What was it? And why, in such a short space of time, had he come to care so much?

Because they'd developed a bond that neither sought, yet it existed. As surely as he lived and breathed, she felt it too. He suspected it frightened her as much as it did him.

A silence fell between them as they sought each other's eyes. Rather than drop his gaze first this time, he said, "She grows roses as well. Blue-ribbon winners. Perhaps the fragrance of the bushes overpowers the marigolds."

His words filled the silence and eased him through the pleasant, unfamiliar feelings of concern she evoked. Feelings that nonetheless unsettled him.

"Roses . . . possible, I suppose," she said quietly.

With a sigh, she moved away from the window to reach for the book that lay open on its face near the foot of the mattress.

"Shall I read to you for a while?"

To entertain him, Caycee had been reading each evening by the light of a coal-oil lamp from the leather-bound version of *Pilgrim's Progress*. He'd been impressed by her education and had wondered aloud concerning her background. He hadn't been surprised when she'd avoided his questions, admitting only that her father had been a professional and her mother a teacher, and that an education had been considered a must in her family. Zackary had concluded from the conversation that Caycee came from unique stock—most influential parents educated the boys and married off the girls.

"No. I think I'm going to try a short walk instead. Suppose you round me up a bar of that soap Klaus has on hand—"

"What are you saying?" Caycee interrupted.

He saw the concern reflected in her eyes. He felt oddly gratified by it.

"That I'd like to try to make it down to the creek. For a bath. With your help."

Zackary rose to his knees.

Caycee closed the book and tossed it onto the mattress.

"The water wasn't all that warm this morning," she cautioned.

"It will be fine," he assured her.

"I should probably get Klaus, don't you think?" she said.

"He's working somewhere out in the fields today. Do you know where?" he asked.

"Not exactly, but I could probably—"

"By the time you find him and get him back to the cabin, the moment will have passed. Besides, I understand it's not that far. Come. Give me a hand, while the idea still sounds reasonable," he said. He extended his hand.

Caycee noticed that Zackary's hand trembled as he reached for hers. He was making an all-out effort to get well as soon as possible. The least she could do was to encourage him. After all, that was what she wanted. For him to get well and move on. Wasn't it?

Well, wasn't it?

For Caycee, who had never had much time for relaxation, life seemed simpler now, essential, elemental, and oddly sustaining, even though existing in the past was like living in another culture rather than the good old U.S. of A. Days had eased into a week as Zackary regained his strength—precious time she feared would somehow affect her

113

chances of returning to her own century.

Along with the hawthorns and the fields of wheat sprouting in soil broken with Klaus's John Deere turning plow, her initial physical attraction to Zackary had blossomed into mutual respect and an uneasy sort of friendship. Their budding personal relationship concerned Caycee. She'd told herself over and over that it was only because she wanted to get home that she'd taken such good care of him. Today, for the first time, she realized she'd lied to herself. The disturbing truth was that she found Zackary increasingly attractive. He made her smile—which wasn't an easy accomplishment, all things considered.

Caycee also realized Zackary was extremely intelligent and that he must be growing suspicious of her. When modern words and phrases slipped off her tongue before she could catch them, he never failed to question her about them. And sometimes when she undressed to slip beneath the covers of her pallet, she had the discomfiting feeling he watched her from beneath partially closed lids. Of course, she chalked that up to simple poetic justice, for she'd often observed him in the same manner.

He stood and began unbuttoning the long johns. Caycee abruptly turned her back on him. He steadied himself with a hand on her shoulder as he stepped out of the underwear. She watched the long johns slide past her boots as he kicked them aside.

She realized he stood behind her without a stitch covering his body; she hurriedly offered him his Levi's.

"Can you get into those by yourself?" she stammered, then wished she could retract the words. She didn't want to help him. She *couldn't* help him. At this point, Zackary no longer felt like her charge.

He felt like a man.

A vibrant man.

A man she felt attracted to in the worst way.

Caycee held her breath. She felt rather than saw Zackary shimmy into his denim pants. She exhaled in ragged puffs.

Unaccustomed to inactivity, Caycee had passed the time several mornings earlier by washing and pressing his shirt. She handed the garment to him, sensing that in his weakened state he fumbled with the buttons. She half-turned toward him.

"Are you sure you feel up to a road trip today?"

"A road trip?"

"An excursion . . . getting out of the cabin, walking down to the creek," she said.

"Positive," he assured her.

"It could cause a setback."

"Not likely. I'm still feeling low, but that will pass."

"You're determined?"

He raked his hands through his hair and took a deep breath. "Yep."

"Okay, let's go for it then."

His gaze clung to hers. Searching. Questioning. "Go for it?"

"That's right. Here. Lean on me." She felt the flush staining her cheeks as she reached for him, angling her shoulder beneath his armpit.

"Thanks for the help, Caycee," he said. His lips were near her ear. She felt his warm breath buffeting her cheek. Her senses tingled appreciatively.

"No problem," she mumbled without missing a beat, consciously controlling the tremble she felt welling inside her.

Somehow she had to come to grips with her reaction to him. Somehow.

They made it down the stairs without mishap. Caycee leaned Zackary against a chair while she collected soap and the rectangular strip of cotton cloth that passed for a towel. Then she slipped back beneath his shoulder, steering him around the furniture toward the door.

She paused on the porch with a dual purpose: to allow Zackary to catch his breath, and to scan the fields one last time. Klaus was nowhere in sight.

They continued down the steps and across the yard, scattering chickens as they went. From the yard, they angled toward an evergreen tree line. Once through the windbreak, they reached the creek within minutes.

The bank gradually descended into a rock-strewn creek. Klaus had fashioned a crescent-shaped, damlike wall from the rocks so that the smooth-flowing water passed in and around it, forming a shallow pool midcreek.

"I'm impressed," Zackary said.

Caycee pulled away from Zackary's embrace. Together they surveyed the bath.

"So was I," she said. "Klaus told me that he did this when he first staked out his land, even before he finished building the cabin. He also told me he'd asked your opinion concerning something he plans to do with the smokehouse."

"He wondered if his idea would work."

She couldn't stop herself. "He asked you because he'd discovered you graduated from West Point. That you were an architect prior to the"—Caycee paused—"to the Civil War. That you were an engineer for the duration of the war."

"I see you've been conversing with Klaus."

I've been doing my homework. "To pass the time. Same as you."

"Couldn't you think of another topic rather than my campaign career?"

"It just sort of happened." *After a minimal amount of prompting.*

"I'll agree that I've built a few bridges in my day."

"For the boys in gray," she prompted.

He took a moment to digest the image.

"I suppose you could call them that," he said.

"Klaus said you were a Confederate field officer." It stood to reason, since Zackary had been born and bred in Savannah, Caycee reminded herself.

"I was."

"So why didn't you go back to your architectural career after the war?"

Zackary began unbuttoning his linsey-woolsey shirt.

He grinned. "You mean why did I take up a dishonest occupation, like robbing banks, as opposed to an honest one?"

"I didn't say that," Caycee said. She couldn't take his grin. It was devilishly inviting. To avoid it, she dropped her gaze to his hands.

"You didn't have to."

"So why did you?" she asked, watching the shirtfront spread to disclose bare skin. She'd made a mistake—his grin wasn't half as inviting as this.

"Suffice to say life isn't a simple proposition."

Zackary shrugged from the shirt and tossed it to the bank. Caycee couldn't seem to turn away this time. She gazed at his handsome chest, mentally assessing it. Not too hairy, nicely muscled, with a puckered scar from the bullet wound that added to rather than detracted from his physical appeal.

You might as well stop playing games, Caycee told herself. As little as you want to admit it, the man turns you on. He has from the moment you dived over the bank counter and into his lap. She wondered why fate had played such a cruel joke on her. Why did Zackary have to look so good? She wanted to use him. Her attraction to him would definitely make that more difficult for her to stomach.

"Nobody ever promised us life would be easy," she said finally.

"I can't afford promises anyway," he said in a voice so low that she almost missed his words.

Their gazes connected for a moment. She felt his eyes on her lips; she almost leaned toward him. Say something, she thought dizzily. Tell him you want to feel his lips against yours. That you've come to appreciate him as a person. That you desire his company for more reasons than one.

For a split second, Caycee sensed that Zackary entertained the same electrifying thoughts. It unnerved her. It must have unnerved him as well, she decided, for they looked away simultaneously.

"The water looks inviting," he said.

"It is," she mumbled in response.

Caycee sensed rather than saw Zackary rid himself of his pants.

"Well, I guess I'll, uh, leave you to your bath. I'll be back in a little while and—" she began, staring at the toes of her boots.

"Stay, Caycee," he interrupted softly.

She heard him splash out into the water.

She glanced up as he sank waist-deep into the pool, afraid to pursue the conversation. Fearful of what she might miss if she didn't.

"Why?"

"We need to talk turkey," he said. "Now is as good a time as any."

Now wasn't as good a time as any. Her senses were afire and she couldn't seem to think straight. But Caycee decided not to express her doubts. Instead, she allowed Zackary to continue.

"Toss me the soap," he called.

She did so. He caught it with his left hand.

Dipping the bar into the water, he lathered first one arm, then the other, methodically working his way across his broad chest.

Feeling as if they were about to share—as if they were sharing—something supremely intimate, Caycee waited.

Finally, Zackary said, "Two, maybe three more days and I plan to rejoin the gang at the Gonzales place." He paused as if he didn't want to impart something to her that he felt he must. "I'll be traveling alone."

His statement of intent was the last thing Caycee had expected. The romantic aura that had surrounded them snapped like an elastic rubber band.

She asked woodenly, "What more do I have to do to prove myself to you?"

"Is that what you've been trying to do, prove yourself to me?" His gray eyes were bright and piercing. They seared her with their heat.

Caycee felt for a moment as if the world had actually stopped spinning and that everything depended on her answer.

"I realize you don't know me from Adam, but Dingus asked that I accompany you," she said carefully. *I need to go with you. Please don't try to leave me behind.*

He shut his eyes briefly. When he reopened them, they were prudently blank. Neutral. Placid. Yet Caycee sensed that something she'd said had somehow hit home. For a brief second, hope soared.

Until Zackary said firmly, "I'm not taking you with me, Caycee."

Appalled, Caycee frowned and stepped closer to the water's edge. The hawthorns were in bloom. Before she knew it, it would be time to harvest the wheat Klaus had so industriously planted. She couldn't hang around for that. What would her father think? She couldn't abandon him like this! Especially since she was an only child. She feared her loss, in addition to her mother's, would devastate him. She must return to her father. To her career. To her own world!

"No?" Caycee asked.

He shook his head.

So much for the soft, womanly feelings she'd been experiencing, Caycee thought as she tamped the emotions deep down inside her.

"You don't care that Dingus expects me to be with you when you arrive? His request makes no difference to you?"

"I'll deal with that when I come to it."

The anxieties from earlier in the day bombarded her. Caycee used anger to counteract her fear and hurt, desperation and confusion.

"Here's your towel, then, Zackary Reece Butler. Catch."

Caycee tossed the towel into the air.

Caught unaware, Zackary belatedly dropped the soap to extend his hand.

The towel missed his lathered fingertips by mere inches.

"Hellfire," Zackary exclaimed as, like a dying bird attempting to catch itself, the towel fluttered briefly in space before landing in the creek. Zackary's gaze swiveled from Caycee to the water-saturated towel and back again.

His voice rose as he accused, "You did that on purpose."

"Did I?" She wasn't sure. Most probably he'd hit the nail squarely on the head.

"Most probably," he said with a scowl, echoing her thoughts. "So . . . what do you suggest I do now?"

The same thing you're forcing me to do. "Wing it," Caycee advised in a voice as smooth as glass before turning on her heel and stalking away.

Chapter Seven

Zackary could feel Caycee watching him as he cinched the Morgan's saddle girth. Her eyes bored into his back, making him conscious of her even though they weren't standing face-to-face.

He punched the Morgan's stomach gently with his knuckles to prompt the horse to exhale any excess air that might cause the saddle to slip when he mounted, then pulled the belt one notch tighter.

The Morgan snorted in protest.

"Whoa, boy," Zackary soothed. He patted the horse's sleek neck, running his hand across his withers and down his brisket.

His mount seemed touchy. The animal probably sensed the impending "road trip" he had planned, Zackary decided. The Gonzales place was located 300 miles from Liberty, Missouri—a bear of a ride under any circumstances. It was a place where outlaw gang members converged to fence stolen gold at a 40-percent discount. A place where life was cheap, and the phrase "No law west of the Mississippi, no God west of the Pecos" meant something.

Because of that, he'd considered staying on to enjoy the peaceful routine of Klaus's farm for a few more days. But he'd regained his strength. And it was time to move on. High time to get back to the job at hand. Beyond high time to leave Caycee Hammond behind.

Strangely enough, the notion bothered him. He wanted to say something to her. To apologize. To try to make her understand. But the words wouldn't come.

Zackary told himself that the nature of his job barred him from emotional displays, but he knew that wasn't entirely true. His job was only a small part of it. He'd sealed up the tunnel leading to compassion with an avalanche of human feelings following Adam's death. Now Caycee was methodically removing one rock at a time to reopen the tunnel. It made her dangerous to him as well as to herself. He couldn't explain anything to her because, like a turtle, he couldn't allow his tender underbelly to be exposed.

"I can see you're not going to change your mind," Caycee said finally, breaking into Zackary's thoughts.

He glanced up and over his shoulder.

"I thought you weren't speaking to me. You haven't in days."

Her eyes narrowed. "I've been thinking."

"Lord above," he muttered.

"I heard that. Lord above, what?"

"Lord above, the idea makes me edgy."

"It should," she said solemnly.

Caycee now had his full attention. He turned his back on the Morgan to deal with an even touchier proposition.

"I'm not grinning, Caycee."

"I can see that. I wouldn't be grinning either if I were you."

"I don't like the sound of that."

"I don't blame you."

"What's this all about?" he said, tugging down his hat brim to shield his eyes from the early morning sun streaming in through the door she'd left hanging ajar when she'd entered the barn.

"I'm going to the Gonzales place with you."

He'd heard a similar declaration before.

Following the war his younger brother had demanded to be allowed to tour the West with him. He'd relented and look what had happened to Adam.

Disturbed that he'd ever permitted his heart to soften toward her, he began, "We've been all through this be—"

"I know," Caycee interrupted. "I was hoping you'd change your mind. But you haven't. And I mean to go with you. So . . ."

Zackary cocked a brow at Caycee. She was hatless and the sun shone against her baby-fine, honey-blond tresses, creating a halolike aura that momentarily captivated him. How could she look so pretty first thing in the morning, with her hair mussed from sleep, and her shirttail half in, half out?

"So?"

She took a deep breath. "If you leave me behind I'm going to hunt Dingus down and apprise him of your secret."

"What are you talking about?" he asked carefully.

"You know."

"I'm afraid I don't."

"The first day we arrived, Klaus told me you were mumbling something about the eye that never sleeps."

"Delirium brought on by the bullet wound," Zackary offered casually.

Caycee shook her head. "I thought so too. Until I realized later that you weren't delirious. Just weak from loss of blood. And rattled."

"A nightmare, then."

"You weren't asleep," she said evenly.

"What are you saying, Caycee?" he asked, thinking that the angel posturing before him had hidden her horns fairly well. Up until now.

"That it took me a while, but I think I've pieced things together."

"What things?"

"I knew I'd heard that phrase, the eye that never sleeps, somewhere before. Actually it's more like a logo, or a trademark. It belongs to the Pinkerton National Detective Agency."

Caycee didn't tell Zackary that the modern corporation supplied guards for banks and corporations throughout the country. Or that Henry, the director she'd been working with for the past few months, had researched the history of the agency in connection to the bank robberies he was filming.

"You have a fantastic imagination," Zackary said dryly.

"I do. But that has nothing to do with the fact that you're an actor of sorts, Zackary Reece Butler. You're playing a part. The part of an outlaw. Somehow you've infiltrated Dingus's gang to gather evidence."

He attempted to sidestep the issue. "Mere conjecture."

Caycee met him head-on. "I don't think so. I figure you were deputized by the local sheriff in Westport. That you planned to witness the robbery, to acquire evidence against Dingus, and to make arrests accordingly. But something went wrong—me, probably. You got shot during the getaway. And Dingus rode off into the sunset, scot-free."

"Of all the leather-headed . . . You're loco. You know that, don't you?"

"Maybe so. But not so loco that I don't know an undercover agent when one dives full-tilt into me."

"Wait a minute. You dived over the bank counter into me."

She realized she'd managed to agitate Zackary, which was no mean feat. She pushed home her advantage. "Only to escape the gunfire ricocheting off the walls."

Zackary swore under his breath. "Caycee Hammond, if you aren't a blister on my rear, I don't know what is!"

"I'm desperate, Zackary. I swear I'll go to Dingus."

She watched him clench and unclench his fists as he asked, "Are you threatening me?"

"I'm making you one of those promises you can't afford."

He lowered his voice to a mere whisper. "What's to keep me from killing you here and now?"

Caycee swallowed. "What would Klaus say?"

"With a pistol pointed at his temple, I suspect he'd help me bury you. Down by the creek perhaps, where the ground is soft. Or in a wheat field somewhere."

Marshaling her courage, Caycee called Zackary on what she prayed was his bluff. "I don't believe you're a cold-blooded murderer."

To her relief, he relaxed slightly.

"If nothing else about you impressed me, your bravado would."

"Can I take that as a compliment?" Caycee asked with a weak smile.

"Impressive or not, bravado can put you ten feet under as quick as anything, blackmail included."

He paused.

Caycee said into the silence, "Does this mean you're going to take me with you?"

"By heaven! You're one of the most forward females—"

Again she interrupted him. "I've been called pushy before now. If you're trying to get me off track, you'll have to take another tactic."

"Do you ever let anyone get a word in edgewise?" he asked in exasperation.

"Not when I'm attempting to make a valid point. I'll lose my train of thought," Caycee answered honestly.

He studied her intensely, saying after a moment, "Blackmail is a low tactic to use on a man."

"Lower than a snake's belly is to the ground," she said on a sigh, using a line from the Western she'd been working on when she'd tumbled into his world.

Zackary took a deep breath. "Why are you doing this? What do you hope to gain?"

"Plenty," she said solemnly, adding almost as an afterthought, "I'm not a woman that needs constant attention. You can see that, can't you?"

His eyes found hers, delving, searching, questioning the motivating factors behind her actions even before he transferred his thoughts into words.

"Who are you running from, Caycee? Perhaps you aren't as innocent as you appear. Perhaps you're an errant wife . . . or a fast woman attempting to escape her past . . . or just plain—"

"Crazy," she finished for him.

He gave a snort. "That's as good a term as any."

She acknowledged that although she'd pretty much figured him out, she remained a mystery to him. That was to her favor—she hoped.

"The only thing you have pegged right is that I'm a woman," she said.

Zackary latched onto her statement like a traveler's burr to cotton socks. "Precisely. And women don't ride with outlaw gangs."

Caycee felt sorely tempted to confess the truth—that she was a reluctant time-traveler, cast in an unknown country, out of her element and time-frame. She wanted to explain that only by remaining with him would she discover the gateway back to the future. But she feared he would dump her for sure if she recounted such an outlandish story. She decided to try another avenue instead.

Recalling the numerous films made concerning famous women of the West, Caycee commented, "Etta Place rode with the Sundance Kid, and Belle Starr's name was—is always linked with Cole Younger's. And no one thought—thinks anything about it."

"I'm not familiar with a woman called Etta Place, but I suggest you tell me more of Myra Belle Shirley and Cole Younger. How did you know he was seeing Myra Belle? Do you know her personally? Where does she live? Is it possible that you've somehow been privy to invaluable inside information concerning Dingus? You wanted to talk, Caycee. So talk."

Caycee instantly realized that she'd gotten carried away. Obviously the Sundance Kid and Etta Place must have ridden, robbed, and bucked the system after Zackary's time. His interest in Cole Younger and Belle Starr doubly confused her. She thought he'd intended to arrest Dingus. What in the world did Cole and Belle have to do with the gloved outlaw from the Westport bank?

"I'll cut a deal with you," she said.

"Cut a deal?"

"Yeah. You let me tag along with you, and I'll tell you everything I know about the gunfighters of the Old West . . . eventually."

"Honest to . . . the Old West? Caycee, I don't know what you're talking about half of the time," Zackary growled.

"So we're even," she said quickly, admitting to herself that she was a thrill-seeker, and that the idea of actually riding with an honest-to-goodness outlaw gang had a certain macabre appeal above and beyond immediate necessity.

"I don't want to shoot you to shut you

up, and I can't afford to have you parading around the countryside spouting off at the mouth either," Zackary said.

Caycee realized he was simply thinking aloud. She responded regardless. "Which means your best bet is to keep me under constant surveillance."

"Apparently so."

"Besides which, you'd have a difficult time explaining to Dingus when you rejoin him at the rendezvous point why "the kid" failed to accompany you."

"You've given this a lot of thought."

"Bunches."

"There's one thing you haven't considered. You don't own a horse. And the Morgan can't continue to carry us both."

It was a last-ditch effort on Zackary's part to dissuade her and Caycee knew it. She'd also calculated the drawback beforehand and compensated for it.

"You're wrong. I remedied that stumbling block yesterday by trading my duster to Klaus for a horse and saddle."

She couldn't mistake the surprise on Zackary's face and in his voice. "Which horse? Surely you don't mean the wagon horse?"

"No. The one in the far stall. Klaus brought it in from the lower meadow last night while you were sleeping."

Caycee pointed to a stall located at the far end of the barn.

Zackary strolled toward the stall, glanced inside, then arched his brows skeptically at her.

"Where did he find her?"

"He says he's had her for a long time."

Zackary hung his arm across the top stall rail, squinting at the mare. "Obviously."

"Since she was a colt," Caycee added.

Curious, the mare nuzzled his arm. Zackary caught at her halter, lifting her lips to survey her teeth.

"She must be twenty years old." He gave her a pat between the ears and released her halter. "Not only that, she's a swayback. In case you haven't noticed."

"I noticed. Klaus told me that was his fault. He said he got anxious and tried to break her too young."

"I suspected as much," Zackary said thoughtfully.

"I've tested her out. Her seat isn't all that comfortable, but she's solid," Caycee said. "And she's got real pluck for an old lady."

"Looks like a plodder to me," he commented.

"Hey, I admit it's not much of a horse, certainly not the caliber I'd choose for myself, but I need a ride in the worst way."

Zackary turned.

"You *are* desperate."

Tears gathered in Caycee's eyes despite her attempt to blink them back.

"I've been telling you that all along. You just wouldn't believe me." She attempted to still the quaver in her voice and failed miserably.

She watched his Adam's apple bob as he swallowed, wondering if he was choking down distaste for her, or emotion. Could she have in some way touched him? She wasn't sure that she wanted to know. It made things almost too personal.

"I don't want to do this, Caycee."

Caycee conceded to herself that she'd backed Zackary into a corner, and that it would be only natural for him to resent her for it. But she felt she had no choice. She also acknowledged that strangely enough she'd developed a fondness for the arrogant, overbearing, sometimes tender, always virile Pinkerton agent.

"I know that."

"But you've got me over a barrel."

"I know that too."

"What makes you think you can trust me?"

"Like you Pinkerton agents, I plan to sleep with one eye open."

"That can get pretty damned tiring over the long haul."

Not as tiring as being stuck somewhere you don't belong. "Who would know better than you?"

"I'm not confessing anything, Caycee."

"Neither am I."

"I suppose that makes us even . . . for the time being."

Caycee didn't like the sound of his words. "What do you mean by that?"

His expression indiscernible, he said, "Nothing in particular."

"I—" Caycee began.

Zackary interrupted her this time.

"Best get your gear together if you're going with me. And make it snappy. We're burning daylight," he said. He turned his back on her and resumed saddling the Morgan.

Caycee couldn't tell Zackary how many times her father had used that very expression. She'd thought he'd gotten it from a John Wayne movie. But maybe not. Perhaps it was authentic. As authentic as the man that stood before her.

As authentic as her fear that if she allowed Zackary to somehow escape her, so would the world she'd known up until a week ago.

Chapter Eight

"How are you doing back there?" Zackary called. He reined the Morgan around and to a standstill.

Eight hours into the journey Caycee had to admit that Zackary had been correct: the mare was a plodder with a god-awful, sloping seat that had her squirming to find a comfortable position. Still, she dared not complain. She'd made her bed. . . .

Without thinking, Caycee gave Zackary the thumbs-up sign.

"No need to be sassy," Zackary commented as she halted the mare alongside the Morgan.

"I wasn't trying to be sassy," Caycee explained. "When you give someone the thumbs-up sign, it means things are great. Fantastic. Couldn't be better."

Their eyes spanned the distance between them.

"I suspect you're stretching the truth a bit," he said.

Caycee straightened in the saddle.

"And I think you're being—what did you call me this morning?—oh, yeah, forward."

An annoyed expression flitted across his face. "You don't lie well."

"You *are* being forward," she said.

He adjusted his slouch hat against the slant of the waning afternoon sun.

"Perhaps I am," he said.

"No perhaps about it," Caycee said, taking his cue and adjusting her Stetson as well. "But I won't fault you for it this time."

He turned to face her. She watched his expression ease.

"Stop sparring with me and tell the truth," Zackary encouraged.

Responding to the lightness of his tone, Caycee grimaced. "Do I have to?"

Being ignored by Zackary didn't bother her half as much as this. She didn't open up to people easily. She'd learned over the long haul to be guarded, to keep her emotions in reserve, to give on an external level while retaining the internal.

But Zackary was breaking down her barriers. Caycee felt herself leaning toward him as a person. It had all started before she'd learned he was a Pinkerton agent and living on the right side of the law. If she'd had any questions as to why he had seemed to protect her in the bank, and later at the ferry, she didn't now. She suspected Zackary to be a dedicated agent. She also believed he was somehow hiding behind that dedication. She'd uncovered one of his secrets by mistake. She wasn't sure she wanted to deepen the degree of their association by removing the mask he wore for the world. She might come to like the man behind the mask too well.

Neutrality was the key, Caycee told herself. Of course, neutrality was impossible in certain situations.

His thick, dark brows drawn in concentration, Zackary said, "They tell me the truth is less taxing than lies."

"I suppose you're an authority," she quipped.

His brows arched and Caycee realized that in attempting to avoid his question, she'd spoken in a tone sharper than she'd intended.

She wasn't surprised when Zackary reacted accordingly, saying dryly, "There's a difference between lies and disguise."

141

He was right.

He was also correct in his comments concerning her horse. Riding the swayback was worse than being poured into a fibrous Nomex underwear suit, masked with asbestos, dashed with alcohol, and ignited. At least you knew a stunt like that would be over when the flames died down—three minutes, tops. She'd mentally calculated that this particular ride would go on for at least six days.

Caycee felt the accredited stuntwoman rise to the forefront. When you were wrong, you were wrong. And she'd been wrong about the mare. The best thing to do was to admit it and move on.

"The honest-to-goodness truth is that I probably should have listened to you—the mare stinks," Caycee said quietly.

His demeanor softened almost instantly. A slow, lazy smile curved his lips and spread to encompass his hypnotic eyes.

Caycee's breath caught in her throat.

Enhanced by the charcoal gray of his linsey-woolsey shirt, Zackary's eyes sparkled provocatively. She decided the man didn't need to be holding a weapon on a woman to assure her compliance. He need only gaze at her with his thick-lashed eyes and, tantalized beyond endurance, she'd follow him anywhere—whether he wanted to be followed or not.

Zackary Reece Butler should definitely be in pictures.

"If you expect anything different from a horse, you're bound to be disappointed," Zackary drawled. His statement was followed by a low chuckle which broke the spell.

"I didn't mean the mare smells. . . . Oh, never mind," she said in exasperation.

Caycee didn't mind being a source of entertainment—back home she'd based her career on it. But she was tired of explaining herself. Tired of riding a swayback horse. Tired of plotting and planning. Tired of worrying about her father. Tired of the sun beating down on her neck. Tired, period. She wanted to lie down and cry.

Zackary cleared his throat.

"Perhaps you'd like to reconsider your decision," he said.

Had her expression given her away? she wondered. Or was Zackary becoming adept at reading her moods?

Caycee stiffened.

"And do what?" she asked. "Turn around and go back to the Becker farm?"

"That's a possibility."

"Not on your life!"

"Here now, no need to get into a huff," he said tightly.

"I'm not getting into a huff," she responded even as she felt her body stiffen for battle.

Seconds passed into minutes. Zackary's probing gray gaze scanned her face. She could almost feel it touching on her eyes, tracing the arch of her nose, resting lightly on her lips.

"I suspect we should start looking for a place to make camp for the night," he said finally.

"I can go on a little longer," Caycee stammered. She could feel the blush creeping across her cheeks as her body relaxed.

"The horses need rest as much as we do," he said firmly.

"Sure," she agreed, careful not to respond too quickly or to sound too grateful for his decision.

Caycee averted her face, glancing down at her saddlebow so that the brim of her black felt Stetson shadowed her heated complexion. He wasn't going to get into a full-scale argument over territory they'd already covered. She wished she could tell him how happy that made her.

Zackary could be so nice when he wanted to be. Too nice. With some people niceness could be a tactical maneuver. She didn't like to think that Zackary would use it as such, but she couldn't take any chances. Trust was a two-way street. Until he trusted her, she couldn't very well allow herself to trust him, could she? she wondered as she followed him down a curving wagon path, through a thicket, and into the forest.

They hadn't traveled 50 yards beyond the thicket when they came upon a white-tailed doe stripping bark from the trunks of a young cottonwood stand. Zackary pulled the Morgan up short, motioning for her to do the same with her mare. The deer remained poised, oblivious to the fact that human beings had invaded its feeding grounds.

Caycee felt the goose bumps rise on her flesh as she marveled at the animal's beauty. With fingers of sunlight reaching through the tree boughs to gild its coat, the doe appeared as sleek to her as a California seal. She hadn't realized before now that deer possessed such soulfully innocent eyes— whiskey brown, long lashed, and mirror clear. The closest she'd ever come to viewing a live deer was when she chanced to pass one on the highway in her pickup truck. Speeding past at 40 miles an hour wasn't the same as seeing a doe up close and personal like this, she thought with satisfaction.

Zackary's world did indeed have its high points, Caycee decided.

"We're downwind," he mouthed, interrupting her thoughts.

Lost in wonder, she sighed and nodded to him without really considering what he'd said.

With a finger to his lips, Zackary wrapped the Morgan's reins around his arm, eased his Winchester from its boot, raised the weapon, and secured the butt against his shoulder. It took Caycee a moment to recognize his intent. She tensed while visions of Klaus Becker's chicken dangling rubbery and lifeless in his hands assailed her.

Unprepared for the consequences of Zackary's actions, Caycee simply and honestly reacted by saying into the quiet of the forest, "Don't do it."

Bark strips dangling from its mouth, the doe glanced up and froze.

Zackary flipped up the rifle's sights, squeezed one eye shut, and slid his forefinger across the trigger.

Life hanging in the balance, Caycee thought. So fragile. So unpredictable. No guarantees. No promises. One minute you were here and the next moment you were . . .

"Please don't," she persisted more audibly, pushing against the rifle's cool, metallic barrel with her fingertips.

Zackary gave no answer, though his grip on the rifle slackened.

The doe took flight during the brief interchange, bounding off to melt into the forest like a fading streak of sunlight at the end of a long day.

Caycee sighed again, this time with relief.

Lips compressed in irritation, Zackary checked his rifle.

"You aren't working with me, Caycee," he said.

"I'm not working against you either," she said quickly. "I just couldn't stand to see you shoot that doe."

Zackary looked genuinely confused.

"What would you have me do with it, Caycee? Wrestle it to the ground and strangle it with my bare hands? I gave up the rigors of bulldogging a long time ago. I'm too old for such as that."

Caycee understood where he was coming from. He didn't have grocery stores to depend upon; she'd never depended on anything else as a source of food. Perhaps the time would come when she could kill something with the idea of eating it, but not today.

"We don't really need the meat the first day out, do we?" she asked.

He made no reply; she continued to plead her case.

"I mean, that's an awful lot of meat to portion out and do something with. Two people couldn't possibly eat it all in one sitting. And how would we keep it fresh for longer than a day? We don't have the salt to cure it. And we don't have the time to jerk it. It just doesn't seem right to waste something so . . . so beautiful," she said, searching for an argument that might make sense to Zackary without causing her to sound like a nut.

He snorted.

"I hope you have a liking for johnnycakes, because at this rate I imagine it's going to be a considerable spell before we taste meat again," Zackary said as he shoved the rifle into its saddle boot. The acidity in his voice could have dissolved iron.

He didn't understand Caycee Hammond and he probably never would.

Resting on his bedroll beneath a tree, his hat shading his eyes, Zackary had been dozing in the shade. Now, wide-awake, he watched as she gathered sticks to start a campfire.

After hobbling the horses with his rawhide lariat in a grassy stand within viewing distance, he'd offered to assist her; she'd refused his help.

It seemed the womanly wiles he'd come to expect when a female wanted her way simply didn't exist in Caycee. She was far from helpless, using her brain rather than her femininity to get her way. Funny, but that only served to make her all the more alluring to him. He couldn't decide for the life of him which one Caycee needed worse, taming or protecting.

Eyeing her back, he said, "See if you can't find some flat stones to surround the fire."

She nodded without turning around, apparently content to stay busy.

Zackary suspected Caycee feared that after the rigors of the day she might fall asleep if she made herself comfortable. And that, after the deer incident, he would lunge at the opportunity to sneak off without her.

I'm dumb as an oyster not to do just that, he told himself.

If not for Caycee, he would be enjoying venison roast tonight. Then again, because of her he was alive and well enough to stew over a meatless meal.

When Caycee had the fire neatly ringed with flat stones, Zackary stood, removed his slouch hat, and tossed it onto his bedroll.

"I don't know about you, but my insides are starting to gnaw on themselves," he said.

"I'm hungry enough to eat a horse," she

commented over her shoulder.

"A horse, but not a deer, huh? I've known men forced to eat their horses or starve . . . tough decision. One I hope I'm never forced to make. The Morgan and I have been together since before the war."

" 'I could eat a horse' is just an expression. I didn't mean it literally. Don't take everything I say so seriously," she said.

"Life is a fairly serious proposition where I'm concerned," he said frankly.

"I think it is for everybody," she muttered.

He heard a soft hiss, saw her toss something into the neatly arranged campfire, and watched as the flames lapped at the dried sticks.

"I see you found the strike-anywheres," he commented.

Caycee pivoted, jamming something smaller than the palm of her hand into the pocket of her corduroys.

"The whats?"

Zackary hunkered down to rummage through his saddlebags for the five-pound bag of cornmeal flavored with soda and salt, and a square of oilcloth. Along with them he retrieved the waterproof case of yellow phosphorus matches, shaved down on one end so they could be easily broken off the wooden block from which they were carved.

He frowned thoughtfully at the case.

"I assumed you'd found the matches I carry in my saddlebags." He tossed the bulky case up in the air and caught it with his left hand. It felt heavy. Obviously the block matches were still inside. "But I see now that you didn't."

She patted her pocket. "I . . . no. I've got my own matches, thanks."

Zackary couldn't help but notice the apparent flatness of Caycee's matches as opposed to his.

"Mighty compact matches," he puzzled aloud.

"Yeah," she said shortly. She punched her hands into her pockets, causing them to fluff like fruit pies in a hot oven while effectively covering the outline of the matches.

"Come to think of it, I don't believe I've ever seen any that compact," he said.

He expected her to pull the matches from her pocket and present them to him. She didn't. Instead she said, "They're called book matches . . . pretty, uh, common where I come from."

Zackary had the distinct impression he was making her uncomfortable. The question of what she'd used to light the fire nagged at him, but he let it go, as he did most things where Caycee was concerned.

He dropped his strike-anywheres on the bedroll beside his hat, collected his canteen, and advanced toward Caycee with the sack of cornmeal and the oilcloth prominently displayed.

"Like I said earlier, I hope you like johnny-cakes."

Zackary poured approximately a pound of meal into the oilcloth and doused it with water from the canteen, then proceeded to blend the mixture. "Might as well make enough to carry over for breakfast," he stated as he kneaded.

When the meal reached the consistency of balled bread dough, Zackary glanced up at Caycee.

"It isn't venison, but it will kill the hunger pangs."

"Can I get the frying pan?" she offered as he portioned out the cornmeal and patted in into half-inch-thick cakes.

"I don't have one. I like to travel as light as possible."

He looked up. This time their eyes connected. They both glanced away.

"You don't use a pan?" she asked.

"Don't need one," he said absently.

"You put the johnnycakes in the fire?"

She had his attention now.

"Not in the fire . . . on one of those flat

rocks beside the fire. They cook up crisp that way."

Zackary sloshed water over a rock, washing away the dirt clinging to it.

"Oh."

"You've never eaten johnnycakes, have you?"

Caycee shifted from one foot to the other. "Not that I recall."

"Never cooked them either, I'd wager," he said, placing the cake on the fire-warmed rock.

Caycee planted both feet firmly on the ground, hands behind her back. "Cooking isn't my bag."

"Where have you been all your life?" he asked without taking his gaze from the bubbling johnnycakes.

"Just because I admitted that I—" Caycee began.

He interrupted her with his own thoughts.

"I suppose, judging by the way you breezed through *Pilgrim's Progress*, you learned to read at some fancy finishing school. Which means there's money somewhere in your background."

"I have an adequate education, if that's what you're getting at."

"From there I'd guess that like most women you went on to an acceptable marriage along with a household of servants. Only you don't seem that kind."

"What kind?"

"Oh, the mollycoddled, social whirl, volunteer-oriented kind."

"What's so bad about that sort of life?"

"Nothing. It just doesn't seem to fit you."

"Did your mother go to a finishing school?"

"As I recall, she did."

"And on to an acceptable marriage?"

"Borderline—my father is a tradesman."

"Does your mother have servants?"

"Yes, but she isn't mollycoddled. She's a strong woman. She'd be the first to roll up her sleeves and pitch in to prove it."

"She likes to socialize, though."

Zackary frowned. "Where's this game leading us, Caycee?"

Excellent question. "I'm pretending to be a Pinkerton agent. I'm gathering information—like you. Humor me."

"That could be dangerous," he said.

"I didn't say it wouldn't be. But you're accustomed to danger. You thrive on it. Right?" she prompted.

Zackary's frown eased. "What was the question again? I've forgotten."

"Does your mother like to socialize?" Caycee repeated.

"Occasionally."

"And I bet she volunteers for all sorts of organizations."

"She does lend her hand where and when it's needed."

"I rest my case. You can't always take things at face value—women in particular. They'll fool you every time. Don't believe everything you see . . . or think you see."

"When you want to, you have a way of twisting the conversation so that I haven't the faintest idea what we're talking about any longer," he said.

"Do I do that?" Caycee asked innocently.

"You know you do. You do it on purpose. I've learned that much about you."

Caycee smiled despite herself at his rather provocative expression. He was attempting to be pleasant even though he knew he'd been duped. The least she could do was meet him halfway.

"I do it to keep you on your toes," she said.

"You do it to keep me off guard," he said.

"Heaven forbid! I have the strangest feeling this means we're beginning to understand one another," she said.

Zackary shot her a rueful smile.

"I suspect it means that by some imprudent and decidedly convoluted route we're getting there," he said.

He rinsed off the oilcloth, fashioned it into a napkin, gingerly scooped up a browned johnnycake from the rock with his fingers, and offered it to her.

Touched by his cordiality, she accepted the cake with a spontaneous thank-you.

Their hands brushed and for a moment, like the deer, they froze in midmotion, warm flesh against warm flesh. Caycee expected Zackary to withdraw immediately. Instead, he deepened the contact by tentatively stroking the side of her hand with the back of his.

Pulse racing and stomach aflutter, Caycee closed her eyes to better enjoy the delightfully unique sensations. Heretofore, she'd never considered that a dance of hands could be so excruciatingly sensual. Perhaps with the right person, all things were possible. . . .

"I hate like hell to walk blindly into things, Caycee," Zackary said after a moment. His voice was solemn, his gaze distant as he slowly withdrew his hand in a bittersweet sort of separation that left her yearning for more intimate and immediate contact.

Caycee realized they were no longer lightly bantering, no longer playing games. Sometime between the first moment they'd met and this moment a bond had formed between them.

"I'm not so sure I know what you're getting at," she said, matching his sobriety.

He stared into the fire.

"I'm asking you if you have a price on your head, Caycee. I'm asking you if I'm going to wish to God before this thing is said and done that I'd never met you. I'm asking you if I'm biting off more than I can chew by giving in to your demands and allowing you to tag along with me."

Johnnycake almost to her lips, Caycee hesitated. She'd dealt with enough of her own lately to recognize anxiety when she saw it.

"I sincerely hope not," she said.

"I hope not either," he said.

Compassionate by nature, Caycee felt her heart went out to Zackary. He hadn't asked for her to come barreling headlong into his life. She wasn't the only one who'd apparently been at the wrong place at the wrong time. He deserved an explanation, but he'd never believe the truth.

Zackary Butler wasn't the only one stuck between a rock and a hard place, Caycee reminded herself.

"I can't give you details right now, and I don't have any assurances—except for the fact that I'm not going to let you leave me behind," she said evenly.

Zackary gave a short laugh.

"I kinda figured that one out for myself."

"I realize I wasn't part of your plans, but some things just happen. I don't know why," she said.

"So you aren't planning to tell me what this is all about."

"I'm sorry, Zackary, but the time isn't right."

"When, Caycee?" he asked.

The tone of his voice pained her, and yet she forced herself to shrug. "I wish I knew."

"I hope to God you don't wait until it's too late," he said.

"What do you mean, too late?" she asked.

His expression pensive, Zackary said, "Nothing, Caycee. Eat your johnnycake before it gets cold."

Glad to leave the intensity of their present conversation behind, Caycee bit into the cake with relish. It tasted just as she'd imagined—like a crisp cornmeal pancake. Light enough to eat several at a sitting. Heavy enough to keep a body from going hungry.

"What do you think?" he asked.

"Mmmm, good," she commented, wondering why food tasted so much better when eaten beside a campfire surrounded by the great outdoors.

"Adequate in a pinch," he responded,

scooping up a second johnnycake and tossing it from hand to hand until it cooled enough for him to join her.

Caycee realized the longer she stayed with Zackary, the more curious he would become about her. His curiosity was pushing the limits now. She was becoming less and less adept at fielding his questions and more and more enthralled by the man behind the questions.

And that could only mean sure and certain trouble for them both.

six nipples after proving to Zackary she could hit a target dead-center at 20 paces . . . and she'd fallen in love.

She had fought her feelings for Zackary constantly: each night as they spread their bedrolls near the fire and talked each other to sleep; at the crack of dawn every morning when they shared a tin cup of oily black coffee and a cold cornmeal patty; all during the day while they rode in quiet companionship, tending their own thoughts as their relationship grew even in silence and seemingly of its own accord.

She had fought her feelings when she'd entertained him one afternoon by doing a fistful of horseback stunts her father had taught her. He'd clapped his approval and enjoyment loud and clear. At that moment, winning an Academy Award couldn't have caused her esteem to soar any higher.

She had fought the tide of her emotions when Zackary killed a scorpion which had been sunbathing between two flat rocks she'd been attempting to collect to use in ringing their nightly campfire. Later, he'd hugged her possessively against his hard chest and admonished in a gruff voice that she must have a care. His words had come to her as if from a distance, for she could think of nothing save his body pressed against hers.

And she fought them now, on their last evening alone together.

"I'll only be a minute," Zackary called to her.

Caycee waved to him in acknowledgment, watching his muscles ripple against the linsey-woolsey of his shirt as he worked to hobble their horses out to graze in a magical meadow overflowing with star grass and studded by thousands of butter-yellow dandelions. She was in love and it felt great! She also admitted to herself that it scared the heck out of her.

Despite the chemistry that raged between them, she and Zackary were products of two entirely different eras, Caycee reminded herself. The conflicts and misunderstandings that had arisen during their brief association proved that. He didn't exist in the world she was attempting to return to; she didn't plan to exist in his any longer than absolutely necessary.

And yet . . .

"There, done," Zackary said, crossing the distance between them. A smile curved his lips, and his gray eyes gleamed with mischief. They had stopped to make camp early and the late-afternoon sun shone on his sable hair, making Caycee yearn to run her fingers through the softly curling locks that brushed his collar.

Glory, he was gorgeous!

He also wore that little-boy, I'm-getting-ready-to-put-ice-down-your-back expression that men often got when they were up to no good.

"What's going on?" Caycee asked warily.

"What do you mean?" Zackary asked innocently, far too innocently, by Caycee's reckoning.

"Don't try to pull that on me. The laugh lines around your eyes are showing. That's a dead giveaway. You're up to something, Zackary Reece Butler," she said.

Caycee backed up a step.

"Who, me? Not me," Zackary insisted.

He flashed her a toothy grin that gave the lie to his words.

"Yes, you," she said.

She backed up another step, shaking her head as if that might somehow ward him off.

"Don't you trust me, Caycee?"

"About as far as I can throw you."

He grimaced. "You've wounded me to the core."

"If I didn't know better, I'd swear you've been drinking. Come on. Let me see your hands," she insisted, expecting at the very least to have a frog jump out at her.

Grin firmly in place, he said, "Nothing in my hands. See?"

Zackary extended his arms, palms out, spreading his fingers wide for her inspection. His hands were empty. Still, he did not slow his predatory advance toward her.

Caycee backed up another step when he unbuckled his gun belt and dropped it at his feet.

"Zackary?"

"Caycee."

He spun his slouch hat like a Frisbee into a bush of wild roses bordering the meadow and slipped his hand in his pocket to extract his watch and drop it onto her bedroll by the campfire.

"I'm warning you," she said, half-serious, half-delighted with his play. He was unwinding toward her. That was good. Wasn't it?

"Warning me about what?" he asked.

"About . . . about . . . This isn't funny, Zackary."

In answer, he began unbuttoning his shirt.

Eyes widening, Caycee pivoted, thinking, A girl had better be careful what she wishes for because she might just get it!

Zackary dove for her.

She squealed.

"Where you goin'?" he asked, scooping her up and over his shoulder like a sack of potatoes.

Caycee's Stetson tumbled from her head. Zackary turned and stepped over it, retracing his steps past the hobbled horses and beyond.

"Where are *you* going is the question? And just where do you think you're taking me?" Caycee asked.

"Think?"

"Okay, so you're taking me somewhere. Where?"

"You'll see."

"I don't like surprises."

"Neither do I," Zackary said. He settled Caycee more securely on his shoulder with a jounce that set her teeth on edge.

"What are you saying?" she asked breathlessly.

"That you've been a dilly of a surprise from the word go."

"I haven't done anything to you," Caycee said, wiggling to disengage her body from his embrace.

"Haven't you?" he asked. He tightened his arm around her upper torso. "I've been counting. You've been blackmailing me for five, no, six days now."

"I—" she began.

Zackary cut her short by changing the subject entirely.

"When's the last time you had a bath, Caycee?"

"You know very well when I last had a bath. At Klaus Becker's farm. In his creek."

"Don't you think it's about time for another one?"

Caycee thought about the terrain they'd traversed in the last several days. She'd seen mountains and deserts and mountains again, but no creeks or ponds large enough to submerge one's body in.

"Speaking of which, don't you think you could use a bath as well?"

"That's the idea," Zackary said, wading knee deep into a pond Caycee hadn't realized existed until now.

"My clothes!" she exclaimed.

"They need washing," he finished for her.

"You wouldn't!"

"Wouldn't I? When we reach the Gonzales place, I can bathe without raising a brow. You, on the other hand, would have a lot of explaining to do. Since you're bound and determined to accompany me, this is the least I can do for you. Wouldn't want you smellin' rank and puttin' the fellows off their food. They've got banks to rob, remember?"

Caycee began to struggle in earnest.

Zackary held on to her squirming body for all he was worth.

"Payback comes when you least expect it, little lady," he said.

With that, Zackary shrugged Caycee off his shoulder and dropped her seat-first into the crystal-clear pond he'd discovered entirely by chance.

It was payback for stepping over the threshold of the Westport bank and ruining a setup which had taken him months of planning to engineer. It was payback for being the persistent type of woman she was—the type that wouldn't take no for an answer. It was payback for daring to blackmail him. It was payback for making him entertain the kinds of emotions he could least afford to feel.

It was payback for making him fall in love with her.

They stared at each for several seconds before Caycee wrapped her arms around his knees.

"Caycee!" he exclaimed.

"Difficult to keep your balance with someone hanging on to you, isn't it?" she said.

Caycee flashed Zackary a catty smile. He saw it seconds before she pulled his knees out from under him and his face went underwater.

Zackary pushed away from Caycee in a strong thrust, gliding to the middle of the pond and the deeper water. He broke the surface for air, maintaining his position by paddling his legs along with his arms. Caycee was on her feet, trying to wring out the tail of her shirt. She glanced up. He bobbed his head beneath the water, thinking perhaps to swim over and tease her further, then changed his mind. She'd probably had enough horseplay for one day, tomboy or not.

When he came up for air a second time, Zackary caught Caycee staring his way.

He ducked beneath the surface again, diving to check the depth of the pond while enjoying the refreshing coolness of the water.

The third time he broke the surface of the water, he couldn't help but notice the stricken look on her pale face.

"For the love of . . ." she exclaimed.

Puzzled, Zackary watched as Caycee yanked off her sopping boots and tossed them in a wide arc toward the bank. He choked from unconsciously sucking in water when she rapidly stripped off her corduroys, balled them in a wad, and aimed them toward the bank as well, displaying a tantalizing expanse of trim, white thigh.

"Hang on, Zackary, I'm coming," she yelled.

The next thing he knew, Caycee was swimming toward him across the pond with the strength of a Savannah paddle wheeler cruising under a full head of steam. He felt her snatch at his waist and spin him away from her like a top. Then her arm snaked out and around his throat, practically choking off his breath as she dragged him along behind her through the water.

"What in blue blazes!" he sputtered, wondering if he'd made her so angry that she meant to drown him.

Zackary turned toward her, treading water while her body bumped up against his. He could feel her breasts through her shirt, her taut nipples teasing at his chest.

"For the love of . . . Caycee?"

"Relax," she said, grabbing at his waist and attempting to position him backward again. "Don't fight me. I was a lifeguard in high school. And I'm a strong swimmer. I can ferry you to the bank. No problem. Just don't panic," she said in soothing tones.

"I'm not in a panic," he tried to explain.

What he couldn't tell her was that he wasn't worried about getting to the bank. He was more concerned about placing some distance between her provocatively supple body and his rapidly hardening one before he did something he would regret. World-weary from the war and the blow of his brother's senseless death afterward, he had been revitalized by Caycee's lust for life. In a few short weeks, she'd managed to do something no one else had been able to do. She'd gotten under his skin, touching him both heart and soul while making him feel whole again for the first time since he could remember.

He respected her for that feat; he also desired her more than he dared admit even to himself.

"Let me go, Caycee," Zackary rasped as his shirttail floated from his Levi's and she brushed the sensitive skin near his waistband with her seeking fingertips.

He placed his palms against her shoulders and forcefully thrust her away in an attempt to regain control of his own emotions. This time *she* went under.

He'd seen grown men drown in less than ten feet of water during the war. Suddenly frightened of losing her, Zackary did exactly what Caycee had warned him against and panicked, lunging to grapple for her beneath the surface of the crystalline pond.

He felt his toes touch the bottom of the pond just as her body bumped solidly against his, propelling him closer to the shoreline. He planted his feet securely in the mud, wrapped his arms around her slender waist, and lifted her out of the water, pressing her torso firmly against the length of his as she slipped her legs around his thighs to catch her balance in water that was over her head.

Their gazes snagged.

Their breathing harshened.

Their bodies tensed.

Caycee closed her eyes first.

And Zackary did what he'd been wanting to do for what seemed like eons, something that felt like the most natural thing in the world to do under the circumstances: He sought Caycee's lips.

His kiss started as a tentative quest. He tested the shape of her lips with his tongue, intimately traveling the gentle, rose-hued contours he'd been studying since that first day in Westport. Her lips proved every bit as tender, as receptive, as savory and encouraging as he'd imagined both waking and sleeping.

Zackary deepened the kiss as he delved beyond Caycee's tough exterior in search of the gentle woman she shielded so zealously behind her boyish facade.

Caycee responded by flicking her tongue across his.

Zackary sucked in his breath, swiveled toward the shoreline, and marched with Caycee in his arms back to the star grass meadow and the campfire she'd built before he'd started the horseplay.

He stood her on her feet. She slipped from his arms. He kept his hands pinned rigidly at his sides, still willing at this point to allow her to escape his mounting passion.

In a way he hoped she would.

In another, he prayed she would not.

Caycee paused, took a deep breath, and reached out to brush his wrist with her fingertips, catching the end of his sleeve and twisting the button loose so that the cuff dangled against his hand. In silence, she proceeded to loosen the remaining cuff. The buttons that closed his shirtfront against her further exploration rapidly followed suit.

Before he knew it, Caycee had peeled his saturated shirt from his chest, pushed it off his shoulders and down his arms, and tossed it aside.

It was an open invitation and all the prompting Zackary needed. Ever so gently he pulled her mouth to his, glad that she'd chosen the prison of his arms over freedom.

"I wasn't drowning, Caycee," he whispered against her lips. It was a lover's peace offering. A token of sorts. A final bid for reprieve—for them both.

"I realize that now," she said.

Caycee pulled away from him only to graze his eyelids, his nose, and the severe line of his jaw with her frantically searching lips. He arched his chin to better accommodate her, surprised when she moved lower still in her ministrations.

"I wasn't then. I think I am now," he said hoarsely as she rained quick, sucking kisses over his shoulders and upper chest.

"Me too," she moaned, seeking his mouth once again, insisting with her tongue that he open his lips to her.

Zackary found the bedroll Caycee had spread beside the campfire while he had hobbled the horses. He lowered her upon the blanket without taking his lips from hers, edging his pocket watch off the bedroll and into the grass.

Caycee followed him down without questioning the adventure she was about to embark upon. It felt right. It felt natural. To deny Zackary would be to deny herself, and in doing so she felt she might somehow cease to exist entirely.

"I want you, Zackary Reece Butler," she said, running her fingertips through his damp hair and down across his back in a sensuous circle.

He groaned, slipping his hand beneath her shirt to caress her chilled breasts with his oh-so-warm hands. Desire spiraled through her and she reached blindly for the buttons securing his Levi's. If she lost this special moment in time, if she let it slip through her fingers, she felt certain it could never be replaced.

The wetness of the denim material made the buttons infuriatingly difficult. Covering her hands with his, Zackary assisted Caycee in working the buttons apart. They removed the Levi's together.

The scarlet chamois hampering his caresses covered her mere minutes longer than his Levi's had his muscular thighs. Her satin panties caused a simple raising of his brows before they too joined the growing pile of clothing at the foot of her bedroll.

Zackary paused when he saw the talisman suspended from its chain. "What's this?" he asked, fingering the polished bone talisman and tightening the chain around Caycee's neck.

"A good-luck charm my father gave me."

"It looks Indian."

"It probably is. Years ago my father worked with a man named Joseph Coyote. He was half Comanche and a good friend to Dad. Joseph swore the talisman held magical properties. He gave it to Dad as a gift, saying it would protect him in his work."

"And your father passed it on to you?"

"Yes, just recently."

"To protect you against evil?"

"No, I think he did it in hopes of bringing me good fortune . . . and it has."

"Perhaps not. Caycee, maybe we should think this thing through—" Zackary began.

Afraid of any second thoughts, fearful of his pulling away from her at this point, Caycee cut Zackary short.

"You taste wonderful," she whispered in his ear, successfully diverting further discussion of the talisman.

"Men don't taste wonderful," he said against the column of her throat, releasing the talisman to gallantly cushion her back against the hard ground with his arms as he resumed their loveplay.

"You do. It's the chemistry," she insisted, tilting her face so that her lips slid across his beard-shadowed cheek, ending in a tender collision with his lips.

"The chemistry?" he muttered against her mouth.

The sable hair on his chest teased her ivory breasts as he stretched his warm, aroused body across the length of hers.

"Yeah, the chemistry between us," she said. "It makes everything—"

"—wonderful," he finished, so softly that she sensed rather than heard the word.

Whimpering, she reached for his buttocks, aggressively tugging him more solidly against her pelvis. She arched against him, expressing her readiness and her need with age-old body language that left no room for doubt.

"Easy. We have time," he rasped, smoothing her hair from her forehead in a caring caress.

"I'm not so sure about that," she managed.

"Perhaps you're right . . . perhaps not," he said after a long pause, burying himself between her thighs and soothing the heavy ache that resided there.

Kissed by the breath of spring whispering against their bare skin, gilded by a rising white moon, and warmed by the flickering campfire light, they explored the shadowy avenues of passion that carried them toward fulfillment.

Hard masculinity driving rhythmically with increasing momentum into soft femininity, he reached the end of her as she reached the beginning of him. Together, they successfully discovered the light at the end of the tunnel. Not once, but twice. She demanded more than he'd ever given; he gave more than he'd thought possible.

Long after they'd exhausted themselves in the wonder of each other, Zackary told

Caycee with a playful wink, "Apparently stunts on horseback aren't the only thing you're good at."

Caycee flashed him a sleepy smile. "Apparently, although I've decided just recently, mind you, and with a good deal of help from a sometimes outlaw, sometimes Pinkerton agent, that a lot depends on finding the right person to share yourself with."

Zackary honored her smile with a radiant one of his own. "Are we right for each other, Caycee?" he asked, tugging her so close that her body rested halfway across his and her head was cushioned against his shoulder.

Feeling a sense of contentment such as she'd never known, Caycee said against the pulse throbbing at the base of his throat, "We're as right and as wrong as two people can get."

He swallowed deeply, almost painfully. "Do tell," he said, using the consciously controlled, smoother-than-smooth tone she'd come to admire.

She made no reply.

He breathed deeply. Once. Twice. Three times. Then he yawned, shifting his weight and tightening his embrace in a way that left no doubt as to his feelings for her.

"So what do we do about it?" he asked. His

smooth tone had the slightest catch in it.

Caycee didn't even attempt to skirt the issue.

"I don't know, Zackary," she said on the tail of a soft sigh.

"Neither do I."

"I guess we're just going to have to go with the flow for a while . . . see where time leads us."

His embrace tightened another degree. She found comfort in the strength of his hold on her.

"Time seems to be an important factor to you," he said.

"It is."

"It keeps cropping up."

"I know it," she said.

"Am I missing something here?"

"Through no fault of your own," she said.

"I suspect it's because you don't care to discuss it in depth with me."

"Please don't take it personally," she said quickly. "It's just that it's not the right time."

"You intend to remain a mystery, even after what we've shared?"

She nodded.

He inhaled deeply, then exhaled.

"Have it your way." He paused before adding, "You worry me, Caycee."

She didn't intend to argue the point.

"I don't blame you," she said. "Once in a while, I worry myself."

They gazed at each other for several moments.

"Do you suppose we'll ever have the kind of time we need?" he asked finally, loosening his embrace and relaxing against her in preparation for sleep.

Would they? She wasn't sure. She was beginning to hope they would. And that concerned her more than anything else had since she'd stepped across the threshold of the twentieth-century false-front bank on a dusty Hollywood back lot and dived headlong into the past, Caycee thought as she snuggled against Zackary, spoon fashion, closing her eyes against the moonlit darkness, and her mind against questions to which she could find no ready responses.

Chapter Ten

Prompted by the aroma of coffee bubbling enticingly in its hinged-lid metal pot, Caycee's eyes fluttered open. She zeroed in on Zackary immediately, where he was hunkered by the campfire and already fully dressed. She noticed her clothes were neatly arranged by the fire and, though wrinkled, appeared nearly dry.

"Have you been up long?" she asked in a sleepy voice.

"Since before daybreak," he answered in the smooth tone that invariably telegraphed tingling sensations throughout her body . . . more so this morning since she had experienced on a personal level the attention to detail Zackary Butler was capable of.

Wrapped from neck to toe in the woolen blanket he used for a bedroll, Caycee sat up on her blanket, which had been spread as a buffer against the meadow's prickly star grass.

"I appreciate your seeing to my clothes," she said around a yawn.

"My pleasure," he responded.

Reaching down to retrieve Zackary's timepiece from its grassy nest beside her bedroll, Caycee said, "Don't forget your pocket watch."

Zackary extended his hand. Caycee dropped the shiny watch into his palm.

"Thank you," he said.

He paused a long moment; then, as if making a decision, he continued. "My younger brother gave me that as a birthday gift. I wouldn't want to misplace it."

Intrigued, Caycee commented, "I didn't realize you had a brother. What's his name?"

"His name was Adam."

"Was?" she asked carefully.

His shoulders stiffened and for an instant Caycee suspected Zackary was considering ignoring the question. Then he rallied, a faraway look hazing his gray eyes.

"Adam was just a long-eared pup when the war ended."

"You returned home to Savannah afterward?"

"Yeah, but the town seemed too tame after years of living hand-to-mouth with the army. I decided almost immediately to travel west. The newspapers were filled with stories of the opportunities awaiting 'bold and daring adventurers.' I thought I'd find out for myself if they were peddling the truth."

"I understand. The call of the wild and all that."

"I suppose. Anyway, when Adam discovered my plans he hounded me to let him tag along. I finally gave in—much to Mother's distress. Adam was a bookish fellow. Mother insisted he would make a wonderful lawyer. Father thought it would be good for Adam to see the world. At that time they didn't have the money to finance a grand tour of Europe, so Adam and I packed up and headed for Kansas."

"And?" Caycee prompted.

His expression composed, Zackary elaborated.

"Adam was minding his own business, window-shopping at a mercantile next to a bank in Kansas City. There was a robbery. He got caught in the cross fire."

The words that followed seemed forced from Zackary's lips.

"Adam died in my arms," he confided.

Caycee didn't know what to say. What could she say?

"How sad," she managed finally.

Zackary cleared his throat. "Senseless," he clarified in a stern voice.

"Things like that are always difficult to fathom."

He nodded. "After seeing Adam's body home, I spent several weeks drunk as a skunk. And then I discovered something among Adam's papers that captured my energy and interest. It was an article concerning America's first private eye."

"Allan Pinkerton," Caycee supplied.

"With a renewed sense of purpose, I took the first train out to Chicago with every intention of investigating the bureau. Within a week, I'd landed a job with the department." He inhaled deeply, then exhaled. "And that was that. I've been working for Pinkerton ever since."

Zackary pocketed the watch.

"You don't get over these things, but you make room in your heart for the pain, Caycee," he said.

"I know," she said, thinking of her mother's lingering illness, and later of her father's disability due to the stunting accident.

"I've dedicated my life to Adam's memory."

Caycee fell silent, wondering what that meant as far as she was concerned.

Zackary's gaze eventually returned to the map he had been contemplating when she awakened.

"Care for a cup?" he asked after an interminable moment, pointing to the coffeepot over the map.

"Sure, in a little while," Caycee said.

She rose to her feet and stretched, glancing up at the cloudless azure sky.

"You know what—it's a beautiful morning," Caycee commented, marshaling a convincing half-smile.

It *was* a beautiful morning, regardless of the disheartening information Zackary had offered her concerning the loss of his brother—perhaps because of it, Caycee decided. For whatever reason, he had opened up to her in a way that made her feel incredibly special.

She would feel good about things.

She couldn't afford not to.

Shading his eyes, Zackary glanced up as well.

"That it is . . . beautiful," he commented.

Caycee realized he was looking at her rather than at the sky.

Suddenly self-conscious, she said, "I must look a mess."

She raked her fingers through her tangled hair. She didn't need a mirror to confirm that without the modern convenience of a blow-dryer to tame it, her baby-fine hair was hopelessly wild. Especially after a swim. In conjunction with a night of lovemaking.

Map in hand, Zackary stood.

"You don't look too bad," he said with a grin, and she realized his mood had considerably lightened.

"What? Tell me. Do my eyes look puffy? Do I have grass stains on my cheeks?"

"It's nothing."

His grin widened.

"It's my hair, isn't it? Come on. Spit it out. I can take the worst. I've been looking at this hair for twenty-six years now. Nothing would surprise me," Caycee said with an answering grin.

"It's just that—" he began. Amusement sparkled in his eyes.

"Just what?"

"The way it dried reminds me of that feisty old rooster Klaus did in for our supper."

"Sticking up like a coxcomb, no doubt," Caycee said, attempting to pat down the crown. "I must look like a fool. It's the cowlicks. I have two that my hairdr—"

Zackary reached out to touch her hand, halting its progress. Linking his fingers with hers, he brought their hands down to rest in a joint fist between them.

"You're no fool and you know it," he said.

Caycee sensed he wanted to say something more. She hoped like heck he wasn't going to apologize for the things that had passed between them. It had been a glorious evening and she sustained no regrets.

"Caycee—" he began.

"Don't tell me that you're sorry about last night, because I'm not," she interrupted.

"That was the farthest thing from my mind," he said, his voice lowering. "You knew what you were getting into. I realized early on that you're experienced in the ways of men and women."

Chin up, Caycee agreed with his statement.

"You're right. I am experienced. I've been married, and I've been divorced."

His brows arched and Caycee realized she had successfully surprised him.

"Not many women would admit that," he said. "It tends to darken their character in the eyes of the world."

"Where I come from it casts only a fleeting shadow," she said.

The magnitude of Zackary's perusal deepened.

Caycee attempted to glance away.

He stopped her by catching her chin lightly with the tip of his forefinger.

"Where *do* you come from, Caycee?" he asked. "After what we've shared . . ."

His words dangled in midair as he awaited her response.

"I can't tell you. Not right now," Caycee said, wishing she could be as up-front with him as he had been with her. But she couldn't share herself with him to that extent. Not yet.

A frown creased Zackary's forehead.

"What's a lifeguard, Caycee? At least allow me that much in the way of an explanation," he said doggedly.

Caycee dropped her gaze and disengaged her fingers from his strong, tanned hand. She must seem to him as if she had arrived from another planet, she thought. She couldn't fault him for being curious about her. She probably made him feel peculiar when she spouted off at the mouth with words he had never heard before.

"A lifeguard is a person who has been trained to attend to other swimmers' safety," Caycee explained.

"You trained in school."

"Yes."

"I see. Yesterevening makes a bit more sense to me now," he said thoughtfully, and she felt the strain between them ease.

"Good. Okay, well . . . I'm just going to go down to the pond now and try to make myself presentable," she said as a way of ending the conversation.

He nodded, allowing her release by returning to his seat near the campfire.

Hugging the blanket to her body, Caycee strolled to the pond, feeling Zackary's gaze resting between her shoulder blades. Without batting an eyelash, she dropped her covering at the edge of the pond and stepped into the water to splash and refresh herself. The juncture between her thighs felt tender, but not overly so. Actually, it was quite a pleasant sensation—just noticeable enough to remind her of the glorious hours she'd spent in Zackary's embrace, Caycee thought.

She glanced up once from her ministrations to catch Zackary watching her. Her gaze met his in an intimate exchange that was not at all disconcerting, considering its intensity and the bareness of her flesh.

Caycee skimmed the water with her hands, playfully splashing droplets up the bank toward him in open invitation.

"I've already had my swim for today," he commented, switching his attention from her back to the map he held open in his hands.

"Have it your way," Caycee called.

She finished her bath and returned to the campfire to collect her chamois and corduroys, moving behind Zackary to don them. When she was done she accepted the cup of coffee he served her, sipping at the strong brew and nibbling at a stale johnnycake while gazing over his shoulder at the map.

Running his finger along a darkened, zigzagging line she assumed to be the trail they followed, he said, "If the map is true, I figure we'll reach the Gonzales place before sundown."

Illogically disheartened by the news, Caycee made no comment. Yesterday at this time, she would have been thrilled to reach the rendezvous point. Today was a different story, even though she desperately needed to return home to check on her father.

In the back of her mind, Caycee wondered if she wasn't fooling herself. Could it be that she wanted to stay with Zackary, not so much for the chance of returning home, but for the sake of spending more time in his company?

When Caycee had finished her breakfast, he said, "I've already saddled the horses. If you would like to roll the blankets, I'll take care of the fire."

"Fine," she said.

Zackary poured water from his canteen to douse the fire, then strolled down to the water's edge to rinse the coffeepot and refill his canteen, leaving Caycee to secure their bedrolls to their saddles.

Within minutes, they were packed and ready to commence their journey. Zackary mounted the Morgan. Caycee gingerly followed his lead.

"There's something I forgot to tell you when we were discussing Adam, Caycee," he said.

"What's that?" she asked.

"That I take my job seriously."

"I realize that now."

"Chances are another robbery will already be in the works by the time we catch up with Dingus," he informed her. "It's going to take my full attention to set up the sort of operation I managed in Westport."

"The sort of operation I screwed up," Caycee provided.

He nodded.

"I can't watch over you this time, Caycee."

"What are you saying?"

"That I want you to stay out of the way."

She reined the mare beside the Morgan so that she could see Zackary's face. His expression told her he was dead serious.

"That's impossible," she said.

"I've told you, I have an agenda that's chiseled in stone," he said in a clipped tone.

If Zackary thought their association would come to a screeching halt once they reached the rendezvous point, he was sadly mistaken, Caycee thought.

"So do I," she said.

"One you won't entrust to me."

"One I can't entrust to you."

"I see you're going to make this as difficult as possible, even after I've broken down and explained myself to you," he said tightly.

"I don't mean to exasperate you," she said.

"And yet you do!"

She refused to meet his eyes.

"So be it, but don't expect my cooperation in relationship to your hidden agenda," he warned.

With a sinking heart, Caycee realized she and Zackary had come full circle only to arrive soundly back at square one.

The Gonzales place, a ramshackle one-room clapboard set on the bank of a river, reminded Caycee of nothing so much as a contemporary pawn shop. She had never witnessed so much junk: wagon wheels, lamps, assorted pieces of clothing, traveling trunks, books, jewelry, jars of beef jerky, guns, cases of ammunition stored under a lean-to, full and empty whiskey bottles in broken-open wooden cases, and stacks of pots and pans and cast-iron skillets.

"That's Gonzales," Zackary said as they dismounted to allow their horses to quench their thirst from the watering trough. "You name it, the man's got it. And if he doesn't, he'll get it. Pronto."

"Which one is Gonzales?" Caycee asked.

Zackary pointed to a rotund Mexican swaying contentedly in a rocking chair positioned in the shadow of a gnarled tree growing between the shack and the horse corral. Dingus, along with a couple of other rough-looking men she didn't recognize, lounged in the shade on bedrolls. Two freckled hounds, tongues lolling, basked in the shade with them.

One of the men, beefier than Dingus and yet resembling him, stood.

"Look yonder. The 'villainous abominable misleader of youth' has finally arrived," he said to Dingus.

Zackary leaned toward Caycee, saying under his breath, "That's Buck. He's Dingus's older brother. Likes to quote Shakespeare."

"I recognize the passage," Caycee said in an equally low voice. "It's from *King Henry The Fourth*, isn't it?"

Zackary raised his brows at her.

"You never cease to amaze me," he said.

Caycee shot him a half-smile. She never ceased to amaze herself either. She had merely dabbled in stage production in college, yet the line by Prince Hal characterizing his friend Falstaff had stuck with her over the years. It was strange, the bric-a-brac that the mind retained.

"I'm glad. That means you won't be prone to underestimate me," she said.

Eyes clouding to a stormy gray, Zackary began, "Caycee, if you think for one minute—"

Rising to stand beside his brother, Dingus interrupted Zackary by calling, "I'd almost given up on the two of you," he called.

"We'll talk about whatever's going on in that head of yours later," Zackary said in a tight voice, tipping his hat toward the brothers.

"Dingus told us what happened in Westport. Tough break. Wondered if you would make it through, shot up like that," Buck said.

"I got lucky. A farmer picked us up on the road. Took us to his hog farm in the Ozarks. Quiet enough to drive a man to distraction, but the solitude did the trick," Zackary said.

"Does it look like the wound is gonna give you any trouble? You know my hand sorta aches when it rains," Dingus said.

Caycee glanced at his hand. Ungloved, it was clear he was missing the tip of a finger.

"None so far. It appears I'm as fit as a fiddle, barring the scar," Zackary said.

"That's pleasin' to hear," the outlaw said, turning his attention to Caycee.

"I suppose we have you to thank for Zackary's recovery," he speculated.

"I can't take all the credit. Zackary's fairly stubborn where his livelihood is concerned. Besides that, his hide is as tough as old boot leather," Caycee said. "Bullets practically bounce off it. Comes with age, I imagine."

Zackary was glaring at her from beneath the brim of his hat, though her comment raised a chuckle among the men.

"Dingus. You didn't tell us the young whippersnapper had a sense of humor," Buck said.

"We could sure use some of that around here," another gang member commented, breaking off a section of the switch he'd been shooing flies with and tossing it toward Buck's feet.

"That's Bob Younger," Zackary said softly. "Watch him. He's as charming as an ivory-toothed, silver-backed comb, but deadly; he's a Missouri bushwhacker born and raised, and proud of it."

Bob Younger's comment concerning her

humor suggested to Caycee two things: that morale was low among the outlaws, and that the gang members were getting restless. That was good in a way, she decided. Perhaps Zackary was correct. Maybe a new bank job was imminent. On the other hand, Caycee felt a sense of uneasiness seeping into her bones. It was a sensation that she couldn't put her finger on and yet she could pinpoint the moment she'd first felt it: when Zackary had leaned over and whispered "Younger" in her ear.

She was missing something here. Something extremely important. She'd stake her life on it.

Dingus's next statement to Zackary confirmed Caycee's supposition concerning his plans for another bank robbery and averted her feelings of unease.

"I've been hashing out a plan for another job. The fellows and I, we've been talking it over among ourselves. But I need your advice, Zackary. Unsaddle your horses and let them out in the corral with my thoroughbred. Then come on in the shack. We'll discuss my idea over a plate of spotted pup." Dingus paused, then added thoughtfully, "And bring the kid with you."

Caycee glanced uncertainly at the hounds.

"Does Gonzales cook dog meat on a regular basis?" she asked under her breath.

Zackary looked confused for a moment, then actually laughed aloud.

"Spotted pup is rice and raisins cooked together, Caycee. It's real common on a trail drive. Gonzales learned to make it traveling with Jesse Chisholm."

"Chisholm?" Everyone had heard of Jesse Chisholm. He had blazed the Chisholm Trail through Kansas. John Wayne had made the man famous by playing him on the silver screen.

"Gonzales rode with Chisholm when he took his wagons southward into Indian Territory and traded along the Wichita River. Gonzales was a camp cook for years."

"Before he turned entrepreneur," she said.

"Exactly," Zackary said.

After the dishes were cleared and the money from the Westport holdup divvied up, Caycee listened while Dingus and Buck, along with two brothers named Bob and John, discussed the upcoming bank job with Zackary.

"We've got a couple more men planning to join us on this one. Cole knows them— Clell Miller and Bill Chadwell. He's bringing them in with him, but I'm afraid he's already warned me they're as green as grass," Dingus said to Zackary as the conversation drew to a close.

"Their first job?" Zackary asked.

Dingus nodded.

"It appears to be. Buck and I talked it over and we figure we need to spend a little time checking out the lay of the land before we spell out the job to the new boys. Cole should be here within the next few days. We'll meet you in town sometime after that."

"Which town?" Zackary asked.

"We've decided to try our hand at the Deposit Bank in Columbia, Kentucky," Dingus informed him. He winked at Buck. "Thought we could take as much as sixty thousand dollars in cash if we're extra careful."

"That's a big haul . . . almost as much as a train robbery," Zackary commented.

"Sure is," Dingus told Zackary. "That's why we can't afford to make any mistakes. And that's where you come in."

Zackary raised his brow at Dingus. "What did you have in mind?"

"Buck and I figured you might oblige us by checking things out before we converge on the town," Dingus said.

"How do you suggest I do that?" Zackary asked.

"After you've rested up for a while, we thought you might agree to ride on down there and pose as a stock buyer. You look the part, and no one knows your face."

"You mean there aren't any wanted posters out on me."

Dingus winked at Caycee.

"That's what I like about your partner. He catches on quick without me having to explain things in minute detail."

"The kid isn't my partner," Zackary commented, scraping his chair across the wooden floor as he pushed away from the weathered plank table.

Caycee frowned. Dingus grinned. Buck watched the proceedings like a Buddha, finally chiming into the silent lull, "Not only that, Zackary, it will give you time to sleep in a real bed before we're forced to run abrush again."

Caycee could only assume Buck meant Zackary would get a hotel room. The idea sounded like a winner to her.

"When you go, I'm going too," Caycee piped up.

The attention of all six men, including Gonzales, who had so far been a silent observer, swiveled her way.

"No, you're not," Zackary countered as if they were the only two people in the room.

"I can be of use to you," Caycee insisted.

"No, you can't," Zackary said firmly.

"Well, I can tell you right now I'm not staying here when I have the option of a real bed," she said.

"Nobody said anything about you sleeping in a real bed," Zackary said.

Though he said nothing, Caycee sensed that Dingus listened closely to their exchange.

"I said I could be of help to you."

Zackary's expression told her he didn't see how in the world she could be anything other than trouble, though he asked, "How?"

She thought back to a scene in a movie she had done.

"With so many people involved, you're going to need help with your horses."

"So?"

"So, I'm great at handling horses."

"We've got a horse-holder," Zackary said dryly.

"No, we don't," Buck interjected.

Zackary's attention left Caycee to rest momentarily with Buck. "What happened to Charlie?" he asked, surprise tinting his voice.

"He's got gout," Dingus answered for Buck. "He won't be meeting us in Columbia. That's one of the reasons I decided to take on the two new men."

"You don't have to worry about old Charlie," Buck said to Zackary. "We told him we would send something to his wife to tide them over until he got back on his feet."

Caycee smiled at the strange sense of honor among outlaws.

Zackary mistook her smile.

"Don't think that means you've won, Caycee, because you haven't," he said. "You're not going to Columbia with me when I go."

Two could play this game, Caycee decided. She glanced at Dingus.

"Why can't I go? I'm smart. I know how to take direction. I'm inconspicuous. And I wouldn't ask for a big cut of the money from the job."

"No," Zackary said. His expression told her he knew what she was attempting to pull off and that he didn't like it one bit.

Well, like it or not, he had no choice, Caycee thought. Her future depended on being in on the bank job in Columbia.

"Now wait a minute, Zackary," Dingus said, playing right into Caycee's hands. "Maybe we can use the kid." He shoved his chair away from the table and stood up. "Step outside," he suggested. "You once showed me some pretty fancy riding. Was that just a fluke? Show us what else you can do. We'll decide afterward whether you're in on this venture or not."

Once outside, Caycee asked, "What do you want me to do?"

Zackary's jaw twitched. Beyond that, he hid his displeasure well. Caycee had to hand it to him—he would make a fine actor.

Dingus whistled once and the horses in the corral began milling around while his thoroughbred perked up its ears. Caycee remembered the sleek animal. She had unsuccessfully tried to escape from the ferry on its back following the Westport robbery.

A second whistle had the trained blue blood prancing near the fence like a show horse on parade. A third whistle alerted Caycee to what Dingus had in mind.

Zackary was alerted as well. He reached for her hand to stop her. Caycee stepped off to one side before he could detain her.

She had done a similar gag before, so Caycee was ready when the thoroughbred sailed over the fence and Dingus yelled, "Catch him, kid!" Muscles tensing, she leapt off the porch, racing at an angle to shorten the distance between herself and the galloping animal. The horse almost yanked her arm off when she grabbed his mane and lifted herself off the ground and onto his bare back.

Hanging on for dear life, Caycee stretched

across his arched neck, snagged his tender upper lip in her fingers, and bent his head around until he was high-stepping in a tight circle. Her captivated audience exuberantly applauded the stunt—all except Zackary.

"Good show!" Dingus shouted.

"If that don't beat all," Buck added.

"You got to give him credit. The kid's got pluck," Caycee heard Dingus tell his brother.

Out of shape, Caycee's muscles screamed out in agony. She had a sneaking suspicion this gag was going to cost her more than Zackary's displeasure.

"You want to call your horse back now before he wears us both out?" Caycee called to Dingus.

"Had enough fun for one day, huh?" Dingus said on the tail end of a hearty chuckle.

"More than enough," Caycee muttered. Her jaw hurt from clenching her teeth, though somewhere along the line she must have relaxed it long enough to bite her tongue, she decided, for she tasted blood.

Dingus whistled and the thoroughbred came to an abrupt and jarring standstill. Caycee slipped gratefully from his back, shaky but exhilarated by her accomplishment.

"I think Dingus meant for you to use a rope," Zackary said when she sauntered shakily up onto the porch. His tone dripped sarcasm, though his eyes showed concern.

Legs like rubber beneath her, Caycee said slightly breathlessly, "As you can plainly see, there was no need for a rope this time."

"It would have made it easier."

"And less spectacular."

"Safer," he said.

"Less impressive."

"You have blood on your lip."

"It's okay. I bit my tongue. That's all," she said.

"You're lucky."

"Luck wasn't a factor. I knew what I was doing. I'm a professional."

Dingus chuckled again, apparently delighted with the exchange. "A professional horse-handler, imagine that." He glanced from Caycee to Zackary and back again. "Looks like you're going to Columbia after all, kid," he said.

Caycee's gaze remained fixed on Zackary's stony-faced expression.

"Looks like I am," she said.

"There's no way I'm taking a wet-behind-the-ears kid to Columbia with me. You can bank on that," Zackary stated flatly, stomping back into the shack.

"Looks like he's put his foot down, kid," Dingus said with a shrug.

"We'll just see about that," Caycee said resolutely, more determined than ever to accompany Zackary to Columbia, Kentucky.

"It appears you've got your work cut out for you," Dingus commented.

"No doubt," Caycee agreed.

Because the Gonzales place was small and relatively busy, customer-wise, the outlaw band made camp a quarter of a mile or so from the shack. Caycee was uncomfortable with the arrangement, but she quickly learned to deal with the gang—more or less.

Two days after her demonstration of horsemanship, Zackary still remained adamant that he would travel to Columbia alone. To enforce his decision, he presented Caycee the cold shoulder at every possible turn. To keep her mind occupied and her thoughts from his censure, Caycee entertained herself by studying the other members of the outlaw gang.

Dingus inevitably rose grumpy in the mornings. Caycee quickly found it best to do as Buck advised and leave him be until he had his first sip of coffee. Dingus spoke often of his farm, of his wife, Zee, and of the wonderful mother she made for their son and daughter. Caycee also learned over the campfire one night when tall tales were being recounted to pass the time that while shooting targets, Dingus had accidently clipped off the tip of his own finger.

That was the also the evening Caycee discovered that Dingus was the outlaw's alias. She had yet to learn his real name.

Buck, on the other hand, seemed fairly even-tempered. He was married as well, but spoke little of his wife and nothing of offspring. He did, however, quote Shakespeare and the Bible regularly . . . and often, whether the passage fit the situation or not.

The Younger brothers and their two compatriots, who had joined the gang on the day following Caycee's arrival, seemed less polished than Dingus and Buck. Caycee was far less charmed by them and consequently more wary.

She was also growing anxious. Each day that passed meant a day lost. She felt her future slipping away into history like sand through her fingers while she stood by and watched it happen.

On the third day following her arrival at the Gonzales place, Caycee could stand Zackary's silence and her own inaction no longer. Determined to talk with him and clear the air, she waylaid him before

the other outlaws awoke from the bedrolls.

An early riser herself, Caycee caught Zackary hunkered down by the campfire making
the morning coffee and frying bacon in a
cast-iron skillet over the glowing red coals.
She decided the timing would never be better.

She knew he heard her advance, though
his back remained fixed toward her. When
she reached him, she stopped, saying over
his shoulder, "I'm not going to get anywhere
with you, am I?"

Without turning around, he responded,
"Not likely."

"You're unimpressed by me," she whispered, trying not to awaken the others. She
didn't relish the idea of being overheard.
She relished the notion of explaining herself
even less.

This time, Zackary turned slightly, and his
gaze touched briefly on her face. With stiff
reserve, he said, "That isn't the issue."

Roughened by the damp morning air and
his stint nighthawking, which according to
Dingus meant standing one's turn at watch,
Zackary's voice sounded raspy. And wonderful.

Caycee swallowed. She'd missed his voice
over the last few days. Their conversations.

His occasional touch. She just hadn't realized how much.

"I'm bound and determined that when you leave for Columbia—and by the way, I hope it's soon—I'll be with you."

He placed the skillet to one side of the fire and rose to fully face her.

"You know my position. I'm bound and determined you won't be with me when I pull out of here."

"Why?"

"We've been through all this before, Caycee," he hissed.

Caycee suddenly realized something that had eluded her before now. She wasn't going to get anywhere with Zackary unless she opened up to him emotionally. He'd confessed that he'd devoted his life to avenging his younger brother's death. Perhaps if she explained the reasoning behind her actions, he would reconsider his position.

"I need to talk to you privately," she said, glancing over her shoulder as one of the outlaws stirred, coughing in his sleep.

"We have nothing to say to one another."

"Maybe you don't, but I do."

Her voice was strained even to her ears, and without consciously realizing it, Caycee reached out and touched Zackary's arm. It was a conciliatory gesture. A woman-to-man gesture. A wait-a-minute-and-listen-to-me gesture. A please-don't-cut-me-off-and-walk-away gesture.

Their eyes met and held.

The cougher in the bedroll stirred and sat up.

Zackary and Caycee sprang apart.

"What's going on here?" Dingus asked, yawning and rubbing the sleep from his eyes.

"Nothing," Zackary said, still gazing at Caycee. "Why don't you roll on out of those covers and keep an eye on this bacon. Caycee and I are going to stroll down to Gonzales's shack."

"What for?" Dingus asked, rising and stretching.

"He's got a strawberry roan in the corral down there. He says if I can break her, Caycee can have her."

This time, Caycee raised a brow at Zackary. Zackary shrugged.

"That roan's a handful. Gonzales made Cole the same offer last year. The mare damned near took his eye out with her teeth."

"I'll take my chances," Zackary said, motioning for Caycee to move along if she planned on speaking to him alone.

"Seems despite the way you've been acting lately, you're mighty taken with the kid to do a fool thing like breaking that roan. Gonzales uses that mare as a talisman against boredom."

Zackary cast a glare in Dingus's direction. Caycee touched the chain around her neck that held the talisman suspended against her heart, thinking of her father and the necessity of returning home to him.

"A man doesn't necessarily have to be taken with someone to accept another man's challenge, Dingus."

"A mite touchy this morning, aren't we? Appears you've been up nighthawking too long and too often these last few days. It's getting to you. You're not as young as you used to be," Dingus commented thoughtfully.

"Idle hands . . ." Zackary said, and Caycee realized he was attempting to defuse the potentially explosive situation that she'd more or less created.

"Yeah, I know," Dingus said. "They're the devil's workshop. Maybe it's about time we made a move on the Columbia job."

"Maybe," Zackary agreed.

"Might be time for you to ride on into town."

"Might be."

"We'll talk later," Dingus said, his tone easing.

"Fine. When Caycee and I return," Zackary agreed.

"Count on it."

Zackary nodded, steering Caycee away from camp by placing his left hand firmly on her shoulder.

"And watch your back with that filly. She likes to kick you in the backside when you're not looking," Dingus called after them.

"She's not alone," Zackary commented, waving his right hand in reply to Dingus.

Thrilled that Zackary had honored her request for a private conference, Caycee launched into speech as soon as they were out of hearing range of the camp.

"Once you asked me what I was running away from and I tried to tell you that I'm not running away from anything."

"I remember."

"The truth of the matter is that I'm trying to get back to where I belong."

Zackary stopped in midstride, removing his hand from her shoulder.

"Caycee, if you're going to start talking in riddles again, I'm going back to camp."

Caycee actually caught his arm and dragged him forward until he was walking in stride with her once again.

"You opened up to me once. You told me about your brother, Adam. Now I'm trying to do the same thing, if you'll just hear me out."

"All right. But this had better be good."

Walking side by side with Zackary, Caycee continued. "A year or so ago, my father was working on a—uh, my father sustained a fall from a horse. It left him paralyzed from the waist down. My mother passed away when I was a teenager and I'm the only family Dad has to depend on."

"Even when you *don't* talk in riddles, you talk in riddles. If your father needs you, what in the heck are you doing here with me?" Zackary asked.

"Don't get all bent out of shape. That's exactly what I'm trying to explain to you. I realize I can't go on masquerading as a boy forever, and I can't live with the constraints that your society imposes on its women."

"It almost sounds to me as if you feel you don't belong in this world, Caycee."

With a deep sigh, Caycee said, "That's precisely what I've been trying to tell you. I don't belong here. I belong with my father. He needs me." Her voice broke on the word *needs*. "If you let me go with you to Columbia, I think I've got a good shot at finding my way back home again."

"Why are you doing this to me?" he groaned.

"You aren't the only one with a mission, Zackary. I have one too," she said in a small, pained voice.

There was desperation in her voice as well . . . and determination. She heard it; he heard it. It was a live thing pulsing between them.

Zackary paused, turning toward her to search her face with his stormy gray gaze, reaching for her elbows and pulling her slowly toward him, his expression mirroring her pain and desperation and determination. For a moment, a heartbeat, a second in time when everything around them stood still, Caycee thought he might kiss her. She even closed her eyes in anticipation of the pressure of his lips against hers.

And then the sound of Gonzales's voice broke them apart.

"What are the two of you up to out there?" the Mexican asked from the doorway of the shack.

Zackary pivoted toward Gonzales. If not for his hand on her elbow, Caycee would have lost her balance entirely.

"We've come to see about the broncobusting the roan," he said evenly.

"Come to see about the roan," Caycee

echoed as her equilibrium reinstated itself and Zackary released her arm.

Gonzales stepped from the shack and escorted them to the corral.

"Go ahead, senor. Try your hand at her. If you succeed, as I've said, the mare she is yours."

Caycee watched in fascination as Zackary unhooked a lasso from the gatepost and climbed over the railing into the corral. The horses stirred. Zackary singled out the strawberry roan and neatly dropped the rope around her neck with a hoolihan loop that flipped up from the ground rather than over the horse's head. Caycee had seen her father do that before. It was a difficult maneuver and she was suitably impressed.

"Seems placid enough," Zackary commented to Gonzales. "How old is she?" he asked, watching as the horse danced against the rope for a moment, then settled down again.

"Four . . . and she is not placid, senor. She is playing with you."

"We'll see," Zackary commented as he drew the horse via the lasso closer toward him.

While Zackary tied the horse to the snubbing post in the center of the corral, Gonzales disappeared into his shack only to return with a single-rigged saddle with only one cinch, a blanket, and a hackamore. Zackary thanked the Mexican, gently slipping the bitless, rawhide-nosebanded bridle over the mare's muzzle and lifting the blanket and saddle into place. The mare snorted when he cinched the saddle girth, but otherwise seemed calm and collected.

Twisting it to distract her, Zackary whispered something into the mare's ear, then slipped his foot into the stirrup and mounted her back. A smile on his lips, Gonzales released the roan from the snubbing post and stepped from harm's way.

Three stiff bucks and the mare calmed down to an easy canter around the perimeter of the corral. Almost before it had begun, it was over.

Gonzales's face told Caycee the Mexican was utterly astonished.

"What did you say to that mare, senor?" he asked after a moment. When he could once again find his voice, Caycee surmised.

"Just that if she behaved, she'd get to take a little trip to town alongside my Morgan," Zackary said, his devilish grin firmly in place.

After several turns around the corral, Zackary dismounted, tying the roan to the fence and exiting the enclosure through the gate this time rather than climbing over the log railing.

Awed by the fluid smoothness of Zackary's broncobusting performance, Caycee asked as the Mexican moved back to the doorway of his shack, "It wasn't as easy as it looked, was it?"

"It never is."

"I know," she said.

"Dingus was right. I'm not as young as I used to be. Every bone in my body hurts. But it looks like it was worth it, 'cause you've got yourself a decent horse to ride into Columbia."

"I'm going to Columbia with you?" Caycee asked softly.

"It looks like it."

"What changed your mind?"

"I'm not sure . . . don't ask. Just loco, I suppose. We're starting to look suspicious together. You're starting to . . . Actually I can hardly keep my . . . No, never mind . . . just loco. That's all."

Caycee didn't ask Zackary to explain. As crazy as it sounded, she understood. She could hardly keep her hands off him either.

"I don't know what to say . . . about the mare, I mean," she said finally.

"Don't say anything. I didn't do it for you," he said, shouldering past her. "I figure the roan will attract a whole lot less attention in town than your swayback mare."

Caycee suspected that perhaps for the first time in his life, Zackary Reece Butler had told an out-and-out lie.

Chapter Eleven

I'm back in the saddle again.

After a week of hard riding, "down and dirty" had taken on new meaning, Caycee thought as she lifted her Stetson and with her forearm dabbed at the perspiration beading her brow.

Zackary hadn't been mistaken when at the pond in the meadow he had commented it might be a while between baths. She could sure use one about now. A hot, bubbly one. One she could submerge her tired body to the neck in and relax her aching muscles until the water grew tepid. A garden tub like the one she had at home. In the weeks she had been away, she had learned to miss those things she had taken for granted, like hot food, cold drinks, the morning paper, a good book. The ring of a telephone, which meant instant communication worldwide at the touch of a button. And last, but not least, her father . . . and the huge garden tub they'd installed after his accident.

Caycee sighed, squinting toward the east.

It looked as if she might be getting a bath soon. But not the kind she wanted.

"I can see a gray curtain of haze in the distance," she said.

Caycee nudged the roan mare up beside Zackary's Morgan, pointing in the direction she had been gazing.

Surface calm hid her inner turmoil as she asked, "Is that a storm heading our way?"

Zackary checked the Morgan, slowing the horse from an easy trot to a brisk walk. Caycee's mare followed suit.

"Yep, it's rain all right. It's closer than it looks too. I can already smell it in the air," he said.

Caycee attempted to withhold the anxiety from her voice, and yet she suspected it trembled ever so slightly as she asked, "It isn't another tornado, is it?" She didn't look forward to going through that experience again.

"I don't see any signs of a tornado. We're in Kentucky now and it's a lot less likely we'll see one here than in Kansas or Missouri," he said.

"Kentucky! When did we cross the state line?" Caycee asked before she could stop herself.

"Day before yesterday. We're only ten miles or so outside of Columbia," Zackary remarked dryly.

"Oh," Caycee said.

She was so accustomed to seeing highway signs and tourist welcome centers that it surprised her she could have crossed from one state to another without realizing it. Of course, there were no markers announcing the passage of miles on the wagon track they followed. With growing respect for his survival skills, Caycee acknowledged that Zackary seemed to instinctively recognize the path without the contemporary trappings she had come to depend upon.

"It amazes me how well you've managed up until now. You couldn't tell a trail marker if it slapped you between the eyes," Zackary continued.

"I won't argue with that," Caycee said. Her words were clipped and careful, as they had been since leaving the Gonzales place.

"What did you do up until now when you traveled?" he asked.

"I depended on a map, like you did to

find your way to the Gonzales place," Caycee said quickly. She did depend on a map—a road atlas that marked each road, each exit, and each rest station. She also traveled at 55 miles per hour rather than 55 miles per day. But she couldn't tell him that. He would think she'd gone off the deep end.

Caycee was also well aware that Zackary still had his doubts about her. He had resisted tooth and nail her request to ride with him to Columbia even after she'd proven her worth to Dingus during the two-week period they'd remained at the Gonzales place. His attitude had softened only after she'd broken down and recounted to him the story of her father. She'd known the tactic of using a common bond would work because she understood about his brother's death and the way it had affected his life. They seemed almost kindred spirits in that respect.

His next words confirmed to Caycee that Zackary's thoughts meandered along the same avenue as did hers.

"I don't know if I've told you this before, but I don't like feeling manipulated, even though we seem to share something in common. Regardless of your father's well-being, I could kick myself for bringing you along with me."

"I realize that," Caycee said, hoping to keep

him talking. Only in that way could she discover the motivations behind his actions. Only then would she know if he truly cared for her or if, stuck between a rock and a hard place, he had taken the line of least resistance in allowing her to accompany him.

"Do you? I decided at the last minute that leaving you behind was more loco than taking you with me."

"Why?" she asked.

"It was a question of safety at that point."

"What do you mean?" she asked.

"Caycee, if you don't beat all I don't know what does. You seem so wise at times, and yet so innocent at others."

Caycee frowned. "I still don't get it. You might as well spell it out."

"All right, I will. Dingus and Buck have a reputation for being true-blue to their wives, but some of the other outlaw members might not be so inclined to conduct themselves courteously should they discover you're a woman."

"Courteously? You mean they might—"

"I'm not saying they would force their attentions on you. I'm saying that I couldn't take that chance. Don't fool yourself. Gonzales saw us together out in his yard. I almost kissed you! He would have relayed the information to Dingus eventually. They would have figured things out sooner or later."

"So you decided the best thing to do was protect me."

"I'd do it for any woman fool enough to get herself into this predicament."

It wasn't what Caycee wanted to hear. She wanted to hear that her burgeoning feelings for Zackary were reciprocated, that he cared deeply for her. That she tripped his trigger in the same manner he did hers. But she suspected it would be a cold day in hell before she heard a declaration like that from Zackary, especially after what she had recently put him through.

The first drops of rain splattered her forehead, scattering her thoughts like feathers in the wind. She tugged on her Stetson, adjusting the brim against the droplets.

Zackary brought the Morgan to a halt, dismounted, and untied his bedroll, extracting a yellow slicker. Caycee reined the mare to a stop, but remained mounted.

He glanced at Caycee, up at the sky, then back toward Caycee.

"I reckon we're in for a fair drenching. You'd best haul out your rain gear."

His expression was expectant.

"That would be difficult to do," she said.

He raised his brows. It was a reaction she

might find charmingly endearing under different circumstances, Caycee thought.

"Do I want to know why?" he asked.

She watched his eyebrows lower. "I doubt it."

"Tell me anyway."

"Because all I had was a duster and I traded it for Klaus Becker's mare," she said.

Zackary shook the wrinkles from the slicker, saying, "I was afraid of that." He extended the slicker.

Caycee shook her head vehemently. "No, I couldn't. Really."

Zackary sighed.

"Don't make this any more difficult than it has to be."

"But I can't take your slicker."

"The last thing I need is a sick woman on my hands. Take the slicker."

"You're the one recovering from a wound," she said.

"Not recovering, recovered. Besides, there's a church a mile or so ahead. There's never anyone around the church except on Sundays. We can shelter there for the time being. If you take the slicker, we might even make it before the worst of the rain catches us out in the open."

On that note, Caycee accepted the slicker. Zackary held her reins while she slipped into it. As she anticipated, like a giant fish after a smaller one, the slicker swallowed her whole. He helped her roll the sleeves up to her wrists and adjust the skirt around her saddle before he remounted without comment.

The rain started in earnest before they had made it a half-mile. Within three-quarters of a mile, hail added impact to the storm. Stinging lumps of ice drove them, horses and all, up the steps and onto the rural church's covered porch. Her memorable experience with the tornado propelled Caycee off the mare, through the whitewashed double doors, and into the cedar-paneled sanctuary, leaving Zackary alone to care for the animals. As an afterthought, she stuck her arm through the doorway and extended the slicker to him.

"I'm all right," he shouted against the drumlike roll of thunder.

"Take it," she insisted.

"Caycee, the horses . . ."

"Take it."

She shook the slicker at him.

He resisted.

"I'm already soaked to the bone."

"So humor me," she said, her voice rising. "The last thing I need is for you to get sick on me again." *The last thing I need is for something to happen to you.*

He took the slicker and shrugged into it, more to placate her than for the good it might do him, she decided as she shut the door against the wind, the rain, and him. She wished she could shut the door to her heart against him as easily.

Within minutes, the door opened and Zackary stepped across the threshold into the church's dusky interior, quickly disposing of the slicker. Caycee watched as it fell into a puddle of yellow on the floor where he had dropped it. Her gaze immediately traveled from the slicker to Zackary's denims, water-darkened and clinging. Then higher to his shirt, which molded his muscular torso like candle wax. And still higher to his hair, plastered against his skull like a luxurious sable cap. Finally, her gaze slipped sideways to rest on the most arresting quality he possessed—his storm-gray eyes.

Caycee experienced a flashback to the evening in the meadow when there had been no holds barred between them, a flashback so powerful it nearly stole her breath away. No, not nearly. It *did* steal her breath away.

She barely had enough air to force the words "You look like a drowned rat" across her lips.

"Thanks," he said.

Caycee ran her hands up and down her

arms. Although she wasn't drenched, thanks to the slicker, she felt chilled. As wet as he was, Zackary must feel like an ice block, she thought.

"I found some candles—bayberry. And there's a potbellied stove, and plenty of kindling and dry logs," she said after a moment. "Do you think the minister would mind if we used some of his supplies to heat this place up a little bit?"

"I doubt it. Helping wayward travelers is one of his prime directives, I suspect."

Without conscious thought, Caycee removed her Stetson and pitched it into the front pew.

"I'll build a fire then," she offered.

"I'd appreciate it," he said.

Zackary dropped his bedroll on the floor and removed his saddlebags from his shoulder, tossing them to Caycee. She caught them in midair without fault.

"The strike-anywheres are in the bags," he said.

"Good. I'll need them. My matches were in my pocket when we went swimming at the pond. They got wet," she said.

Their gazes connected.

"Did we just have an exchange without questioning each other?" Zackary asked.

Caycee felt a smile tugging at her lips.

228

"You know, I think we did. What does that mean?"

"I'm not sure."

"Neither am I."

"Sort of scary," Zackary said.

"Yeah, it is," she agreed, watching as he undid his belt buckle, tugged his shirttail from his Levi's, and stripped out of his shirt.

"What are you doing?" Caycee asked, breaking off one of the wooden block matches and swiping the head along the striking plate of the waterproof case. The match burst into phosphoric light and she ignited several of the bayberry candles sitting in brass candlesticks on the podium. The aromatic properties of the candles blended with that of the cedar paneling, sending a bittersweet scent wafting throughout the church.

Zackary paused.

"I'm getting out of these wet duds."

Passion rising at the thought of what lay beneath his "wet duds," Caycee abruptly turned her back on him.

As if he had read her mind, Zackary said quietly, "I don't plan a repeat of the meadow, if that's what you're thinking. It was a big mistake. We both know that."

No, she didn't know that, Caycee thought, not quite prepared for the pain his words inflicted. At the time, their coming together had seemed the most natural thing in the world. As right as rum and coke. It still did, regardless of the moments that had passed between them since then.

"Sure we do," she managed.

"We're getting too close to each other for comfort—like old vaqueros."

She swallowed her pain. "I agree."

"It's not prudent," he said.

Few things in our case are. "No, it's not."

"So we agree?"

"You betcha." The words felt as if they had been torn from her lips.

Lost in thought, Caycee busied herself with lighting the fire while Zackary finished undressing. She heard rather than saw him throw his soggy clothes over the back of a pew and shake out his woolen bedroll. By the time she got the fire going well, he was beside her, hands extended palms-up toward the orange-red flames.

Listening to the rain pelting the roof of the church, Caycee gritted her teeth, wondering how long the storm raging outside would last. She suspected a much shorter amount of time than the one rampaging within her.

and turned it into an open-air bathhouse. The stalls have tubs in them rather than horses. It's really a rather ingenious idea when you think about it."

Caycee glanced down the main street toward the shops and buildings that comprised Columbia, Kentucky. It was a cinematographer's dream town. A few people milled about outside the open doorway of the dry-goods store. She heard a saw and realized that somewhere nearby stood a wood mill and that perhaps that made up the economy of the town. Farther down the unpaved street a group of children played ball. Still farther, she could just make out the signs for the sherriff's office, a two-story saloon, and a hotel called the Golden Arms directly across the street from the Deposit Bank.

The bank's most prominent feature was the row of squeaky-clean front windows which reflectively traced the afternoon sun's zenith like signal mirrors. Oddly enough, the windows reminded Caycee of the Westport bank and the dangerous shards of glistening glass that had exploded around her, sending her sailing in fear of her life over the teller's counter—and into Zackary Butler's lap.

Columbia in general sparked the memory of the Hollywood set she had been working on before she had traversed the time barrier and landed in the past. Henry Lawrence, the director of the Western, had requested that the set be constructed in replication of a nineteenth-century border town. Her skin tingled at the thought that the gang's upcoming bank job could be her ticket home.

Deja vu, only in reverse.

"The bathhouse smells like horses, even from here," Caycee commented absently.

Zackary's mouth twitched.

"So do I . . . only not for long. You, however, are another story," he said.

"Why?" she asked.

"Read the sign, Caycee. It says, 'Gentlemen Only.'

Zackary flipped his reins toward Caycee. She caught at them, missing them by a mile. When she reached out to grab at the Morgan's bit, the horse sidestepped, bumping into her mare. The mare kicked at the Morgan. He nipped at her. Caught in the middle, Caycee finally managed to get them under control and tied to the hitching post only after Zackary interceded with muscle and brawn.

"I could have managed," she stuttered afterward.

"Managed what? To get stepped on or maybe something worse? Don't ever grab at the

Morgan's bit. He has a sensitive mouth and he'll balk every time. You have nerve. I'll grant you that much. But I'm not too certain about common sense," he said with a wry smile.

"Where would you have me catch his bridle?"

"You would do better to snag the nosepiece or the cheek band. He'll stand still for that."

Zackary reached for Caycee's hand, placing her fingers on first the nosepiece, then the cheek band. The Morgan remained calm. Caycee wished her heart would do the same.

"I'll remember that next time," she said.

"See that you do," he said.

"I will," she shot back.

They sounded like squabbling children. They realized it simultaneously. Caycee blushed. Lips compressed, Zackary released her hand and stepped away from the horses.

This time Caycee was grateful for the margin of distance between them. A girl could only take so much tension without snapping. Even when she was miffed with him, and he with her, Zackary sent her into an undulating pool of sensations. She supposed until now she hadn't really realized what passion was all about. At least not the kind that existed between a man and a woman—if they were exceptionally lucky.

Zackary took a deep breath.

Caycee let out a sigh.

"Can you handle them now?" he asked finally from the wooden-planked sidewalk.

"Does a hen lay eggs?" she asked in a dead-pan voice.

He smiled. Almost.

"You sound like Klaus Becker," he said gruffly, effectively stifling any hint of a smile.

"I stole that line from him."

"The time we spent at that old hay shaker's farm, wound and all, was . . . pleasant, wasn't it?" Zackary said.

Zackary had a faraway look in his eyes and Caycee realized that she need not reply, but she did so anyway, for his statement was the last thing she had expected.

"Memorable . . . and yes, pleasant in an odd sort of surrealistic way."

Zackary's gaze snapped back to the present and Caycee felt the tension that had momentarily relaxed between them resurge.

"You never answer anything straight on, do you, Caycee?" he asked. "There is always something carefully hidden. Something you don't want anyone to see, to touch on. What is it? How can I trust you when I don't know what's going on with you half the time?"

"Trust is a difficult proposition at best. I didn't ask you to trust me," she said.

"No, you didn't." Zackary paused. "What is it that you want from me, then?"

What did she want? "Your help."

"I've got a job to do, Caycee. You know that." He lowered his voice so that she had to strain her ears to pick up the words. "I've told you about Adam, and about the agency. I plan to go through with this come hell or high water, and you aren't making it easy. I can't afford another fiasco like Westport."

Her heart went out to him and she said softly, "I know that."

His eyes darkened.

"Don't soften your voice, Caycee."

Caycee couldn't avoid his stare nor the hint of urgency in his voice.

"I didn't."

"You did."

Caught in the spell of his ever-changing eyes and the gamut of emotions reflected there, Caycee said, "Not consciously."

He was caught too. She knew it as surely as she knew her heart was beating when he said, "Don't do it unconsciously. You sound too much like a . . . woman. Someone will hear. They'll know."

Caycee glanced around. "No one can over-hear us."

Zackary glanced around as well. "You can never be too cautious."

Caycee's eyes sparkled conspiratorially as she said, "Maybe I should go in the bathhouse with you, throw anyone who might be watching off the track."

"Maybe not," he said sternly.

She was pushing it and she knew it, but she couldn't help herself. She needed to know how he felt. At this moment, it seemed more necessary than air.

"I could scrub your back," she offered.

His face remained bland, but his eyes sparked fire and heat and desire at her.

"Definitely not," he exclaimed.

Her thoughts reeled. He cared, regardless of the things he had professed to her in the church: that their encounter in the meadow and then again at the Gonzales place had been two of the biggest mistakes of his life! But she was getting in too deep for the streets of Columbia. Her heart hammered with the revelation, her palms felt suddenly clammy, and her head was spinning.

It was her turn to back off, which she did with all due haste.

"I'm teasing," she said in a rush.

"You're not attempting to throw the people of Columbia off track. You're trying to avoid my question!" he said.

"Caught red-handed."

With a tight laugh that held no humor, he said, "For the love of . . . It's like pulling teeth to get a straight answer from you, Caycee. How can I help you if you won't tell me what you need?"

Caycee heard the frustration and anguish in his voice. It pained her to know she had created such havoc in his life. Of course, her life hadn't exactly been a bed of roses lately either. A bed of thorns, maybe . . .

"We've been over this before," she said.

He nodded. "Often, without much progress as far as I can see. I spill my life history to you; I'm lucky to know your name," he said, his tone hard and accusing.

"I need time, Zackary," she said. *I need time to correct its mistake. To put me back where I belong before it's too late. Before I lose the willpower to return to the future because of you.*

"You're obsessed with time!"

It appears time is obsessed with me. "Perhaps. Besides, every time I break down and try to explain things to you, you cut me short."

Muttering something about dirty, scrawny kids and the unpredictable trouble that had dogged him since meeting her, Zackary turned his back on Caycee and stalked toward the entrance to the bathhouse.

Carefully hiding her displeasure, she called just before he disappeared into the bathhouse, "Hey, what am I supposed to do while you're in there?"

"Wait!" he barked over his shoulder without slowing his step.

Hurt and angered by his abrupt dismissal, Caycee checked the horses' reins. They were tied securely—no problems there. Lower lip caught between her teeth, she pivoted in the direction of the Deposit Bank. You must remember that your father needs you, she told herself. She must get out of the past while the getting was good. She could leave Zackary if and when the opportunity presented itself. Certainly she could.

Maybe.

Possibly.

Perhaps.

Remember how mad he makes you, she thought. Remember how contrary he can be. Remember that he's a part of the past and you're a resident of the future.

The steps that took Caycee down the street to the bank started out positive, but by the time she reached the sidewalk outside the bank they lagged. She stalled completely at the threshold of the Deposit Bank.

What if she didn't need a robbery to propel her back to the future? What if she need only cross the bank's threshold to return to her own time? she wondered.

Caycee paced the sidewalk outside the bank, her bootheels tapping out a rhythmic tattoo on the uneven planks.

Was she ready to go now, this moment? More importantly, was she resolved to leave Zackary behind? Certainly he had exasperated her enough over the last few days for her to disappear from his life without a trace.

But could she actually take the necessary steps to do so? Without confiding in Zackary first? After what they'd shared, he deserved some sort of warning, didn't he?

Caught in a quandary, Caycee chewed thoughtfully at her lower lip.

Your father, she reminded herself once again. Think of your father. Zackary is strong and independent. Your father would like to be, but isn't. He's stuck in a wheelchair.

Chin up, shoulders back, Caycee forced her legs to carry her inside the bank.

Absolutely nothing happened.

The teller watched her with a curious smile pasted on his lips as Caycee tried again. Still nothing happened.

Caycee actually sagged in relief.

"Can I help you?" the teller finally asked.

"Uh . . . no, thank you," Caycee stammered. "I thought this was the dry-goods store."

"No, sir. The mercantile is down the street on your left." He pointed out his directions.

"It is? Oh, thanks. Thanks a lot," Caycee said, backing stepping toward the door.

She exited the dark interior of the bank, blinking as the bright Kentucky sunlight hit her in the eyes. She felt dismayed and yet relieved that it was apparently going to take a robbery to transport her back to the future.

Caycee retraced her steps back to the horses. Hat in hand, frown in place, Zackary awaited her return outside the bathhouse. She hadn't counted on him finishing so quickly.

"You clean up pretty well," she commented, eyeing him up one side and down the other. He had on the same clothes, but his hair was washed and slicked back, and his face clean-shaven.

"Compliments won't save you a dressing-down," he said.

"I wasn't—" she began.

"You've been down to the Deposit Bank, haven't you?"

"I—"

"You must have had an interesting conversation with the teller." He nodded in the direction of the bank. "He followed you to the door and watched you amble back to the horses."

"I didn't say a thing to him," Caycee said, suddenly alarmed. "Really. He said hello and asked if he could help me. I told him I was looking for the dry-goods store."

"And then you walked right past the mercantile without stopping in."

"I didn't think," Caycee said.

"I'm not the only one who noticed. The teller did as well."

"I apologize," she said.

"We can't afford to make those kinds of mistakes, Caycee. I wish you hadn't taken it upon yourself to visit the depository."

He seemed so disappointed in her that she couldn't help herself. Caycee found herself saying, "I had to see if for myself. I think that bank depository may be my route home to my father."

"Caycee, you're not making any sense," he said, his words clipped.

"What if I told you I was a time-traveler looking for a way back to my own century?"

"What do you mean?"

"I mean that by joining in this . . . escapade . . . I think I may succeed in my quest, and that I believe the Deposit Bank is my ticket home?" she said, her voice strained with quiet desperation.

He ignored the strain.

"I'd say that you must think I'm as dumb as an oyster, and that you're up to some new type of mischief . . . like that crazy horseback stunt at the Gonzales place, only worse."

"That's just what it was—a stunt. I knew what I was doing or I wouldn't have attempted it."

"Would you have me believe this thing concerning time-travel some sort of stunt as well?"

Hands on her hips, Caycee said defensively, "I knew that would be your reaction when I tried to tell you the whole truth and nothing but the truth. That's why I've refused to fully explain myself to you before now."

Zackary felt as if he were being royally duped. It made him furious with Caycee but more so with himself, since he had allowed his feelings for her to expand into something that he couldn't control. The more he distanced himself from her so that he could examine their situation objectively, the more absorbed with her he became. Caycee was a mystery that only grew more tantalizing with each passing day. He didn't so much distrust her as he did his inability to remain detached where she was concerned.

Why, he had almost experienced heart failure when she had pulled the trick with

Dingus's thoroughbred, endangering her life just to remain at his side! He had never been so angry . . . or so proud. She had shown calm deliberation in the face of danger. He couldn't help but admire that. Dingus was right on the nose. The woman possessed pluck along with an incredibly provocative imagination.

Attention veering back to their conversation, Zackary expressed that singular thought aloud.

"Caycee, you have a fantastic imagination."

"I do, but that's not the case in this instance. I'm not making this up," she said.

By now, several men had sauntered from the bathhouse to lounge near the entrance and smoke cigars. Zackary untied the Morgan's reins and motioned to Caycee to do the same with her mare.

"Let's stable these animals."

"You're not going to discuss this with me, are you?"

Their gazes locked in silent communication. Zackary finally reluctantly withdrew his gaze from her face and momentarily closed his eyes. When he reopened them, he said, "We're attracting undue attention by airing our differences in public."

Caycee glanced toward the men.

"I'm not blind," she said.

"Dingus wouldn't like it if he knew about the teller."

"He might call off the job," she said quietly.

"He might do worse than that. He doesn't care for wagging tongues," Zackary said tightly. "Someone could get hurt. Maybe the teller. Maybe you. Maybe me."

"I wouldn't want that to happen."

"Neither would I."

"Truce then," she offered.

He nodded. "Truce, for the time being."

"Shake on it?" Caycee asked as they walked their horses down the main street of Columbia.

"Bargains are sealed with a handshake."

"Right . . . no need for lawyers between friends. My father still believes in living that way," Caycee said thoughtfully.

"We aren't friends, Caycee."

"What are we then?"

"I'm not sure."

"Neither am I . . . so shake on it anyway."

They strolled in silence for a moment before Zackary said dryly, "You're carrying this show a bit too far, aren't you?"

Caycee shrugged.

"Let's just say I have a flair for the melodramatic."

"That you do," he agreed, sensing the tension between them dissipating.

"Besides, it appears we're playing to an audience," she said, the gaze she cast over her shoulder pinpointing the men with the cigars.

"Like you did at the Gonzales place," he said, acknowledging that the bond between them was once again slipping into place despite everything.

"Right on, partner," she said.

"You're doing it again," Zackary said, extending his hand sideways to her.

"Doing what?" she asked as she accepted his handshake by crossing her arm at the waist.

"Talking in tongues," he said. He released her hand and at the same time himself from the sensual sensation of her touch.

Shoulder to shoulder, they were standing too close.

Strolling too companionably.

Talking in normal voices.

Almost as if they were enjoying each other's company.

It was almost too much for a man to take and remain sane.

He needed all his facilities unclouded and in good working order to get through the next 24 hours before Dingus joined them in Columbia, Zackary thought. He planned to arrest the outlaw this time, but he must also protect Caycee as well as himself in the process. He felt convinced that the only way to accomplish the deed was to maintain a healthy distance between himself and the woman walking at his side.

Anger was the key, he decided. If only he could keep Caycee stirred against him long enough . . .

Chapter Thirteen

"I could use a home-cooked meal. How about you?" Zackary asked.

"I sure wouldn't turn it down if you're buying," Caycee said. The idea of fresh, home-cooked food such as her father prepared daily made her mouth water.

Zackary pointed to a building sporting a sign which dubbed it the Delmonico Diner with "the best fixin's in Kentucky."

"Why am I not surprised?" she muttered.

Delmonico must be a generic term for diner, Caycee decided. She had seen it used in almost all the flicks her father had played in, from gangster to huckster to cowboy movies.

"What?" Zackary asked.

"I was just saying what a nice ring the name Delmonico has to it," Caycee said.

They entered the restaurant with its neat red-and-white-checkered curtains and matching tablecloths.

Existing in the past reminded her of getting married, Caycee thought. Something old, something new, something borrowed . . . something blue.

They barely had time to seat themselves before a pretty young redhead wearing a blue serge dress and a yellow apron sailed over to their table. A bright smile hugging her lips, she said, "What's your pleasure, stranger?"

How cliche, Caycee thought, watching as Zackary reciprocated the waitress's smile with one of his most blinding.

"I'm not sure," he said. "How about going over the specials for us today?"

A frown of concentration creased her perfect brow. "We have steak and potatoes, corn on the cob, bread, butter, milk if you want it, or coffee, your choice, and apple pie to top it all off," she recited.

"What's it going to cost me?" he asked flirtatiously.

Zackary winked across the table at Caycee as if they were sharing some sort of joke. She felt a real urge to gag.

"Twenty cents apiece plus the tip," the waitress said.

"Is the tip yours?" Zackary asked.

"It sure is."

"Sold then."

Zackary counted the coins out onto the table, surprising Caycee by paying for the meal before they were served.

"Are you buying for your young friend too?" the waitress asked, glancing down at the coins.

"I suppose so. He looks as if he could use a good meal, don't you think?"

Zackary wasn't fooling Caycee. He was annoyed with her, and he was playing the part of a flirt to get under her skin. He was doing a pretty good job too. The young waitress was basking in the light of his attention. Then again, what woman wouldn't with a man like him? Caycee wondered.

"I wouldn't know about that, but he'd be plain foolish to turn down a full-fledged lunch that's bought and paid for out of somebody else's pocket," the young woman responded.

"You're absolutely right. He would." Zackary studied Caycee a moment before saying, "I'll have coffee with my meal. Bring the kid milk. I'm of the opinion he could use some fattening up."

He had called her scrawny out in front of the bathhouse. Now he was rubbing it in. Zackary Butler had better watch out. He was playing with fire. Only he didn't know it yet.

"He looks just fine to me," the waitress said coquettishly. She batted her eyelashes at Caycee. "But since you're the one that's forking out the money, milk it is."

The waitress sashayed around their table and disappeared into the kitchen.

Zackary nodded toward Caycee, his devilish grin firmly in place.

"I think she likes you," he said.

"I didn't notice," Caycee said stiffly, glancing at the change on the table. Now she understood why Zackary had kicked up such a fuss when she'd given Klaus Becker the 50-dollar bill. In her world, 50 wouldn't pay for a night's stay in a bed-and-breakfast, much less a square meal plus dessert and drinks. In Zackary's eyes, she had gifted the farmer with a month's pay in exchange for common hospitality. She had also possibly knocked Zackary out of a considerable amount of money. Money he probably needed to live on.

Of course, he had his loot from the Westport robbery. But perhaps that was evidence. Or he might even be planning

252

to return it to the bank. Caycee had no idea. Whatever he was using for spending money now, she was glad he had it because she was starving. Not having a refrigerator available was more inconvenient than one would imagine.

"You make a fairly convincing boy," Zackary commented, bringing Caycee back to the moment at hand.

If you'll recall, I make a better girl. "She doesn't like me. She likes you," Caycee countered. She glanced at the nickel he had added above and beyond the total cost of their meal. "Probably because you're such a high roller."

Zackary pursed his lips together and they remained that way until the meal arrived.

Caycee had to admit that the food smelled delicious, tasted even better, and should have soothed her frazzled nerves. But it didn't. They passed the meal in silence, both too absorbed in the savory flavor of the food to make small talk. Afterward, Zackary indicated he planned to quench his thirst with a beer.

In an increasingly foul humor, yet revived by the meal and determined to stick to Zackary like glue, Caycee trailed him to the smoky saloon situated next door to the diner.

Again, the saloon was decorated as she had expected, with a stand-up bar, card tables, brass spittoons, wooden tables and chairs, and mirrors on three walls.

It too reminded Caycee of hundreds of similar stage sets she had glimpsed during her career. Only this was the real McCoy, she reminded herself as Zackary purchased a "long nine" panatela cigar from a voluptuous cigarette girl.

"Smells pretty bad in here, doesn't it?" Zackary commented several moments later.

Caycee nodded.

"Now that you mention it, yes. What is it?"

"Those god-awful short sixes they give away for free here."

"Short sixes?"

"Free cigars, Caycee. Free cigars. The management can't sell them, so they give them away to men that lack discriminating taste."

"As a boon for business."

"You catch on quickly," Zackary said.

"That's the *one* thing you can depend on," Caycee said, wondering if they would ever find a table so she could put her back to the wall.

Zackary eventually found a table that suited him—near the stage, front and center.

"They have a full quart bottle of malt whiskey for a dollar. Or perhaps you would prefer beer?" Zackary asked as they sat down across from each other.

Caycee sensed Zackary was testing her, pushing her to the limits, trying to make her so angry she would throw up her hands and stalk away from him and the bank job. She couldn't and wouldn't do that, she told herself.

"I think I'll pass," she said. She needed a clear head and a sharp eye to keep up with Zackary.

"Suit yourself," he said, raising his arm in the air and pointing a finger toward the ceiling. Almost immediately, the bartender delivered a five-cent bottle of Brandenberg's New Jersey Beer and a glass to the table while a blowsy cancan dancer that had eyed him when they strolled into the saloon finished her stage routine only to posture on Zackary's lap afterward and kiss him on the lips.

The distracted expression on Zackary's face as he twisted off the wire from around the cork bottlecap with one hand and sloshed a hefty portion of beer in his glass told Caycee that he didn't know the woman, but that he was enjoying the attention. She had a burgeoning desire to punch out Zackary's lights for encouraging the woman's advances by offering no protest—not a telegraphing stunt-punch like the roundhouse right in which you stepped into the punch and without bending your elbow swung your arm and fist in an wide arc that invariably missed your opponent's chin, but a skin-contacting one that would make him sit up and take notice of his surroundings . . . and of her.

Since Zackary's hands were otherwise occupied, Caycee reached over and retrieved his beer glass, sipping at the dark liquid in hopes that it might cool down the blood boiling through her veins.

"Take it easy. That's a pretty strong brew," Zackary warned.

Caycee couldn't see his face for the broad expanse of crimson-red, satin-covered bust blocking her view. In rare form, she drained the glass. The warm beer went immediately to her head.

Several moments passed during which Caycee experienced jealousy for the first time in her life. She didn't like the feeling in the least.

Bolstered by the alcohol, Caycee swiveled in her chair and stood up, almost toppling her chair in the process.

"That's all I can stands. I can't stands no more," she said, using her best Popeye imitation as she steadied the chair and shoved it beneath the table.

"I suppose that means you're ready to call it a night," Zackary said, blowing at the feather boa dancing near his face.

"You betcha. High time to blow this honky-tonk," Caycee remarked.

"Perhaps I'll stay for a few minutes longer," Zackary said. He was standing as well now, but his arm rested lightly around the cancan girl's waist.

Silently fuming, Caycee forcefully tamped down her jealousy and called his bluff.

"Suit yourself. Perhaps, since my watch-dog is otherwise occupied, I'll stroll over and check out the Deposit Bank."

"Perhaps you shouldn't do that alone," Zackary suggested in a low voice.

Caycee raised her brows at him.

"Looks like the kid here thinks it's time to say adios. And I always listen to the kid," he told the woman.

Zackary tipped his hat to the cancan girl and stepped away. Caycee led the retreat from the smoke-filled saloon.

Out in the streets of Columbia again, Zackary took charge.

"You were getting mighty uppity in there," he commented. "And by the by, what in the heck does 'blow this honky-tonk' mean?"

Caycee couldn't help but notice that the tightness had crept back into his voice.

She shrugged. "It was the beer. It makes me talk funny. That's why I don't drink often."

"Good thing, too . . . could get you killed quicker than you could spit. Say the wrong thing to the wrong man and he's likely to take you to task."

Caycee halted abruptly. "Are you threatening me?"

Zackary stepped all over her heels before his brakes finally kicked in.

"I'm telling you the hard, cold facts. In a place like that saloon, one imprudent move and . . ."

Zackary let the sentence dangle, but Caycee caught his drift loud and clear.

"This is no place for you, Caycee," he continued. "I should have left you—"

"No place you know of is the place for me!" Caycee said in acute frustration.

Zackary inhaled sharply.

"What the hell is it with you, Caycee? Why won't you trust me? Why are you holding back?"

"Trust you! I'm blackmailing you, remember? That's the only reason I'm standing beside you now."

"You're overwrought."

"I'm angry." *I'm lost. I'm frightened. I'm*

258

homesick. I'm weary. And I'm in love with you.

"You need rest. I'll get a room."

Suddenly deflated, Caycee said, "Sure. Whatever."

Caycee trailed Zackary across the dusty street to the Golden Arms Hotel, which was conveniently located across the way from the Deposit Bank.

Zackary signed the register at the desk under the alias of Mel Gibson, paying for the only available accommodations in the house. Caycee followed him up to the third floor and an attic, corner room with exposed beams whose arched gable window created a picture-perfect frame for the bank.

"Lucky us," Caycee commented, gazing with detached interest at the Deposit Bank.

"Yeah, lucky us," Zackary agreed over her shoulder.

He spun away from the window, moving to turn up the oil lamps before swinging to face Caycee.

"This isn't working out," he said flatly. The light created by the oil lamps danced around them, creating caricatural shadows of them that danced larger than life across the flowered wallpaper.

"I know," she said.

The tension in the room was a palpable

thing. A creature with sharp fangs gnawing at them both and making them act out of character.

"We're getting on each other's nerves," Caycee continued. "You would think we were married or something."

She was trying a stab at humor. The line failed miserably. They both knew it.

"Listen, Caycee. I need some time alone to cool off. I'm going downstairs to play a game of billiards and smoke the long nine panatela I purchased in the saloon. Try to get some sleep," Zackary suggested.

Caycee glanced at the brass bed, single in size and sloping in the middle. The idea seemed dubious at best.

"But—" she began. Anything to stop him from leaving her alone in a strange room, in a strange town, with most of the night left for thought.

"I'm not going to slip off like a thief in the night, if that's what you're worried about," he said. "I've got too much invested to do something that loco. I figure Dingus and the rest of the gang will be here by tomorrow morning. I can almost assure you that all this will all be over fairly soon now."

Caycee realized Zackary spoke the truth, though she was positive that instead of shooting a game of billiards as he had said, he intended to further his relationship with one of the women they had met earlier in the evening. Much to her chagrin, Caycee admitted that she couldn't stand the thought of him locked in the embrace of another woman.

Left alone in the room with only her thoughts for company, Caycee absently glanced into the wavery cheval mirror stationed at the foot of the brass bed. The woman staring back at her looked like a stranger. Her hair, always fine and flyaway, reminded Caycee of strands of corn silk caught in a windstorm. She had lost ten, perhaps 15 pounds, so that when she untucked her no-longer-scarlet chamois from her far-from-cinnamon corduroys and tugged it upward to gaze at her torso, she could readily count the bones of her rib cage.

No wonder Zackary had called her a dirty, scrawny kid. If anyone could use sprucing up, she could. Besides, a hot soak would do her a world of good. She hadn't felt warm water against her skin since her shower the morning of the stunt crouper she had planned so meticulously with Henry Lawrence.

Caycee glanced at the cracked porcelain washbasin, wrinkling her nose in distaste. A sponge bath simply wouldn't do this time, she decided thoughtfully, zipping the talisman up and down along on the chain encircling her neck until it actually felt warm against her skin due to the friction she'd created.

No, sirree. A sponge bath wouldn't do at all! She could feel the trail dirt that had seeped through the fabric of her clothes and covered her skin in a heavy, perspiration- and oil-based film.

Still slightly tipsy from the beer, Caycee tripped out into the hall. Finding no one in sight, yet determined to indulge herself, she strolled down to the second floor and flagged down the housekeeper.

"I'd like to order a bath with lots of hot water," Caycee said.

"Which room?" the housekeeper chirped.

"Corner room. Third floor," Caycee said, pointing above her head.

"That's mighty uncommon—a bath on the third floor," the housekeeper said hesitantly.

Perplexed by the offhand comment, Caycee asked automatically, "Why?"

"That should be fairly evident. It takes a lot of toting to get water up there."

Of course, no pipes, Caycee thought. It was amazing, the things one took for granted.

"Regardless, I'd like a bubble bath in a deep tub if you have it. With *real* towels—

not like the burlap potato sacks I saw them airing out on a line at the bathhouse."

"Sacks work fairly well," the housekeeper commented.

Caycee cringed inwardly at the idea of rubbing her tender skin raw with a potato sack. It might be okay for the men who bathed at the livery stable turned bathhouse, but she wasn't a man. Not really. Not on the outside if you looked closely enough to notice, and certainly not on the inside. Especially with the way she was feeling tonight.

"As far as I'm concerned, sacks are out. I'm going all the way and I want real towels with my bath. Nail clippers. A razor. And another Brandenberg's New Jersey Beer. Can you get all that for me?"

"I can."

"I'll help carry everything up," Caycee said.

"No need," the housekeeper said, obviously softening toward Caycee due to her unexpected offer. "I have a boy I can get to help do that, but I'll need to know who's paying for this celebration before I start ordering *real* towels from the Chinese laundry down the street," she said.

Caycee smiled, thoroughly enjoying herself.

"Charge it to Mel Gibson's bill."

Chapter Fourteen

Zackary returned to the hotel room to discover Caycee dozing in a hip bath filled with a dense layer of foamy white bubbles, her knees in the air and visible, the rest of her body submerged to the neck. A half-empty bottle of Brandenberg's New Jersey Beer rested on the floor within fingertip reach while the light of an oil lamp gilded the well-worn furniture with its age-softening glow.

He eased the door open wide enough to step through, then closed it gently behind him. He wasn't sure if he did it so as not to disturb her, or because he wanted her to remain as she was for a few moments longer so he could enjoy the enticing picture she presented.

Reclining in the tub with her eyes closed and her expression relaxed, she appeared a hundred times more beautiful, alluring, intriguing, and maddeningly seductive than Zackary remembered her from their brief encounter in the moonlight-spattered meadow. It was because the tension in her expression was softened in relaxation, he decided. Even her delicate snore attracted rather than repelled him.

He was smitten with her, sure and certain.

Why had love come to him now, when he could least afford emotional involvement? Why now when he was so close to achieving his objective?

Caycee Hammond did things to him, caused him to entertain thoughts, kindled desires in him no man in his position could afford. His passion for her jeopardized all his well-laid plans. More importantly, she was blatantly jeopardizing her own safety in the process by visiting the bank without his permission. Not only that, she had now graduated to feeding him fantastic tales when it suited her. Tales that no man in his right mind would believe. Tales like she'd tried to tell him at the Gonzales place. Tales like she'd started to tell him outside the bathhouse—before he'd stopped her because to acknowledge her story was to risk losing her. And he couldn't face that proposition just now.

Who was this enigma of a woman that had lunged over a banking counter and into his life, uncapping his bottled-up emotions as easily as he'd uncapped his beer, emotions that ideally should have remained sealed? He'd opened up to someone for the first time since his brother's death and now he was paying for it in spades.

Anger washed over Zackary and his normally even temper soared. He stalked across the room and tapped Caycee on the knee. Her eyes flew open.

"Where am I?" she stammered groggily.

"You know where you are, Caycee. The Golden Arms Hotel," he managed, thinking her skin appeared as blushingly pink and felt as velvety soft as the skin on the peaches his mother grew in her garden in Savannah. Life had been much simpler then. Before the war. Before he'd lost Adam. Before Caycee.

"I was dreaming I was Dorothy and that I'd finally gotten my hands on the ruby slippers and was on my way home," she said.

Zackary recalled that Caycee's lips tasted as succulent, as honey-sweet as the juice-laden peaches his mother nurtured. As tempting as the fruit he'd scrambled up slick-barked trees to pluck from the boughs and quench his thirst on hot summer days.

Far too seductive to ignore.

Without preamble, Zackary reached through the bubbles to grasp Caycee's upper arms and haul her to her feet. The water surged and bubbles poured from the tub, soaking his boots.

"For God's sake, put on some clothes, Caycee," he growled.

Her eyes widened.

"I can't. I asked the housekeeper to have them sent down the street to the Chinese laundry to be washed. A gofer is supposed to leave them at the door when they're dry and pressed. It might be morning before—"

"A *gopher!* How the hell is a ground squirrel going to deliver your clothes from the laundry to the hotel?"

Zackary watched Caycee suppress a giggle that escaped through her teeth and across her lips regardless of her attempts to imprison it.

"A gofer is what we call an employee whose duties include running errands," she explained. Her eyes sparkled in amusement. It added to rather than detracted from her allure.

"We who, Caycee?"

"The cast and crew of the movie company

I'm currently working for," she said matter-of-factly.

Zackary gently shook her.

"Wake up, Caycee. You're talking nonsense again."

The bubbles that clung to her body, discreetly covering her prominent breasts, gently slipped down toward her stomach, then still lower to plop onto the surface of the bathwater. Without her film of bubbles, Caycee was left shimmeringly bare and doubly enticing.

Zackary swallowed hard against the sudden dryness of his throat.

Caycee faced Zackary, proud, defiant, and uninhibited.

"I am awake. And I'm not talking nonsense. I'm stating a fact. At least I'm trying to."

"Look, Caycee. I can't take much more of this. Two Pinkerton agents have already died in the line of duty while attempting to apprehend Dingus and his outlaw gang. You've got me so addled, I can't think. How am I supposed to protect you if—" he began.

"Don't worry about me," she said, suddenly contrite.

"How could I not worry about you?" he groaned. "Caycee, you've accomplished the impossible. After a game of billiards, I went over to talk to that saloon girl again and—"

Again she interrupted him. "I knew you would."

"Let me finish. I went over to talk to her, and all I could think of was you. Do you understand what I'm saying?"

Caycee shook her head. "Not exactly."

"I'm telling you that I've lost my mind. I'm saying that . . . I've fallen in love with you, Caycee."

Before he realized what was happening, she leaned into him, stretching her arms around his neck to nuzzle his throat. It was a genuine response to his declaration.

When she arched her body to press feather-light, teasing kisses along his jawline, her nearness brought on a physical trembling. Desire, swift and startling, assailed him.

He moaned deep in his throat, administering a tentative kiss to her cheek.

"Don't start something tonight you don't intend to finish," he warned.

"I'm not."

"What is it you want from me?"

"Release," she said.

"You blackmailed me," he reminded.

"That's not the kind of release I mean," she said.

He rocked her in his arms.

"I want you, Caycee."

She arched her pelvis against his swelling hardness.

"I want you too," she said.

That was that. On that simple note, he was lost.

Zackary lifted Caycee from the tub and placed her, damp and trembling, on the bed. She yielded to him and the passion that bound them as they shared an ardent kiss that left nothing to the imagination.

She couldn't find the buttons of his shirt quickly enough. He ended up pulling it over his head. She fumbled with his belt buckle and with the buttons on his Levi's. He popped the top button off assisting her. It flew up and hit the ceiling with a soft ping before falling in some shadowed corner of the room.

Zackary and Caycee ignored the button, as they did time. Minutes merged into hours as they took pleasure in the secret wonders of each other's body. He tugged her nipples into peaks with the gentle sucking motion of his mouth. Her hands roamed freely over his body, introducing him to the heights of intimacy.

Breath ragged, Zackary took the initiative from her, stroking Caycee's skin with gentle caresses while his manhood stroked her womanhood to a quick and fulfilling climax. Again. And yet again.

"Enough?" he whispered against her ear when they were nearing exhaustion.

"It won't ever be enough," she responded softly, too tired to do more than turn her cheek into his throat and rest in his embrace.

"This time I'm inclined to believe you," he said on a sigh, his eyes fluttering closed.

Zackary hugged Caycee tightly to him and they slept until the vibrant Kentucky dawn blazing through the thin hotel curtains awakened them to the harsh reality of day.

Chapter Fifteen

As dawn pinkened the Kentucky sky, Caycee and Zackary watched arm in arm from the hotel window while Dingus and the other outlaws converged on Columbia from differing directions.

"I've stationed an operative inside the Deposit Bank and sent a coded telegram reporting to Allan Pinkerton at the agency headquarters in Chicago that things are continuing as planned," Zackary informed her, turning away from the window and releasing her hand. "The Jessie Woodson James Gang should be in jail by nightfall."

"I knew there was a piece to this puzzle missing . . . something I wasn't quite grasping! No wonder you took such notice that day at Klaus Becker's farm when I mentioned Belle Starr and Cole Younger! I didn't realize then that your interest stemmed from the fact we'd been riding with the legendary James gang that day in Westport," Caycee said.

Despite her surprise at his revelation, she couldn't help noticing how enticing Zackary looked shirtless and with his Levi's slung low on his hips. The tip of his big toe was bruised black-and-blue where he'd bumped into her outside the saloon the night before, and his eyes were red-rimmed from lack of sleep. His sable hair was tousled. And his cheeks were darkly shadowed with a day's growth of beard.

With all that, he still made her heart pound and her pulses race. It was true, she decided—love did strange things to normally well-balanced people.

"I don't know if I'd call them legendary," Zackary said. "A more likely description is troublesome and dangerous."

"And ruthless," Caycee added, perching on the edge of the brass bed. Folklore pictured them as western-style Robin Hoods, which she knew from experience to be a false representation. "If I'd realized who they were before now I could have given you information that would have saved you loads of time and worry."

"Caycee, I don't have time to play games."

"I'm not playing a game."

"I don't have time to discuss any incriminating evidence you might think you have on the gang. They're going to be making their move soon and in front of the whole world. I'll have everything I need to finally put them behind bars. So I'd best get going," Zackary said, reaching for his shirt.

"I don't want you to go like this," she said in a small voice.

Zackary sighed.

"I'm not saying all this to hurt your feelings, Caycee."

Near tears, she said, "I know that's not your intention. You're saying it because you think it's the truth."

"It *is* the truth," he said firmly. "I've got them this time. Right and tight."

"Not really. Not if history plays true," Caycee said, caressing the talisman around her neck.

Zackary caught her under the chin with his forefinger, gently tipping her head back so that he gazed directly into her eyes. Caycee dropped the talisman to place her hand upon his.

"I've already tried to explain, I don't have the time for this. We'll talk later," he promised softly.

Her heart constricted and all she could do was nod as he released her and turned to don his clothes.

While she watched Zackary dress, Caycee slowly recalled the story of the Northfield disaster, how the James gang had been blasted to bits in front of the First National Bank in Minnesota. In her mind's eye, she remembered sitting in a director's chair and watching her father perform the stunts for a major scene in a famous Western which premiered in the midseventies. He had doubled for one of the actors supposedly shot to death outside the bank.

"Don't go yet," she said as he adjusted his slouch hat on his head. She heard the desperation in her own voice . . . hoped he heard it too and wouldn't discount it. "I want to tell you something that's going to prove important. You don't need to put your life in jeopardy over the James gang. I know how they'll wind up."

Zackary paused.

"We all know how they'll wind up after today. At least we hope we do," he said.

"That's not what I mean. Today won't determine the eventual outcome."

Zackary frowned, taking off his hat to rake his fingers through his hair.

"You're doing it again, Caycee. I swear, I

don't understand a word you're saying."

"That's because I'm not doing a very good job of this." Caycee's gaze fell to her hands, resting lightly in her lap. "You've asked me repeatedly to confess," she said without looking up. "You've wanted to know who I really am and what I'm running away from."

When she did look up, Caycee met his steady gaze.

"I tried to tell you at the Gonzales place that I'm not running away from anything. I'm trying to get back to where I belong," she said. "And I figured you were the key."

Caycee felt the bed sag as Zackary joined her.

"I give in. Go on."

Linking her fingers together, she continued as he'd suggested.

"I was working on a film, preparing to do a simple stunt on horseback. I stepped through the doorway of a false-front bank, and the next thing I knew—"

Zackary promptly interrupted her.

"I understand tricks on horseback. But I'm not sure what you mean when you say film. Are you talking about a photograph?"

"Sort of. A film, or movie as people call it, is a series of pictures projected onto a screen in such rapid succession that they appear to be in motion. Actors and stuntpeople like me perform in them. I'd like for you to live to see one. Of course, they won't be around for another twenty-five years or so."

"You're spookin' me, Caycee," Zackary exclaimed. "Have you been at the Brandenberg's again?"

"You know I haven't," she said softly.

"But—"

"Just hear me out."

Zackary nodded.

"As I was saying, I was performing in this film and stepped over the threshold of a make-believe bank. Somehow, I managed to step outside of my twentieth-century world and into the past. You're the past, Zackary. You're . . . history. That's how I know what's going to eventually happen to the James gang. In my time, they're legends. Children read about them in books. People visit their farm. It's a historic site."

"You were right. This is the craziest thing I've ever heard. Why are you doing this, Caycee?" Zackary asked.

"Because it's time to do this. It's the truth. And I'm attempting to protect you from getting involved in something that's really unimportant."

"All right. Let's assume that . . ." He paused, apparently searching for the appropriate words.

Caycee filled them in for him. "Time-travel."

He nodded. "Let's assume that time-travel is possible. Why did you pick this particular time and place?"

"I didn't. Time picked it for me. I figure it was some sort of fluke. A portal between the past and the present opened up just as I was stepping through the bank door. I shot through it like a bullet through glass."

"You can't expect me to believe a story like this without some kind of proof," he exclaimed.

"I'm the proof," she said. "Besides, I can tell you things about the James gang that no one else could know."

"For example?"

"I know that the James and Younger brothers will ride together for the last time during the famous Northfield, Minnesota, raid. I know that Jesse James won't be caught today. He won't go to trial. He won't die for ten years. When he does, it will be in his own home, shot dead by one of his gang members, Bob Ford, while straightening a picture on the wall. Frank James will serve a prison term and live to be an old man. He'll meet his Maker as free as you or me."

"And the Younger brothers—Bob and Cole and Jim?"

"If I remember correctly, they'll get shot up pretty badly, but they'll survive to be captured a couple of weeks after the Northfield raid. They'll spend a considerable amount of time in prison making amends for their lives of crime. I think Clell Miller and Bill Chadwell died at the scene."

"You could be making all this up. You have a great imagination."

"I could but I'm not," she said.

Caycee scrambled across the bed toward the nightstand, gathering up the pile of items that had rested in her pockets before she'd sent her corduroys and chamois to the laundry.

"Remember the day on the trail when you thought I'd discovered your strike-anywheres, only to find them in your saddlebags?" she asked him. "You wondered how I'd ignited the campfire and I told you I had my own matches."

She plucked the pack of red-tipped book matches from the hodgepodge of items clutched in her hand.

"Look. You haven't seen anything like this before because they don't exist yet."

Caycee pressed the book matches into Zackary's hand.

"There's a phone number written on the inside with ballpoint pen," she informed him.

"I wrote it—it belongs to my director, Henry Lawrence. The name of the restaurant where I picked up the matches is advertised on the front of the book. The address and telephone number of the establishment is embossed on the cover in gold and black lettering."

Zackary flipped them over and over in his palm, examining and reexamining them. Finally he peeled off a match and struck it against the plate. Nothing happened.

"Mine are better," he commented.

"Naturally. Mine got wet when we went swimming in the pond. They're not good for much of anything now beyond proving that I'm who and what I say I am."

Zackary shook his head. "I don't know, Caycee."

"I have more." On her knees now in an almost prayerlike position on the bed, Caycee shuffled through the items, extracting her change purse. Flipping it open, she flashed her charge card with the expiration date at him.

"Look at this. It has 1998 stamped on it. Why would it read that way if it wasn't true?"

Zackary reached for the card. "What is that?"

"Plastic money. Buy now, pay later. If you don't pay up later, your creditors will use

281

those phone numbers I told you about to call and drive you wild."

"In that case I don't understand why you'd want to use plastic money."

"You live and learn."

She dug for further proof.

"And how about this? I have a few pennies, which most of the time is all the cash I carry around."

"Since you have plastic money," Zackary interjected.

Caycee grimaced.

"Yeah, well. Anyway. One of the pennies is dated 1966, the other 1985. Why would the U.S. Mint do that if it wasn't so?"

"I don't know."

On a roll, Caycee was determined not to give up until Zackary conceded that she was indeed a time-traveler.

"Last but not least, I have a driver's license. It has my birth date, and expiration date, and a color photograph of me on it. I *know* you've never seen a color photograph before."

Zackary carefully examined all the evidence. Still she witnessed the skepticism in his eyes.

"Look, you're a Pinkerton agent, right?" she asked.

"If I weren't, you would not have been able to blackmail me as you've done."

"If it were possible for you to travel to my world, you would be amazed by the strides that have been made in the detective business. They use fingerprinting to catch suspects. The police force employs forensic specialists who can relate medical facts to legal problems in explicit detail."

She sucked in a gulp of air and continued.

"There are interconnected police alarms and hidden bank cameras that remedy the need for the sort of operation you've been forced to use to catch Jesse James redhanded. You'd have his image captured on film—no fuss, no muss."

"Even if all the things you've said are true, the fact remains that the James gang is preparing to rob the Deposit Bank. Innocent people like my brother Adam could be gunned down. I can't stand by and see that happen."

Zackary rose from the bed, adjusting his hat on his head and moving toward the door.

"I've got to go down there," he said.

Zackary opened the door, tossed her brown paper–wrapped laundry inside, and stepped from the room before Caycee had time to collect her thoughts.

Chapter Sixteen

Caycee heard the click of the skeleton key turning in the lock. She dashed to the door.

"Zackary?" she questioned.

"You're better off this way, Caycee," he said through the wood that separated them.

"Open the door," she said, placing her ear against the wood to better hear his reply.

Rather than his voice, she heard the keys jangle as Zackary pocketed them.

She twisted the doorknob back and forth, placing her foot against the wall and rattling the door on its hinges. She quickly realized physical force wasn't going to free her from the hotel room.

"I'll tell the manager to release you in an

hour or so," she heard him say.

Hands on her hips, Caycee planted both feet firmly on the floor.

"You're not coming back?" she asked through the door.

He made no reply.

"Zackary, are you still there?" she asked as she fought down panic.

"Yes, I'm still here, Caycee."

"I've told you the outcome of the gang."

"Even if the things that you say are true, and I'm beginning to believe they are, I can't wait until the Northfield holdup to apprehend the James gang. Justice must prevail. The risk of the lawbreakers further endangering innocent lives outweighs all other considerations."

"What's going to happen to them is history. You can't change that," she exclaimed.

"We'll see."

"You can't!"

"If nothing else, I hope to make a small difference in their career . . . for the sake of all the young Adams out there who won't have a prayer if I don't try."

"But I'm the official horse-handler. I'm supposed to be with you."

"I'll tell Dingus you're sick from drinking too much beer at the saloon last night."

"You'll do no such thing, Zackary Reece Butler."

"I want you to know something . . . to remember something. It's the most important thing that I've got to say to you today." He paused. "Are you listening?"

"Yes."

"I want you to know and to remember that I love you, Caycee."

The cold day in hell has finally arrived, Caycee told herself as her heart bunched in knots along with her stomach so that she couldn't tell one from the other.

Caycee acknowledged the silence that followed on the other side of the door. She knew Zackary was waiting for her to reciprocate in kind. She bit her tongue to stop herself. It was too much like saying good-bye. And she absolutely refused to tell Zackary good-bye.

"See to my watch," he said after a moment.

Zackary pushed his watch through the crack at the base of the ill-fitting door. Horrified, Caycee watched it slide toward her bare toes.

"No, I won't see to your watch!" she said on a sob. "I won't wind it on Sundays. Do you hear me? I swear I won't do it!" She was down on her knees now, talking under the door, trying to push the watch back to him against his hand.

"See to it, Caycee," he said quietly. Persistently. Refusing to retrieve the pocket watch. Sliding it back under the door each time she managed to dodge his fingertips.

Finally, she realized it was no use. He'd made up his mind and he wasn't going to change it.

"Don't leave me, Zackary," she said brokenly. "Please don't. . . ."

Her voice trailed off as she sensed him rise to his full height. Minutes later, she heard his footsteps receding down the hall.

Caycee rose to her feet as well and flew to the window, watching as the outlaw gang converged in the street below. Her panic escalated as they joined Zackary to saunter casually toward the Deposit Bank.

To a Hollywood stuntwoman who had based her career on illusion, Zackary seemed more honest, more down-to-earth, and more real than reality itself.

She simply couldn't let him do this. But how in the world, in this world, his world, was she supposed to stop him?

A sick feeling settled in the pit of Caycee's stomach.

In a quandary, she feared that if she interceded before the robbery took place, she might well risk her only opportunity to return to the future. On the other hand, if she didn't involve herself immediately, she reasoned she might never see the man she loved alive again.

She had been clobbered with breakaway furniture and plaster of Paris bottles, fallen from a helicopter, done car rollovers and rooftop chases, and been set afire in a special protective suit where the temperature reached 200 degrees. Escaping from the hotel should be child's play.

Caycee dressed quickly, jamming her possessions in her pockets as she planned her next moves detail for detail in her mind.

Pocketing Zackary's watch last, she tied back the frilly curtains and raised the double-hung window as far as it would go, then eased out the hotel window to the roof exactly as she'd done in dozens of movies. Scooting along the slippery shake-shingled roof, she tried not to think about the fact that she was performing a dangerous gag without a body harness and air bags to cushion a fall.

Caycee felt gratified upon reaching the spreading oak tree that grew next to the hotel.

So far so good, she thought.

Now all she had to do was sail through the air like a flying squirrel, attach herself to a sturdy branch, and shimmy through the leaves and twigs to the ground.

She could do that.

She had to.

Caycee braced herself. Counting under her breath to get the timing right, she took aim and jumped. She hit the bough with a *whump*, scratching her cheek against the rough tree bark, breaking two fingernails, and jarring her spine from her neck to her tailbone.

"Jeez, doesn't take long to get out of shape," she muttered as she scrambled through the branches, pleased when she reached the ground in relative safely.

Caycee rounded the corner of the Golden Arms Hotel just as Dingus extended his gloved hand to Zackary. The fact that he was missing the tip of the middle finger on his left hand seemed glaringly apparent now that she knew for sure the outlaw's birth name.

She marveled that she, Caycee Hammond, had ridden with the James gang along with the Younger brothers and their cohorts and lived—so far—to tell the tale.

Caycee wasn't close enough to hear what they were saying to each other, but she watched them shake hands as if they'd reached some sort of satisfactory agreement between them. Then Dingus motioned toward Cole and Bob, who were holding the horses out in front of the saloon. Zackary shrugged. Dingus nodded as Buck joined them, jovially spouting a line from Shakespeare's *Hamlet*. Before she could reach them, the trio disappeared across the bank's threshold.

Something instinctive and terrifyingly powerful assailed Caycee. A premonition of sorts. She didn't know what she was going to do, but she felt compelled to act, so she followed the men at a dead run, bursting into the bank just as Dingus drew his Navy colt and placed the barrel through the cage under the cashier's nose.

"Stop. Please don't do this! This is all so unnecessary!" Caycee exclaimed.

She had used the same line before when she'd asked Zackary not to kill the doe stripping bark from the trees in the forest. Only now, rigid with determination, she said it more forcefully.

She was talking to Zackary's back, but he recognized her voice instantly and swiveled toward her. Dingus assumed she was speaking to him. He turned as well.

"I'll be. You've surprised me again, kid."

"I never intended this," Caycee stammered.

"And I never figured you for a double-crosser," Dingus said. His blinking blue eyes narrowed and he aimed a second revolver at Caycee's heart. With calm deliberation, Jesse James, alias Dingus, thumbed back the hammer.

"Duck, Caycee!" Zackary yelled as he dived between them.

Caycee instinctively reached for Zackary's hand. Their fingers brushed once, then brushed again before their hands connected and he entwined his fingers with hers. But the sensation of touch was fading fast and she realized her fondest wish was in the process of being realized—time was sucking her into the future.

Caycee didn't want to release Zackary and yet her fingers were slipping as if she had no will of her own. She was losing him and she knew it in her head, sensed it her heart, and felt it deep down in her soul.

The last thing Caycee saw before she felt herself being propelled back into the future was Zackary going down in a hail of gunfire.

"No!" she cried. "No. No. No. No. Oh, God, please, no. Don't let this happen."

She couldn't think, she couldn't feel, she couldn't breathe . . . could barely see. Yet with her last ounce of strength, Caycee did the only thing that seemed to make any sense. She yanked the talisman from around her throat. The chain dangled from her fingers as she pressed the piece of polished bone into Zackary's fading palm.

Caycee recalled that while still in the hospital recovering from the stunting accident, her father had questioned Joseph Coyote concerning the talisman. He'd complained that even though he'd been wearing it, it had undoubtedly lost its magic because he had been left paralyzed. Joseph had responded that the bone talisman still held the potential for miraculous effects because her father had survived the accident rather than succumbed to his injuries.

She hoped Joseph Coyote's rationale had been correct. She prayed the talisman still held the power to avert bad fortune and that, because she could not, it would somehow protect Zackary from the yawning jaws of death.

Chapter Seventeen

Hollywood, California
Spring, 1995

The air surrounding her seemed so thick,
Caycee felt as if she fought her way out of a
plastic sandwich bag. Heartbroken, gasping
for breath, and clutching Zackary's pocket
watch for dear life, she stumbled out of
the false-front bank and across the back lot
toward the white-hot set lights and movie
cameras, totally ignoring the horse patiently
awaiting her stunt mount.

"Cut!" the director yelled.

Caycee blinked in confusion. When had
she wrested the watch from her pocket? She
couldn't remember. But it felt good in her

hand. Comforting. Real. Solid.

Caycee blinked again. Her broken chain dangled from her fingertips, but the bone talisman was nowhere in sight. She glanced frantically at the ground beneath her feet.

Did Zackary have the talisman in his hand? God, let Zackary have the talisman! Let him be all right. Wherever he was and whatever he was doing at this moment, he *had* to be okay. She couldn't bear to think otherwise.

"What the hell's going on here? What's wrong with you, Caycee? And what have you done with your duster? You're out of costume!"

Face flushed bright red, Henry Lawrence threw his hands wide.

"Would someone please tell me who cued Caycee to shed the duster in the robbery scene? I specifically told wardrobe that the stunt double should be wearing a duster when exiting the bank. It's right here in the script."

Henry started flipping wildly through the pages of the script, tapping out the words with his finger as he read them aloud.

"Aha, there it is! I knew it! Duster, d-u-s-t-e-r," he said.

Caycee could only stare at the crowd beginning to cluster around her and the director. It appeared she'd been away from her world only mere minutes while she'd spent months in the past with Zackary.

How could that be?

Grief-stricken, Caycee ignored Henry's tirade entirely, pivoting back toward the false-front bank. The people from her world seemed determined to crush her, to suffocate her by pressing in with their concern like dark shadows from another lifetime. She must get away from them ... must return to Zackary and the light of his world!

Perhaps if she retraced her original steps ...

When Caycee crossed the threshold of the bank, nothing happened. She tried it again. Still nothing.

Gazing sadly beyond the bank's facade and out across the rear of the studio lot, she acknowledged the gateway to the past had vanished.

"No," Caycee whispered brokenly.

"No!" Henry squeaked. "No, you can't do the crouper? Come on, Caycee. My reputation is riding on this picture. Don't cop out on me now!"

She swayed from the bank and out into the waiting arms of her own era, feeling hollow-chested and certain that she'd left her heart in the past with Zackary Butler.

"Jeez, are you all right?" Henry continued to jabber.

Caycee nodded numbly as the shadows lost their threatening quality, separating and evolving into individuals she recognized by name.

"I'm not so sure about that," Henry said. "You're as white as a sheet!" He turned to his assistant, demanding, "Call makeup and wardrobe . . . we're going to need a retake of the stunt mount . . . hand me a cup of water for her . . . and get in touch with that story consultant we hired . . . the one that's familiar with data and pictures from the Pinkerton Security Services' rogues' gallery of Western outlaws. Something has gone wacko here!"

Caycee grabbed at Henry's hand.

"Did you say Pinkerton agent?" she asked urgently.

"Yeah. We've been using him over the last few weeks. He's a real intellect. Knows a heck of a lot about the Old West. Worked for Pinkerton's for over ten years."

Caycee's heart soared. Maybe, just maybe . . .

"Get him on the set, Henry," Caycee insisted.

"Exactly. Just like I said." Henry once again turned to his assistant. "Get that Pinkerton man down here. Pronto!"

* * *

An hour later, Caycee watched a tall, well-built man wearing cowboy boots, faded Levi's, and a white, pocket T-shirt beneath a black sports jacket saunter onto the set. He was bareheaded, perfectly tanned, and professionally coiffed.

Caycee swallowed at the hard knot in her throat.

"Is that the Pinkerton agent?" she asked in a small, dejected voice.

"It sure is. He took his own sweet time getting here, too," Henry said.

Tears gathered in Caycee's eyes. He might be a Pinkerton man. But he wasn't, as she had hoped against hope, Zackary Reece Butler.

Nothing difficult is ever easy. Can't is a four-letter word. Courage is like a black dress. And you *will* get over Zackary Reece Butler, Caycee told herself as she steered her battered pickup into the gravel driveway, eased it into Park, and shut down the motor.

Fingers gripping the steering wheel, Caycee sighed.

"Sure, you'll get over him—the day you draw your last breath," she said softly.

The effort necessary to climb from the truck seemed suddenly momentous. For several moments, Caycee simply couldn't muster the gumption. She remained motionless, gazing out the windshield toward the rustic California home she shared with her father.

Her forehead soon joined her hands on the wheel.

A month away from Zackary had left her drained and wanting. A woman's happiness wasn't supposed to be dependent on the man in her life. Personal happiness came from within. She was independent. Resourceful. An advanced thinker. Great at making the best of a situation. Strong.

So why did she feel like a used-up, washed-out dishcloth? Why the despondency? The must-literally-force-yourself-to-function attitude?

Because she yearned to feel Zackary's arms around her. Because he brought out the best in her. Because he was her friend and her confidant. Because she missed his company with every fiber of her being. Because she was head over heels in love with him even though she'd avoided expressing her feelings verbally.

And because she felt guilty.

She should have told him she loved him before it was too late. She should have expressed it aloud if only once during their association.

So, you can't change things at this late date, she told herself. Stop the whining and get on with your life.

Caycee lifted her head from the wheel, blinked back the tears, inhaled deeply, pocketed her keys, and exited the truck. As she reached the side porch, she could see her father through the screen door. He was unloading leftovers of a previous night's dinner from the refrigerator: foil-wrapped roast beef, a Tupperware dish filled with seasoned new potatoes, asparagus spears atop sliced, home-grown tomatoes. The plastic tea pitcher was perched on the table along with beverage glasses filled with ice cubes and garnished with freshly sliced lemon wedges festooned with sprigs of mint.

"Dad," Caycee warned as she stepped through the door and into the black and white stylishness of the contemporary kitchen. "Don't go to all that trouble for me."

"Hi, Caycee," he said.

Head muffled by the refrigerator, his comment sounded garbled and distant to Caycee.

"Listen, it's been a grueling day. We worked in the blazing sun for over three hours without pulling off the gag to Henry's satisfaction, and I'm not really hungry. I think I'll get a shower and call it a—"

Her father cut her short.

"Not goin' to the trouble for you alone, honey," he commented in a preoccupied tone as he reached around a jar of mayonnaise to retrieve the remains of a walnut-topped mango salad.

"You're hungry. I'm sorry. I wasn't thinking," Caycee said hurriedly.

She knew her father looked forward to their evening meals together. He spent so much of his time alone since her mother's death, Caycee reminded herself.

"No need to apologize," he said, handing her the salad over his right shoulder. "I'm not really hungry either. I'm not doing this for us. I'm doing it for him."

He ducked out of the refrigerator to nod down the hall toward the living room.

Perplexed, Caycee placed the dish on the table with the other leftovers.

"I think I've missed something here. Him who?" she asked.

Her father closed the refrigerator door, wheeled his chair to the table, and began slicing the roast beef with an electric knife before responding.

"Don't know, really. Says he's a friend of yours from way back. Arrived about an hour ago lookin' as if he'd been ridden hard and put up wet."

"What does he look like?" she asked.

It felt to Caycee as if her father took an eternity to reply, though she realized mere seconds had passed.

"Wasn't sure until he took off his slouch hat," he said thoughtfully. "You know, I'd forgotten how the broad brim of one of those suckers shadow a man's face."

Almost afraid to hope for the impossible, Caycee felt as if she might explode before he got down to the nitty-gritty.

"Come on, Dad! Save me the suspense. What color is his hair? Are his eyes stormy gray? Does he look well? I mean, you know, reasonably healthy?"

Her father cut her a shrewd glance.

"He's the reason you've been so down in the mouth lately, isn't he?"

"Dad. Please! I don't mean to sound anxious, but this is really important to me."

"Okay, okay, honey. Calm down. Man has dark hair . . . almost black. Gray eyes, I think. About my height. Like I told you, looks like he could use a good meal and a decent night's shut-eye. Otherwise, he seems in pretty good shape, as far as I could tell."

Caycee couldn't speak for the lump forming in her throat. Her father obviously took her silence as a cue for him to continue.

"I have to admit, though, there are times

you remind me of your mother—associate with some peculiar characters."

"Mom always called you a peculiar character," Caycee mumbled, her thoughts racing a mile a minute.

Could it possibly be Zackary? God, let it be Zackary!

"That's beside the point. You should have seen this dude's expression when I offered him a glass of tea. Stared at the ice cubes as if he'd never seen frozen water. And when I turned on the tube to watch my game shows, he nearly jumped out of his skin."

"He did?" Caycee asked, bemused.

"Yeah. I was sort of put off at first. Wondered if he might be on drugs or something, but after talkin' to him for a while I decided he was all right. Knows a heck of a lot about horses. Told me he's spent the last few years ranch-handing in Kansas and Missouri. Seems this is his first visit to sunny California. I, uh, wound up asking him to stay for supper. I hope you don't mi—"

Heart pounding, Caycee didn't remain to catch the end of her father's sentence. Out of the kitchen and down the hall like a gunshot, she stumbled into the living room breathless with anticipation.

* * *

Their guest relaxed in her father's worn leather wing chair, hat hanging on one knee, empty beverage glass balanced on the other, his head back and his eyes closed. He remained motionless, though she felt positive he'd heard her enter the room.

Caycee stopped just across the threshold to drink him in.

Finally, when she could stand it no longer, she asked, "How did you find me?"

His eyes fluttered slowly open; Caycee's heart constricted. Her father was right. Dark circles shadowed his piercing eyes and stubble patterned his cheeks and chin. His clothes needed pressing. His posture appeared careworn.

He'd never looked so incredibly fabulous.

He gazed at her for a long moment, his expression appreciative as he perused her open-toed pumps and spaghetti-strapped sundress. For once, Caycee was glad she'd taken the time to change from her costume to civilian clothes following a shoot.

"I am—correction—*was* a Pinkerton agent. I can follow clues. And you left a dilly behind—a book of matches with a California restaurant's address printed on it that I slipped into my pocket when you weren't looking."

"And you pursued me through them."

"Like a posse on the trail of a despera-
do." He reached into his shirt and extracted
the polished bone talisman which he wore
on a strip of leather around his neck. "This
helped more than a little bit."

"My talisman," Caycee said, her eyes shin-
ing.

"Yep," he said, untying the leather strip
and removing the talisman. "After you vanished, I figured this might have have giv-
en fate a little push. You kept talking
about me and the bank robberies and por-
tals into the past being the key to your
return home. I decided that in your determination to reenact the events that landed
you in the past, you might have over-
looked something important. I figured it
might be the talisman. I did some in-depth
research." He paused. "Did you know it's
supposed to be carved from the skull bone
of an Indian medicine man?"

Caycee shook her head. "Joseph never
shared that with us," she said.

"I think I can understand why."

"So can I. Who would willingly agree to
wear a piece of someone's skull around their
neck, even if it was supposed to be good for
them?" she asked.

"Exactly."

"So . . ." Caycee prompted.

306

"So as far as the Comanche chief I spoke with was concerned, and incidentally talking with him wasn't the easiest thing I've ever accomplished, the talisman possesses endless magical powers when worn encircling the neck. After I offered him my six-shooter, he discussed them in depth with me." Zackary turned the talisman over and over in his palm as if examining it anew. "It seems few people experience the talisman's full potential. He said we were truly lucky . . . blessed, actually."

"I see," Caycee said, even though she didn't. How had Zackary traversed the time barrier by using the talisman? And how had she returned without it? she wondered, deciding just as rapidly that it really didn't matter. She had returned home to her father, and Zackary was here with them now. In the scheme of things, how he had accomplished the deed was entirely inconsequential.

"I believe he was right," Zackary said finally.

"So do I," Caycee agreed.

"We are blessed."

"You betcha."

Caycee lifted the watch dangling from a gold chain clasped around her neck and lovingly thumbed the engraved metal case.

"I said I wouldn't take care of it, but I lied. I've kept it wound for you. Every Sunday. Rain or shine," she stated softly.

His lips curved into a warm and tender smile.

"I never doubted you for a minute."

Caycee hesitated. There were things she wanted to say. Matters she needed to clear up.

"I wish I could say the same thing about you. I suppose I slighted you more times than you can count by avoiding sharing the truth with you . . . my truths . . . until it was almost too late."

"I've never felt slighted where you're concerned, Caycee. I learned soon after the Westport robbery that you're the kind of woman that needs hard, fast proof before you'll trust someone to share your deepest, darkest secrets. I needed to prove myself to you—and I think I have. Besides all that, there's a price to pay for everything and you're well worth the trouble you've caused me."

He was teasing her, attempting to ease her conscience where he was concerned and she knew it. Her eyes sparkled in response to him. He was one of the kindest men she'd ever known.

"Am I?" she asked.

He nodded. "Darned right."

They were slipping into their old camaraderie as easily as if they'd never parted, Caycee thought. There was something between them. Something special. Something enduring. A chemistry so right it made her ache inside.

"So, what do you plan to do about it?" she asked.

"Simple—give you whatever you need."

"Jeez, how I need," she moaned.

He carefully placed the empty beverage glass on a coaster on the coffee table alongside the talisman, tossed his hat across the sofa, and opened his arms wide.

"It feels like forever since I've held you in my arms," he said.

Caycee crossed the room in three strides and sank into Zackary's lap, showering his face and throat with enthusiastic kisses.

"Remember . . . your father," he rasped between pressing quick, firm kisses against her lips. She noted his mouth was chilled from consuming the ice in the glass; she concentrated on heating his lips with hers.

"Not to worry," she assured him later, when they came up for air. "Dad is going to like having you around."

Zackary chuckled against her lips. "Is he now?"

"Yep. But not nearly as much as I am." She paused for a moment. Commitment to this man would never be difficult. He appreciated and respected her for who and what she was. He wouldn't ask more than she could deliver; he would never deliver to her anything less than her wildest expectations. "I love you, Zackary."

Capturing her flushed cheeks between his palms and forcing her to be still, his eyes searched hers.

"You've never admitted that to me before now," he said.

With trembling hands, Caycee kneaded Zackary's shoulders through his linsey-woolsey shirt.

"Sometimes you don't know what you've got until it's gone," she confessed quietly. "Sometimes you don't even realize what's in your own heart until you lose something precious."

"Am I precious then, Caycee?"

She could not overlook the catch in his smoother-than-smooth voice.

"The most precious thing I've ever known," she whispered.

He cleared his throat and slipped his hands from her cheeks to encompass her waist.

"I suppose you'll be expecting me to stay for supper as well," he said on a sigh.

Her smile expanded.

"You can bank on it."

"Next thing I know, you'll want me to speak to your father—ask for your hand and everything else that goes with it." A devilishly teasing grin replaced the tender smile as he settled her more securely in his lap.

Delirious with happiness, she winked at him. "Most probably. When you feel . . . up to it."

Zackary cleared his throat again.

"Oh, I feel up to it, all right. Of course, I suppose that means I'm going to have my hands full for a long, long time."

"Only if you want them full," Caycee said, her tone suddenly serious.

His voice solemn and filled with promise, Zackary responded, "It's the answer to my most heartfelt prayer."

Epilogue

"Would you mind explaining this to me one more time?" Zackary asked. "I'm sort of new at this, you know."

Caycee smiled. Dressed in a black tuxedo, with his hair neatly slicked back, and his shoes polished to a deep shine, Zackary Butler literally took her breath away. Of course, that was nothing new, she reminded herself.

"The principle players were released yesterday due to other commitments. This is called a distance shot. It will be edited into the film later during cutting. We don't have any lines. All we have to do is stand here in costume and look pretty while the cameraman circles around us. We're body doubles for the major stars."

313

"Like Mel Gibson." He winked as he smoothed down the lapel of his coat and inserted a red carnation in the button hole, and Caycee's smile broadened.

"Now that you know who he is, do you suppose I'll ever live that one down?" she asked.

"I expect by next week—when I slip a wedding ring on your finger and do this for real," he said.

"Next week," Caycee said, echoing his words. "I can't believe we've managed to pull everything together so quickly. So much paperwork, so many details, so many complications."

"We've worked magic with the help of your father and his friends in high places. But it's all done now—nothing more to worry your pretty little head about," he said, tracing with his fingertip the edges of the bone talisman she wore suspended on a gold chain around her throat. "Besides, it seems time is on our side," Zackary said. His gaze took in her dress—white silk with yards and yards of cream-colored lace. His expression softened, almost melting her heart. Zackary loved her, and she loved him—for all time.

"Okay, guys. Cut the chitchat. Time to get to work. Let's roll 'em," the cameraman advised.

"Time is on our side—finally," Caycee agreed as Zackary tugged her into his arms and soundly kissed her for all the world to see.

"So between them love did shine. . . ."
—Shakespeare
"The Phoenix and the Turtle"

Prologue: Call back yesterday

Louisiana, 1864

The woman stood alone before the huge stone monument, which lay nestled under a massive oak tree dripping with Spanish moss.

She was dressed in black, from the lace veil that covered her fashionable black hat to the slippers that covered her feet. Trickles of perspiration ran between her full breasts. It was late September, and the hot, humid weather gathered around her like another layer of clothing. Even now, with evening fast approaching, the sultry temperatures gave no sign of abating.

Gently, she knelt upon the ground, the

black silk of her skirt spreading out around her, and placed the bouquet of white roses against the carved stone front. She reached out a black gloved hand and traced the letters in the name so handsomely carved into the marble—*Matthew Justin Devereaux*. Beneath that was the inscription. *And flights of angels sing thee to thy rest.* Then, she shyly touched the relief sculpture of an angel above his name.

Before folding her hands in prayer, she made the sign of the cross. She bowed her head, the mother-of-pearl rosary in her hands gleaming richly against her black lace gloves.

Oh Matthew, she thought, tears coursing down her pale cheeks, we had so little time together. It isn't fair.

Do you know what I regret most, my love? she asked silently, lifting her head and staring at the marble. That I never knew the joy of waking up in your arms, of having you hold me so close to your body that our flesh was one.

I can feel no shame, she confessed to herself honestly, for having these thoughts, my love. My only shame is that I never gave in to the depth of my feelings for you. How I wish that I had. Perhaps then I would have memories to cherish rather than an aching, empty heart. Or I could possibly have had your child. Your son or daughter would have been such a comfort to me, something of you to hold and keep. For that, I would have risked any shame, any scandal.

But forgive me, I did not realize that then, my love, she thought. I believed that I could hold myself above the wants of the flesh. I believed that we had all the time in the world for the promise of tomorrow. And I believed you when you told me that you would come back. I trusted you, Matthew! Bitterness at the cruel twists of fate rose within her. You said that not even the war could keep us apart. That we were meant to be together—forever.

She looked down at the rosary in her hands, tears stinging her eyes. It was torn in two, the silver links rent.

Like her heart, it was irretrievably broken.

She lifted her veil, kissing the crucifix before she wrapped it slowly around the roses. One last token, she thought. One last remembrance. He'd given her the rosary, an heirloom from an ancestor.

She touched her gold initialed locket, which gleamed against the dark material of her bodice, her fingers clenching it tightly.

Matthew had given that to her also, just before he'd gone away. Their portraits were inside.

Moving closer to the stone, she placed her lips against the surface of the marble, tears spilling freely.

Farewell, my love.

I shall never, ever forget you.

She stood up, walking away from the past, yet knowing that she would always carry it within her heart.

As she moved slowly toward her waiting carriage, she couldn't resist turning her head and giving one last glance at the stone sepulcher.

Someday, somewhere, somehow, Matthew, she vowed silently, we will be together again. If there is a justice for lovers, it must be so.

PART ONE:
ONCE UPON
A DREAM

Chapter One

"Savannah, you can't marry my brother!" the man shouted, bursting into the wedding chapel just as the minister had asked the question, "Is there anyone here who knows just cause?"

"Joshua," the petite brunette sighed, dropping her small bouquet of wedding flowers as she watched the tall man stride down the aisle. Tears welled in her eyes. "Oh my God, it can't be you," she said, her face blanching from the shock of seeing her supposedly dead husband come back to life. Two years. Two long years. If this was a dream she didn't want to wake up. She couldn't possibly go through this once again. Losing him had been too painful.

The man standing beside the woman watched as his brother rejoined the living. Damn! Jack Benson thought. Just a few minutes more and Savannah, the woman he'd loved so deeply for years, would be his. He'd finally persuaded her that it was time to start living again, and the best way to do that would be to marry him. And now Joshua, his bastard half brother, had risen from the grave. He should have known—Joshua had always had a flair for the dramatic.

Joshua, his white teeth flashing in an engaging grin, reached out his tanned hand and caressed the woman's soft cheek. "It's me, darlin'," he said and bent his head, capturing the woman's mouth with his, kissing her passionately.

Savannah Creed nearly swooned with delight to be back in her beloved Joshua's strong arms again. No one kissed her quite like Josh—so savagely tender. She would know the feel of his mouth. No one could fake that. Wasn't that how she'd exposed the man who'd pretended last year that he was Josh, albeit with a surgically altered face? One taste of the impostor's lips and she'd known that it was a setup, that someone was trying to get control of Josh's enormous fortune.

"Oh, baby," he said, his warm baritone delivering the lines in a husky tone, "I missed you so much. Dreaming of you is what kept me alive all that time in the jungle."

Savannah, tears flowing even more freely, slowly pulled the engagement ring, an overly large diamond, from her finger and handed it to Jack. "I'm sorry, Jack, but I can't marry you. I know you understand. I could never love anyone the way I love your brother." She kissed Jack's cheek fondly and turned her attention back to the long-haired, jean-clad man before her. "If you hadn't stopped this, I would have made such a mistake, Josh," she said softly.

Josh smiled again. "I told you, darlin'," he explained, his large hands cupping her gamine face, "no matter what, that I would always come back to you. Nothing, and no one, could ever keep me from you." He drew her to him for another deep kiss.

"Camera two, close up," the director called out in the control booth. "Hold it just a moment longer. Terrific! Cue theme music." He ground out his stub of a cigarette. "Okay, that's a wrap. Great job, everyone."

The actors relaxed as the cameras went dark. The taping was complete and another episode of the award-winning, number-one soap, *Tomorrow's Promise*, was history.

The stage manager, Bob, checked a few last minute details with the director via his mic linkup and smiled broadly.

The cast and crew gathered around the set. Instead of the actors moving toward their assorted dressing rooms to change to their street clothes, and the crew seeing to their duties before everyone called it a night, they all remained where they were, joined by others from nearby sets and the personnel from the control booth. One actress adjusted the terry bathrobe she'd donned to cover up the skimpy teddy she wore beneath, her feet in thick, knee-high socks, as she entered, followed by her TV lover, who wore jogging shorts and a well-worn T-shirt that hugged his massive chest.

The actress playing the role of Savannah Creed burst out laughing. "What a fashion statement, Meg," she said, giggling.

Meg shrugged her shoulders, replying with a wicked grin, "Gee, I thought so." She grabbed for the baseball cap her TV brother wore and plunked it upon her strawberry curls. "Now where's that photographer?" she called out.

"Right here, Miss Carmichael," the thin man said, emerging from the shadows, camera ready, snapping a photo of the actress, who jumped into the arms of another male costar, a venerable older man who played her father. She kicked one leg in the air and waved.

"Well, that ought to get you a feature, at least," stated the smiling, tall blonde who walked onto the set.

"Hell," Meg crowed, "I was hoping for the cover," she responded as she was passed to the brawny arms of her love-scene partner.

The blonde chuckled. Rebecca Gallagher Fraser's rich, warm laugh and good looks could have made her a star on daytime dramas, if she'd chosen. She'd been a fan of soaps since she was a teenager, but for her, the lure had been writing for soaps, not acting in them. That had been her ultimate goal, and through hard work and talent she'd achieved the position of head writer on *Tomorrow's Promise* just a little over 18 months earlier. She'd taken the soap from near the bottom of the daytime ratings to the number-one show for the last four months. Rebecca was damned proud of what she'd accomplished, and she had expected to be with the show for a few more years, at least.

That had been the plan, until the network approached her two months ago with a job offer she couldn't refuse. She would be given her own show to develop to replace an hour's worth of unworkable talk shows currently clogging the network's daytime arteries. Today was her last offical day on the set of her soap.

So, in recognition, the cast and crew were throwing her a farewell party, complete with photographers from the leading soap publications to record the event.

A huge cake was wheeled in, with a congratulatory message and a slightly risque couple pictured in frosting. The assembled crowd broke out into wild guffaws at the confectionary treat.

"Somehow, I don't think you'd better get a close-up of the cake, fellas," Rebecca said to the photographers, "at least not for publication. But," she added dryly, "I'd like one for my scrapbook."

Champagne corks popped and glasses were passed around so that all could join in the toast.

"At least it's finally the real thing." Ally James sighed as the bubbly was poured into her fluted glass. "If I had to drink one more glass of sparkling cider I was gonna puke, I swear it," she grumbled good-naturedly. She was truly sorry to see Rebecca go—for many reasons. It had been Rebecca, while she was an associate writer, who'd created the character Savannah Creed. That part had garnered Ally a daytime Emmy, several best-actress awards from the major soap-opera publications, and bags of fan mail. It had provided her with a role she relished playing, a hefty income, and the man she was engaged to marry, Rebecca's former husband, Ben Tyler.

Rebecca cut the cake. "Chocolate?" she said with an ingenuous look on her face. "How did you ever guess?"

That broke up everyone. Everybody who knew Rebecca knew of her weakness for anything chocolate. Caffeine and chocolate were in abundant supply in her office. They were the two things that she swore got her through a day—especially on a day when her office was the scene of an actor demanding to know, "Why am I being put on the back burner, storywise?" Or another saying, "Rebecca, I've got a surprise for you. I just found out that I'm pregnant. Can you write that into the script?" And there were always the actors who came to her with the ever popular: "I loathe the fill-in-the-blank I'm doing a love scene with. Please can't you help me?"

She'd grown fond of her group, with all their various idiosyncrasies, but the challenge of creating her own soap from scratch was much too good to pass up. She would have six months to come up with the concept and see to the rest of the details.

"Congratulations, Rebecca."

She turned around to see a man standing there, a wide smile on his pleasant face. "Ben," she said, taking his outstretched hands in hers and leaning over to give him a friendly kiss on the cheek. "How great of you to stop by."

"Well I certainly couldn't miss your last day at the factory, now could I?" he asked, raising one thick blond eyebrow.

Rebecca grinned at his use for her favorite term regarding work—the factory. It was one of their personal jokes. She stepped back and gave her ex-husband the once-over. Ben looked healthy and happy, and every inch the successful corporate lawyer that he was. His endearingly boyish face often fooled opponents into thinking him less experienced than he was, often to his, and his clients', benefit. "You look terrific," she stated.

"So do you, my dear." Ben slipped his arm about Rebecca's waist, enjoying the feel of the silk blouse that she wore. "Now," he asked, "is there a new man in your life?"

Rebecca groaned. "Oh, Ben, not you too?"

He smiled. "Don't give me that, Rebecca." He leveled his tawny-brown gaze at her

330

through his thin wire frames. "I only want you to be happy."

She hugged him. "I know you do, Ben."

"Then tell me. What gives? Are you at least dating someone?"

"No," she admitted, giving a small shake of her head.

"I have a friend—"

Rebecca rolled her blue eyes. "Oh my God, Ben. Spare me. My ex trying to fix me up?"

Ben gave her a fixed stare. "What's wrong with that? You did the same for me if you'll recall?" he prodded.

"That was different," she protested.

"Bullshit," he shot back, taking the edge off his word with a smile. "You know I still care about you, Rebecca. There's nothing wrong in my wanting to see you taken care of."

"You're sweet, Ben, really you are, and I appreciate your concern," she said with a smile, "but I'm okay."

"Just okay, Rach?"

"Please," she responded, "don't get overly distraught about my love life, or lack of one. Right now I have my work, and that's enough."

"I certainly hope that you're not trying to convince me of that fact, my dear, because it won't work. Remember, I'm the man you were married to." He squeezed her hand, a touch of regret in his voice for the past. "I just wish that I could have been what you were looking for, Rebecca. I really do."

Rebecca returned the squeeze. "Maybe I don't know what I'm looking for," she said with a graceful shrug of her shoulders.

"Oh, but you do, my dear," Ben assured her in a smooth tone. "You most certainly do."

Rebecca was left pondering Ben's remark while he went to find his fiancee, who dashed into his arms, kissing him wildly before all. Rebecca was glad that Ben had apparently found what he was looking for—the right wife for him. A woman who had no problem with passion or showing it. She'd be willing to bet that Ally had no problem with surrendering herself to Ben's lovemaking.

Rebecca's lips curled into an ironic smile. Passion was a part of her business, the life-blood of the storyline. She wrote love scenes that were erotically charged; she wrote of passion denied, of passion quenched; she crafted dialogue of high drama, ringing every ounce of emotion she could from her actors and the audience.

But Rebecca felt no such great passion in her life, except for her work. Even love-making had only been, at best, a merely pleasant experience. She'd admit that she had little real knowledge, having only had one lover, Ben. And she couldn't fault Ben. He'd done his damnedest to elicit some kind of deep response from his wife.

Had she desired further practical lessons in sex, she could have very well taken several of the actors who worked for her, or whom she'd met at various functions, up on their offers. Handsome, virile men were abundant in her business. And some of them Rebecca had found extremely attractive. However, Rebecca wasn't interested in a mere sharing of bodies for either a few hours or a few days or even a few months. She couldn't imagine being intimate with anyone she didn't truly care about. A fantasy was one thing; cold reality was another.

Just once in her life though, Rebecca had wanted to feel the longing, the completeness of total oneness with another person.

In the back of her mind she wondered: Was there someone just for her, waiting, searching, somehow, for her?

When she was younger, she'd thought that person was Ben. But she'd been wrong, mistaking friendship and caring for the soul-shattering dream of love she'd harbored deep in her heart.

*   *   *

When she unlocked her spacious apartment on New York's Upper West Side, Rebecca collapsed back against the door, thankful that her last day on *Tomorrow's Promise* was finally over. After the cake and champagne had come the presents. Some were gag gifts; others were expensive tokens; a few were chosen with care, the givers knowing Rebecca's taste.

Rebecca placed two large fancy gift bags on the floor and sorted through her mail. Nothing that couldn't wait till later. She noticed that the red light on her phone anwering machine was blinking like a warning beacon, and she pressed the button to retrieve her messages.

She began to laugh at the number of calls she was getting from either actors or their eager agents wanting a chance to be in her new show. Since the announcement had been made, Rebecca had been flooded, both at the office and at home, with tapes of actors, male and female, asking to be considered for a role in her new soap.

Oh, God, she groaned, how long would this keep up? She listened to the calls as she stepped out of her flat brown leather shoes, wiggling her toes. How was she even to begin to think about actors when she still didn't have a notion of where she was going with a storyline? she wondered as she moved toward the spacious kitchen and put on her coffeepot. Several ideas had been perking in her brain, and yet none hit her with the resounding force that would make her say, "Yes, this is it." She wanted something that was different, something that would grab an audience right away, something that had a feel, not only of the present, but of the past. Timeless. Solid. Connected.

Leaving the kitchen, she made her way down the hall into her bedroom. Rebecca heaved a sigh. This was her sanctuary. Like all the rooms in her apartment, it had a high ceiling, giving the feeling of space. A massive queen-size sleigh bed dominated the room, piled high with an eclectic assortment of pillows in all shapes, sizes, and fabrics. To the right was a TV set and a collection of video tapes in several piles on the bare floor. Rebecca favored the romantic movies of the past, mostly what were then labeled the women's movies—pictures that ranged from screwball comedies to high drama, from Westerns to sophisticated mysteries and rousing swashbuckling adventure. On the opposite wall was an old framed movie poster of *The Mark of Zorro* with Tyrone Power and Linda Darnell. Next to it was a smaller one of *Casablanca*. She smiled when she thought of the new addition that Meg had given her today—*Robin Hood* with Errol Flynn.

Rebecca removed the hunter-green tailored trousers she wore and the cream silk blouse, anxious to get into relaxing clothes, hoping that the change would somehow ease the tension she felt.

That accomplished, she went back to her kitchen, popping a frozen pizza into the microwave and pouring herself a generous mug of coffee. She sprinkled a little dash of cinnamon into the rich brew and added cream.

Perhaps she should have taken Ben and Ally up on their idea to go out to dinner?

Rebecca shook her head. No, she decided, that really wouldn't have been a very smart idea. To be out with her ex and his soon-to-be bride was asking for trouble, especially with the mood she was in.

And just what the hell kind of mood was that? Rebecca pondered as she removed the pizza-for-one from the microwave, cutting a slice and devouring the pepperoni and sausage.

Unsettled was the closest word she could come up with.

Chapter Two

Now, Rebecca thought as she fixed herself a cup of coffee the next morning, just what was it that she had to feel unsettled about?

She heard the sharp ring of the phone and let the machine pick it up as she walked into her living room. She was glad that she had. It was only another agent calling for two of his clients, promising that tapes of them would be sent to her by messenger later that day.

Rebecca sipped her coffee. Was this what she had to look forward to for the next six months?

She curled up on her sofa, listening to the sound of the rain as it beat upon the leaded glass windows. It felt so strange not to be at work, having staff meetings, reading some of the viewer mail, going over changes that had to be made, or just watching the taping.

Restless, she returned to the kitchen for another cup of coffee and the phone rang again. As soon as she heard the voice of her doorman, she picked up the receiver.

"Another package?" she said with a weary shrug of her shoulders. "Just bring it up, if you wouldn't mind."

Rebecca walked to the door and heard the old-fashioned elevator make its way up. She stood there, a bright smile on her face for the doorman. He was a retired cop in his late fifties, and his presence made the tenants of this building feel all that much more secure.

"Thanks, Mr. Slovak. I appreciate your doing this."

The big man, standing over six feet two inches, gave her a wide grin. "Happy to do it for you, Miss Rebecca," he said, his voice betraying his Bronx upbringing.

She took the large envelope and felt its weight. Another video cassette. "I have a feeling that you're gonna find that I'll be getting a few more of these kinds of packages today," she told him. "If I do, just keep them downstairs and I'll get them later. Believe me, there's no big rush on these things," she said.

"Okay," he said, going back to his duties as Rebecca added the newest envelope to the pile on her hall sideboard.

She looked at the growing collection, blankly staring at them for a minute until a quick flash of an idea hit her.

Rebecca dashed into her bedroom and went straight to her closet, pulling out one of her suitcases. She quickly opened drawers, flinging clothes into the case, along with a few paperbacks from the nightstand. She added several pairs of jeans, some thick sweaters, and a couple of practical shirts to the mix.

She'd be damned if she was going to stay cooped up in here with the incessant ring of the phone and the constant stream of video cassettes and faxes arriving. She'd never get any serious work done that way.

What she needed was a change of scene, someplace where she could be alone to think and work away from this maddening crowd, and she knew just where to go.

A late spring snow blotted the landscape white as Rebecca pulled up into the driveway of her family home in Stowe, Vermont, later that day. A large, sprawling stone farmhouse stood bathed in the light of the moon and snow combined, giving it a glowing presence. Smoke curled from the main chimney.

Rebecca smiled as she parked the car in the large garage that was separate from the house, added only about 40 years ago. Several lights were on, giving a welcoming feel to the place. When Rebecca had stopped for a late lunch, she'd called her neighbors, the Robertsons, and asked if they would light a fire in the largest of the fireplaces, the one in the living room, and turn on some lights.

She fit her key into the lock, pushing her suitcase inside, and went back out to fetch her laptop computer. Shutting the door, Rebecca breathed a deep, contented sigh. Here she had no doubt she would find peace.

Rebecca loved this house. It was where she'd grown up, and it had been in her family since the early 1800s. It was hers now, her parents having deeded it to her when they decided to retire to the sun of New Mexico a few years earlier. She used it infrequently of late, since she usually remained in New York due to her heavy and hectic workload.

But now she could relax and appreciate it. Time was finally on her side.

The smell of something aromatic cooking drew her into the kitchen. The floor was brick, with a large bird's-eye maple table centered there. Several braided rugs were scattered throughout the room, giving it a homey touch. A deep green crockpot was plugged in on the counter. Rebecca lifted the glass lid and sniffed the contents. Fresh chicken and rice soup, with hearty chunks of vegetables, simmered inside.

It was then that she saw the handwritten note next to the crockpot. Removing her coat and hanging it over the back of one of the chairs, she picked up the slip of paper and read:

Dear Rebecca:

I thought that you'd probably be hungry when you got home and in no mood to fix a proper meal, so here's a little something for you. There are corn muffins in the basket and I stocked the fridge also.

If you need anything else, don't hesitate to call. When you get settled in, come on over for lunch or dinner—that's up to you.

Rebecca saw the small basket decorated with ivy leaves and covered with a lace cloth. Nicole Robertson was an artisan, whether she was doing her own line of recycled, handpainted stationery (the piece Rebecca held had a small red squirrel at the top) or fixing a basket so that something plain was made delightful or making a delicious home-cooked meal. Rebecca envied her the last skill, as her own repertoire in the kitchen was severely limited.

Since it was after nine in the evening, and the drive in from New York had been a long one, Rebecca wanted only to get out of her clothes, curl up in front of the fireplace, relax, have a bowl—or two—of the soup, and crash.

She did just that.

"I will come back for you."

Rebecca awoke quickly, looking around. Had she really heard that masculine voice? Or had it been a dream? She shivered with apprehension. It had sounded so real, as if whispered fervently into her ear.

She shifted slightly, listening for any noises.

God, she was getting paranoid. It was just a dream, for heaven's sake. If it were an intruder, she doubted seriously that he would announce himself to her.

But the voice had been so clear, so distinct—a deep voice with traces of an accent. Rebecca's brow wrinkled in concentration. It had been a smooth Southern accent, slow and melodious. And the speaker had been vehement, as if he'd been making an impassioned promise, a solemn pledge.

The rest of the dream had been vague. She could only recall warmth and the intoxicating smell of jasmine.

Rebecca stood, stretching to ease her cramped muscles. It was definitely time for bed, she decided, taking care of the fire in the hearth. Casting a glance at the empty soup bowl, and the half-finished bottle of white zinfindel, she concluded that it must have been her imagination working overtime.

Gathering up the tray, she carried it back to the kitchen. The clock on the wall read one a.m.

When she finished tidying up, Rebecca made her way up the stairs. Entering her bedroom, she saw that the bed was unmade. She'd completely forgotten to check before she'd eaten.

Rebecca didn't really feel like going to the trouble of making it up just then, being far too tired. All she really needed was one of her mother's many antique quilts, collected over the years and stored in the third-floor loft, to throw over herself. Rebecca recalled that, when she was younger, she'd loved exploring up there, selecting the treasured pieces of work that they would use for the bedrooms, and for decorating the various sofas.

One of Rebecca's favorites was a very old quilt that had been sewn by her great-great-grandmother in tribute to her homeland of Ireland. It was a special piece of work done in shades of white and green with embroidered roses. It was that quilt she had to have tonight.

Climbing the short flight of stairs, Rebecca flicked on the light and walked into the room. She located the cedar-lined mahogany armoire that stood against one wall. Here her mother stored all the precious linens and quilts.

Running her palm against the wood, as if absorbing the memories stored there, Rebecca finally opened one of the doors, comforted by the smell of cedar, fresh and crisp inside. This armoire was an antique also, the property of her great-great-grandmother, Rachel. The name of the maker was still visible inside—P. Mallard, New Orleans—etched on a brass plate.

She went through the stack of quilts, locating the one she wanted on the very bottom of the pile. When she slipped her hand inside to pull that one out, Rebecca felt another small object. Her fingers touched a piece of metal, and she drew it out along with the quilt.

It was a key on a slim velvet ribbon.

Curious, Rebecca examined the key and wondered what it was for and why it was hidden. She couldn't remember her mother saying anything about a key before.

Yawning, Rebecca knew she was too tired to search the room for whatever it was that the key would unlock.

She shrugged her shoulders. There was always tomorrow. There wasn't any particular reason why she should be in a hurry. Better to explore this room in the daylight when she could give it her full, wide-awake attention.

She placed the key upon the top quilt and, on a whim, opened one of the bottom drawers. Inside, wrapped in tissue paper, were several nightgowns, all made of cotton and lace. Rebecca smelled a hint of jasmine as she lifted one from the drawer. Jasmine— the fragrance in her dream. She held the nightdress up; it was delicate and very simple with a square neck and hem edged in a small band of lace.

Why not wear it tonight? she asked herself.

Because I'll probably freeze my butt off, she responded.

The garment was made for a hot, sultry night, guaranteed to raise the temperature of any man privileged to see the woman in it. Not because it was overt; rather, Rebecca judged, because it was a nightgown suited to the tempting innocence of a bygone era. It revealed while it concealed, wrapping the wearer in seductive modesty.

Perhaps some other time, Rebecca promised herself. But not in mid-April in Vermont. That wouldn't be a very wise move.

She returned the nightgown to the drawer and scooped up the quilt. Stiffling another yawn, she reluctantly closed the door to the loft.

Tomorrow would suffice for explorations.

The next morning Rebecca awoke late. She turned over and picked up her watch from the bedside table, noting the time. It was after eleven o'clock. Rebecca couldn't recall the last time she'd slept past seven. One night here had already altered her usual frantic pace. She felt refreshed, revitalized. She had energy to burn.

After having a long, hot shower, Rebecca dressed and made her way downstairs for a late breakfast. The wide windows in the kitchen provided a spectacular view of the

346

Green Mountains. She could see the sheen of snow covering Mt. Mansfield and imagined a few die-hard skiers were enjoying the spring bounty. Her hometown made a lot of its collective living on servicing the ski trade. Mike, Nicole's husband, had a superb French restaurant nestled in the woods. During ski season, it was staffed by men and women drawn to the superb conditions that the mountains offered.

Rebecca picked up the phone and dialed the country restaurant, thinking that Nicole might be there. She was proved right when her friend picked up on the second ring.

"Hello," Rebecca said, pouring a large mug of freshly brewed coffee and adding cream. "Glad I found you there. I wanted to thank you for the care package last night. That soup really hit the spot." Rebecca took a sip while Nicole talked.

"I'm glad. So what brings you up here now?" Nicole asked, knowing that Rebecca's normally busy schedule didn't leave much time for visits back home.

Pride threaded through Rebecca's voice. "I got a fantastic job offer," she said. "I get to create a new daytime drama for the network."

"Oh, Rebecca," her friend responded enthusiastically, "I know how much that must mean to you. To be able to do what you want, how you want."

"Yes," Rebecca said, "I'm a very happy camper."

Carol considered the situation. "Then why aren't you holed up in New York working your buns off?"

"Because I got so damned tired of my phone ringing nonstop with agents and actors calling and wanting to be considered for the new show. And," Rebecca said, then paused to take another sip of her coffee, "I needed a respite from all the audition videos arriving at my door. My apartment was beginning to get swamped with the stuff. I left word that anything else was to be put in storage and I'll see it later.

"Hell," she said with a sigh, "I don't even know what I want to do with this hour yet. How am I gonna tell who would be right for what if I don't have a clue yet myself?"

Nicole laughed softly. "Oh, yes, I guess it must be so"—she drawled that word out—"tough to sit down and view those hunky dudes all day long. Gee," she said with an exaggerated sigh, "if you need any help in forming an opinion, please don't hesitate to call."

"As if you'd ever look at any man other than Michael," Rebecca teased.

"Hey there, friend, I'm married, not dead," Nicole said emphatically with a hearty laugh. "No harm in looking." Her mouth curved into a smile. "Besides, you know the only man who could really tempt me would be Frank Langella waltzing into either my shop or this restaurant. Other than him, old Mike is pretty safe." Nicole, seven years older than Rebecca, had seen the actor give his mesmerizing performance on Broadway in *Dracula*, and ever since then, she'd harbored a very soft spot for the handsome, sensual actor. "Now," Nicole said, "if you could find an actor who looked like him and cast him in the soap in a prominent role, that would be a real treat."

Rebecca laughed. "I promise that, should I find anyone who even remotely resembles him, I'll give you a copy of the tape."

"You'd better," her friend insisted. "So are you free for lunch?" Nicole asked, switching topics.

"I only got up an hour ago," Rebecca confessed, "and I'm just having breakfast now."

"Okay," Nicole responded, "how about coming over for dinner this evening?"

"That sounds great," Rebecca said. "I want to get things together here, and by the time I'm finished, a meal out will be most welcome." Rebecca didn't mention that she was planning on scouring the attic to find whatever it was the key unlocked.

"Shall I arrange to have an extra man at the table?" Nicole asked.

Rebecca shook her head and stifled a groan. Another matchmaker. "That won't be necessary," Rebecca said, her tone of voice conveying to her friend just what she thought of that idea.

"I get the message, Rebecca. I promise, no surprises," Nicole stated. "Is eight okay for you?"

"Yes, that should be fine," Rebecca agreed.

"See you then."

Rebecca poured herself a refill and headed back up the staircase, eager to explore. When she entered the attic loft again, she pulled the key from the pocket of her jeans. Just why this was so important to her, she couldn't fathom. It simply was.

Rebecca looked around the room for something the key might open, poking her head around boxes, shifting a large trunk, but with no luck.

In the corner was a white iron daybed piled with accent pillows. Rebecca knew her mother had often put things either underneath or behind the daybed, out of the way. She walked to it and checked, bending down and looking underneath, smiling when she discovered a small wooden chest hidden in back of it. She reached for it and drew it out.

Sitting on the daybed, Rebecca tried the key in the lock. It was a perfect fit. She opened the lid and a delighted gasp of surprise burst from her lips. Inside the cedar box were several notebooks. Rebecca opened one and saw the date, 1860, and the place, New Orleans, written inside, along with the name of the writer—Rachel Gallagher. A bundle of letters, the faded ink almost indecipherable, were wrapped in a lilac velvet ribbon that matched the ribbon that held the key. Several scraps of material also filled the crowded treasure box. Picking up one, a midnight-blue silk, she found it protected a single photograph. Stamped on the back was the name E. Jacobs.

Rebecca turned it over. She was riveted by the handsome face that stared back at her, a hint of a smile on his mouth. It was the eyes that captured Rebecca's attention most though. She couldn't tell what color they were, of course, but for some reason, she presumed that they were a shade of blue. They were penetrating, seductive eyes, set in a most hauntingly masculine face, with a wide, high forehead and thick, slashing dark

351

brows and curling dark hair. Altogether, a man most women would stop and give a second glance to and, she suspected, a third look as well.

Several minutes ticked by before Rebecca could tear herself away from the photograph and the vague sensation that the man wasn't a stranger to her.

And that, of course, was ridiculous. He was long since dead and gone, judging by the clothes that he wore, and the date beneath the photographer's name, 1861.

But who was he?

Rebecca knew that it wasn't her great-great-grandfather. She'd seen an old photograph of Barrett Fraser and his wife, Rachel, and he looked nothing like the man in this picture.

Finally tearing her gaze away from the picture, Rebecca explored further, finding a delicate lace-edged handkerchief with a butterfly motif embroidered on the material. Inside was a locket of gold on a slender chain. It was a marvelous piece of jewelry, with a filagreed set of intitals intertwined: R and M. Rebecca pressed the snap and it opened, revealing two miniature portraits— a man and a woman.

Rebecca recognized the woman—it was her great-great-grandmother, Rachel—and the man was the one in the photograph.

Rebecca shivered. The artist had captured a color so richly blue that even after all these years, the man's eyes were still riveting. And Rachel's hair was the same shade of natural golden blonde that Rebecca possessed.

Unable to resist, Rebecca picked up the locket and placed it over her head, letting it nestle in the hollow of her breasts. She closed the snap with a soft click.

She picked up one of the leather-bound diaries and momentarily debated whether or not she should read it. Would she be invading her ancestor's privacy?

Well, yes, technically, she mentally answered.

But, Rebecca reasoned, if Rachel hadn't wanted them to be read, she could have destroyed them.

Maybe Rachel wanted them to be found eventually. Perhaps her writings contained some hint as to the identity of the man in the portrait and the photograph. The man Rachel hadn't wed.

She must have loved him very much, Rebecca thought. Or maybe I'm just being fanciful, seeing something with my writer's imagination that isn't really there at all.

But Rebecca knew that she was right. She felt it, deep in her heart. Rachel had loved this man enough that she never forgot him, even though she wed another.

Rebecca envied that kind of love.

She made herself comfortable on the iron daybed and began to read:

Today I met the man whom I want to be my husband.
Oh, faith—I know that sounds foolish—
I've just laid eyes on him, but 'tis true.
Nothing will ever be the same for me again.

How can that be? My heart has met its keeper. . . .

Chapter Three

Louisiana, 1860

Rachel Gallagher watched the man ride across the lush grass on the back of a spirited stallion. It was one of her papa's best horses, she thought proudly, and a perfect match to the rider. They moved as one. She stood there, under the shade of a live oak dripping with Spanish moss, the warmth of the day wafting around her, along with the scent of the jasmine that grew nearby.

The masculine rider put the animal through its paces, discovering what the horse could handle. Rachel's breath caught in her throat as she watched the man move the big red horse toward the three large stone jumps, each one successively higher than the previous. Horse and rider took each one cleanly, sailing over the obstacles with a minimum of fuss, much to the cheering of the spectators, both black and white, who had gathered around the whitewashed fence.

"Faith," boomed the big voice of Connor Gallagher, Rachel's father, "I knew the lad could handle that bloody stubborn horse. See, me darlin'," he said to his daughter, pointing to the rider as the man took the mount over the jumps again, this time at a gallop. Vicarious pride rang through in his voice.

Rachel's white-gloved hands were clenched at her sides in fear. He was taking too great a risk. What if the animal balked? He could be hurt or, worse, killed. Even as fear gripped her, Rachel couldn't look away. Her unblinking eyes followed the man and the horse until they'd cleared the last hurdle, again to overwhelming approval from the assembled crowd.

She blinked then and let out the breath that she'd been holding. Her papa was right, as he usually was in matters pertaining to horses: The rider was magnificent.

"Would mademoiselle care for some refreshment?" a smooth-as-honey feminine voice asked.

Rachel turned and stared at one of the most beautiful women she'd ever seen. Tall, with a turban of cherry red wrapped around her head, she had skin the color of cafe au · lait and eyes of deepest gold.

"Why, yes, I would, thank you," Rachel murmured, accepting the tall glass filled with crushed ice and lemonade. Ice was a precious, and expensive, commodity in the South. It was shipped down the Mississippi and carefully stored so that the rich planters could make use of it in their households, especially on days like that day.

Rachel sipped the drink, enjoying the sweetly tart taste on her tongue. For a girl who before had drunk only milk or tea, each new beverage she'd sampled since her arrival in New Orleans only six months before was a delight to be savored. The rich taste of the coffee found at the Cafe du Monde had quickly seduced Rachel; now she insisted on drinking it upon waking each morning.

Almost everything about this section of Louisiana, and New Orleans especially, was fascinating to Rachel. Life here was so different from what she was used to at the boarding school she'd attended in her native Ireland. There, she'd belonged in a very feminine world, with little or no contact with the masculine sex, save for the occasional farmboy or village elder.

Here too the men were different—excitingly so. Gallant. Willing, if this man were any indication, to take a dare or a challenge. They were, she'd observed, both courtly and charming.

"Name your price."

At the sound of a rich, masculine voice, Rachel raised her head and looked up into the face of the man on the horse.

What she saw there was her destiny. She knew it as she knew her own name. In that instant, everything changed in her life. Love had accomplished that transformation. Swift, sudden, and sure.

With that man, there would be no boundaries, no even keel. It would be all or nothing.

"Five thousand, just as we agreed," Connor Gallagher replied, pleased that the horse and man suited each other so well.

"I would have paid twice that amount," the man stated honestly, dismounting, one of his hands stroking the stallion's neck and cream-colored mane.

Rachel was fascinated by his large, tanned hands and long, slender, strong fingers. She could well imagine such hands wielding a fencing weapon with great skill, lifting a delicate wineglass, dealing a deck of cards, or holding a woman close as they danced beneath a sultry Louisiana sky.

" 'Tis well aware I am that you would have, lad, but when Connor Gallagher gives his word on something, that's as it shall be."

"Done then," came the tall man's reply as he extended his hand toward Connor.

They shook, and it was then that the man saw Rachel standing there. He smiled, revealing even white teeth against his tanned face. It was a generous smile, lighting up his very blue eyes.

"May I present my daughter, Rachel, monsieur," Connor Gallagher said, his face glowing with pride as he introduced his offspring. "Rachel, this is Matthew Devereaux."

Rachel wet her dry lips with a quick flick of her tongue. She had heard his name before; he was the scion of one of Louisiana's first families. A wealthy young Creole-American of impeccable lineage who was first in the hearts of the marrying mamas. She could scarcely believe that this man actually existed, so lengendary was his prowess. He could dance longer, ride faster, shoot straighter, and hold his liquor better than any ten men in any parish in Louisiana. Whispers of his skill with an épée abounded, as did rumours of a beautiful quadroon mistress in Rampart Street. All this and more Rachel had gleaned from some of the younger American female residents of the Garden District, who couldn't resist the stories connected with and about a Devereaux.

"*Enchanté*, Miss Gallagher," Matthew Devereaux said, taking her gloved hand and bringing it to his lips.

Rachel trembled, even though his mouth hadn't actually made contact with her bare flesh. She was afraid that she was blushing, so warm did she feel.

"I am ever so pleased to make your acquaintance, Mr. Devereaux," she responded, giving him a tender smile.

"Won't you both stay and join me for luncheon?" Matthew asked.

Connor hastily sliced a glance in his daughter's direction before answering. "Be happy to, my boy," he said in his direct manner.

"Good." Matthew Devereaux turned and called to a lanky lad of about 14. "Jason, come here."

The boy did his bidding quickly, a wide smile on his dark face.

"So what are you to be naming this fine beauty, Mr. Devereaux?" Connor inquired.

Matthew regarded the big red stallion with a thoughtful gaze. He considered for a moment before he spoke. When he did, his blue eyes gleamed with a devilish light. "Would you care to do the honors, Miss Gallagher?"

Rachel raised her gaze to Matthew's, heat suffusing her face. "If you wish?" she asked.

"I would be most pleased," he responded warmly.

Rachel thought for a moment, giving her attention to the proud-looking animal. "Cimarron," she said.

Matthew Devereaux gave Rachel a rakish smile, showing his agreement with her choice. She'd come up with the Spanish word for wild, untamed. A clever name for this animal, he thought. He gave her a small nod of his head, thick black waves of hair curling about his face. "*Merci trés bien*, Miss Gallagher, for your most inspired choice."

"Take 'Cimarron' to the stables, Jason," Matthew said, giving the reins to the young groom, "and see that he has an extra treat in his feed." He smoothed his hand along the big stallion's flank. "Give him special attention with the currycomb too."

"Yes, sir," Jason responded, leading the horse away, speaking softly in a soothing patois to the large animal as he did so.

"If I may?" Matthew asked, holding out his arm so that he could escort Rachel.

She looked toward her father for permission. When Connor nodded with pleasure, Rachel placed her arm atop Matthew's, and they made their way to the plantation house. She was conscious of the fact that he shortened his long strides to hers and of the warmth that emanated from him. Beneath the fabric of his pale gray frock coat, Rachel could feel the rippling play of muscles in his arm.

As they sauntered along the path, Rachel sensed that there was something wild and untamed, much like the stallion, about this very picture of Southern manhood.

The house itself was bigger than anything Rachel had ever seen since coming to this country. It was a grand home, with stately moss-covered oaks flanking each side, like guardian sentinels. Massive columns held up the roof of the second floor; a long balcony with grilled black ironwork surrounded the upper level on three sides. This provided shade for the first floor, where red bricks also ran the length of the house on the three sides. French doors adorned both levels, several open now to catch the languid breeze, white lace curtains fluttering gently. Sunlight dappled the lush grass as they approached. A large dog stood to one side of the house, warily watching before he sprang toward them.

Rachel halted, her eyes wide as she watched the huge beast race the few feet that separated them from the porch. The dog stopped and barked in recognition, pushing its head towards his master's hand.

"What is it?" she asked, standing still, her eyes never leaving the beast.

Matthew laughed. "A little bit of this and that," he said. "I won him in a card game two years ago."

"You gambled for a dog?" she asked incredulously.

"On this occasion, yes, I did. The dog had been mistreated and I wagered the owner five double eagles for the animal."

At Rachel's curious look, Matthew said, "A double eagle is a twenty-dollar gold piece, Miss Gallagher."

Rachel was impressed. "You were willing to risk losing that sum to save the dog?"

Matt shrugged his broad shoulders. He didn't elaborate on the story.

What a strange, interesting man, Rachel thought as he ushered her into the cool depths of the house.

"Angelique," Matt called softly, and the red-turbaned woman came gliding into the room.

"*Oui*, monsieur," she asked, her voice a soothing balm.

"Take Miss Gallagher to one of the upstairs bedrooms so that she may freshen up before luncheon. Are Mama and Marguerite within the house?"

Angelique gave Matthew a knowing smile. "The mistress is with your papa in their room, and your sister is playing with her dolls."

Matt chuckled. "*Eh, bien*, Angelique." He relinquished Rachel's arm and tilted his head toward Connor Gallagher. "Mr. Gallagher, can I interest you in a glass of wine while we conclude our business?"

"You may indeed, my boy," he answered, giving his daughter's gloved hand a reassuring pat as she ascended the huge winding stairway to the second floor.

Rachel's gaze lingered on the portraits of Matthew Devereaux's ancestors that lined the walls. One woman in particular caught her eye. The painting depicted a handsome woman in her later years, stiffly proud, yet with a glimmer of humor in her blue eyes and a touch of wickedness to her mouth.

Angelique paused, watching. "That was monsieur's great-grandmother, Baroness Madeleine-Anneé de Chartier. She was a great beauty and much loved by her family."

Rachel could detect the family resemblance between the baroness and Matthew Devereaux. Each seemed blessed by the ability to draw people toward them, to intrigue with the merest hint of a smile.

They continued their way to the top of the stairs, where Angelique showed Rachel into a large, comfortably appointed room, with a massive canopied bed of walnut dominating one wall. Sheer white bed curtains, which were used at nightime to protect the sleeper from mosquitoes, were pulled back with a thin, gold-braided chain of silk and tied loosely to the carved bedposts. Marble-topped nightables stood at each side, a silver branch of candles atop each. An armoire stood at one side of the capacious room, and a tufted aubergine velvet chaise on the other.

"Faith!" Rachel exclaimed, marveling at the loveliness of the bedchamber. Her room in the boarding school had been plain and utilitarian. There, excessive frills were discouraged in favor of practicality. This, Rachel thought, was absolutely luxurious.

"I shall return with water for your toilette, mademoiselle," Angelique said, a warm smile on her face.

Rachel blinked. "Yes, thank you, Angelique. I would appreciate that," she said, feeling almost overwhelmed by the room.

With the door shut, Rachel cautiously explored the room, not wanting to disturb anything. Her mama would love this room, Rachel reflected. It was the pampered domain of a woman who loved beauty. Removing her gloves, she trailed her fingers along the sheer bedcurtains—soft, so very soft. She adjusted her wide skirt and sat carefully upon a small sofa at the end of the bed piled with petit-point pillows. She examined the embroidery and smiled in appreciation of the skill of the worker. A spaniel decorated one pillow; another held a forest-glade scene of a doe and fawn.

A soft knock sounded at the door and Angelique reentered. She carried a copper pail of water and poured it into a porcelain washbasin. She removed a small bottle of purple-colored glass from the deep pocket of her skirt and uncapped it. "Essence of violets, mademoiselle. Do you have any objections?"

"None," Rachel responded.

Angelique poured a small amount of the scent into the warm water. She gave a delicate sniff and was satisfied with the results.

"Do you have need of anything else, mademoiselle?"

Rachel couldn't think of anything and said so, removing her bonnet and placing it upon the vacated sofa.

"I shall leave you then and come back within a half hour. The family will be down then for their midday meal."

"Thank you so much, Angelique."

Another warm smile was Angelique's response to Rachel's words of praise.

Rachel made her brief ablutions and felt refreshed. As she buttoned her bodice, her thoughts drifted once again to the man known as Matthew Devereaux. Her pulse quickened with the memory of his face, with the thought of his deep, intensely seductive blue eyes.

Fortune's wheel had turned, and he was the one: her own Prince Charming, her brave knight, her heart's true measure. Without warning, he'd captured her love, for now and, she knew, for all time.

Rachel's generous mouth curved into a secret smile. He might not know it yet but that was of no consequence. She did.

THERE NEVER WAS A TIME
GAIL LINK

"Gail Link was born to write romance!"
—Jayne Ann Krentz

Sitting alone in her Vermont farmhouse, Rebecca Gallagher Fraser hears a ghostly voice whisper to her. But not until she stumbles across a distant ancestor's diary do the spirit's words hold any meaning for her.

Drawn by inexplicable forces, Rebecca journeys to the once resplendent Southern plantation where her forebear loved and lost a Union soldier. And there, on a jasmine-scented New Orleans night, she discovers that passion unfulfilled in one lifetime can defy fate and logic and be reborn so much sweeter in another.

_52025-7 $4.99 US/$5.99 CAN